Dolores vaulted onto the other side of the tube, sending Ramsey's body crashing into hers. Their faces were only an inch apart.

"Thank you, Dolores," Ramsey spluttered at her. "I feel much more relaxed after that graceful approach."

"Did you like that, Shortcakes?" Dolores smiled as she delivered a quick kiss on Ramsey's lips. "I thought I'd just give you a preview of what lies ahead."

"Get me out of here!" Ramsey yelled as Lisa pushed their tube out into the river.

"Oh, relax, Shortcakes. You'll have the time of your life," Dolores said as she put her arm around Ramsey.

"Maybe the *last* time of my life," Ramsey groaned as the tube spun around several times as it met the river's current.

ON THE ROAD AGAIN
THE FURTHER ADVENTURES OF RAMSEY SEARS

Elizabeth Dean

Madwoman Press
1992

This is a work of fiction. Any resemblance between characters in this book and actual persons, living or dead, is coincidental.

Cover by Lauren Kurki
Typesetting by Atomic Design

Edited by Diane Benison and Catherine S. Stamps

Printed in the United States on acid-free paper

Library of Congress Cataloging-in-Publication Data

Dean, Elizabeth.
    On the road again : the further adventures of Ramsey Sears / Elizabeth Dean.
        p. cm
    ISBN 0-9630822-0-5 (alk. paper)
    1. Lesbians --Fiction. I. Title
PS3554.E16205 1992
813'.54--dc20

                                                                92-60820
                                                                CIP

To George

Also by Elizabeth Dean

As the Road Curves

Written with Linda Wells and Andrea Curran
Cut-Outs and Cut-Ups
Cut-Outs and Cut-Ups Coming Out!

Written under the name Amy E. Dean
Night Light
Lifegoals
Letters to My Birthmother

INTRODUCTION

Ramsey Sears and I have been pleased with the opinions of the majority of the critics of her introductory travel-adventure novel, *As the Road Curves*. These critics have, for the most part, lavished praise upon Ramsey's character and upon me, the writer.

But there are some critics who have felt that two circumstances in the first novel were too incredible to be part of a fictitious story (which has made me question their definition of fiction). The first was the snowmobiling contest in Marbleton, Pennsylvania. As most writers know, inspiration is often based on a formula comprised of one part creativity and one part reality. Thus, in fact, there *is* such an event as the snowmobiling contest I described. I attended this event, not surprisingly run and participated in solely by males, several years ago in Stow, Massachusetts. My inclusion of this event in the story was often criticized as being "too unbelievable."

But if there's one thing I've discovered in writing for the diverse lesbian community, it's that I'll *never* be able to predict the response my work will generate. (However, I can always rest assured that my writing will evoke some kind of response!)

The second component of the first novel that my critics had difficulty with was not only the existence of such a magazine as *Woman to Woman*, but also its ability to make a profit. I think the common belief that most, if not all, lesbian publications are marginal, if not outright unprofitable, and, additionally, are rarely in existence for more than a short period of time, are unfortunately, true.

But my book isn't! Fiction being what it is, the existence of *Woman to Woman* was and, as you'll read in this book, still *is* a fun dream on my part.

So now, let's focus on the *really important* issues in Ramsey's second story — like where the Wanderlust will wander to next, who Ramsey's next sleeping companion will be, and so on.

PART I.

DEEP IN THE LONELY HEART OF TEXAS

Woman *TO* Woman
MAGAZINE

June Issue

We Are Family

Sisters, tell me, what's your definition of family?

Remember that I asked you this question in last month's column? Now it's time to look at your responses. So now, from my "femailbag," here are some of the replies I received ...

"My family is my lover Sylvia, our cat Cheshire, our dog Bonkers, and my kid sister Joyce who lives with us."

"To me, family is all the people in the book club, who I've been meeting with regularly, third Friday of every month, for the past twelve years. When I get the book for the month, I hold it in my hands or look at it lying on my nightstand and I think, 'Everyone else is reading this book, too,' and that thought gives me a great deal of comfort. Like, we're all in sync with each other, we share something in common, even if we've got our own separate lives and don't socialize with each other outside the group. Then, when we meet together to discuss the book and I look around the room and listen to the thoughts and opinions of women who I've grown to care for over the years, I feel content and at peace. We are family in my book club."

"Family is when my lover and I share special holidays together. Celebrating such times with her makes me feel closer than I feel to my family of origin."

"I like the way my mother, father, and sister have accepted me and welcomed my lover into the family. I feel this especially over Labor Day weekend, when all of us rent a house on the Cape and play cutthroat croquet games. We laugh together, prepare meals, take walks on the beach, and look forward to this one weekend as a time when all of us can be together."

"Family is when I walk in the bar and the bartender says 'hi' and hands me my drink and we don't need to say anything more to each other."

"My motorcycle is family

to me. It never talks back, tells me what to do, or fucks me over. I treat it right, and it treats me right. We get along well, and it's all I'll ever need."

"Family is happening to me right now. My lover's hand caresses my swollen belly — there's a life growing inside me — and we spend hours decorating the baby's room. My lover and I talk endlessly about our baby's education and upbringing, and how we will truly become family when the child is born."

"My grandmother is my family. She's the only one who seems to understand what Doris means to me. She tells my mother, who doesn't understand, to leave me alone."

"Family is my friends. Family is my ex-lovers. Family is my lover. My parents aren't my family. They just raised me."

"When I look at the community calendar in the gay newspaper every week and read the listings of groups for all people, that's my family."

"Family is my brother, who has AIDS, his buddy, his lover, and their friends. Sometimes I think gay males accept me and love me more than my sisters do."

"The ocean is my family. I always feel safe when I look at it."

"Family is love. It doesn't matter who or where it comes from. As long as I can feel love, I have family.

From Ramsey Sears's column, June issue, *Woman to Woman*.

Chapter 1

"Fifty-nine bottles of Poland Spring mineral water with lime essence on the wall, fifty-nine bottles of Poland Spring, you take one down and pass it around, fifty-eight bottles of Poland Springs on the wall," Ramsey sang at the top of her lungs as she cruised at a steady sixty miles per hour on the open highway in the camper she called the Wanderlust. On the passenger seat next to her, a pile of cassettes lay scattered and out of their cases, having been listened to repeatedly over the three hundred miles she had driven since she had left New Orleans earlier that morning.

"I'm so bored, I'm so bored, I'm so bored," Ramsey cried out as she hit her blinker lever and steered the Wanderlust into the passing lane to overtake a tractor trailer.

"I'm so tired, I'm so tired, I'm so tired," Ramsey complained as she hit the blinker again and moved back into the middle lane, ahead of the truck. "I must have averaged four hours of sleep a night with Paula. Well, not *with* Paula, not in the conjugal sense, that is," she commented with a smile, "but with her in the sense that we stayed out until the wee hours of the morning in bars and coffeehouses. Then we'd get up early each morning to go on a run through the streets of New Orleans. What that means now is that I'm one lethargic lump of a lesbian. And how do you spell relief for such a lesbian? I spell it, S-L-E-E-P."

As Ramsey sped along the highway, she thought about the events that had led her to be traveling on Route 10, through the Lone Star State. Less than a month earlier, Rita Hayes — the wealthy, attractive, and teasingly single — owner and publisher of *Woman to Woman* magazine had given Ramsey Sears, star writer for the magazine, permission to embark on a cross-country trip to explore lesbian destinations and events in order to give her sagging writing a lift. Ramsey had left the duplex she rented in Fairfield, Massachusetts in a borrowed camper she had renamed the Wanderlust and embarked on her trip. She stayed a week in Marbleton, Pennsylvania, where she met full-time farmers Nan and Pam and their friend, Bert Hightower, who won the coveted first prize in a unique snowmobiling contest from archrival Tough Tina. Then Ramsey had moved on to an idyllic, ocean-front campground in Shylerville, North Carolina, where she had met seventeen-year-old Janna Lee Hull, a softball player and aspiring writer who played the bases on — and off — the field quite well.

"And then there was Paula," Ramsey said aloud with a smile. "I never thought I'd be able to say her name again without an ache in my belly. But looking her up after such a long time had passed — after all, she was the older woman who had brought me out at summer camp when I was only seventeen — and being able to talk with her about the abrupt ending to our relationship helped me to put the feelings I have for her in perspective. I found out that I love her, but not in the same way I loved her all those years ago; not as a lover, but as someone who will always be special to me, because she was my first love. And now she's my friend."

Ramsey grinned. "I've made a lot of friends on my travels so far. And who knows what new faces will come into my life!"

"I'm in the San Ygnacio Campgrounds," Ramsey shouted into the telephone receiver as she pushed a finger into her other ear and leaned closer in the open telephone booth as a way of bringing the voice on the other end of the line closer to her. "God, Bernice, I don't know how to spell it. For that matter, why do I *have* to spell it?"

Bernice's response faded into a lulling murmur, then suddenly boomed out of the telephone receiver at a decibel level slightly higher than a rock concert.

"Yikes!" Ramsey shouted. "Bernice, the line just cleared. You don't have to shout anymore. Can you repeat what you just said, but at a lower volume?"

"I said, you've got some mail here and I didn't know if I should send it to you. I thought if you could tell me how to spell San Yigglewhatever, I'd get it to you."

"Oh. Well, I guess I'll be here for a couple of days. That way I can coordinate meeting Shane at Healing Hills," Ramsey replied, wiping the sweat from her brow as she stood in the late afternoon sunlight and sweltered in the 90-degree plus heat. "Although I don't know why I'd want to stay here for more than five minutes. It's hot, it's dusty, and it's dull."

"I'm glad you're having such a good time," Bernice's voice shouted back at her.

Ramsey shook her head. "You obviously didn't hear a word I just said, did you?"

"Fine, fine," Bernice responded.

Ramsey gave a quick laugh into the receiver. "What a fun conversation we're having. Don't you think so, Bernice?"

"What's that, Ramsey?"

"Nothing. Listen, here's the address for the campground." Ramsey pressed the receiver to her ear with one shoulder as she held onto the brochure she had picked up at the campground's front office and recited the address to Bernice.

"Got it," Bernice said. "I'll Fed Ex these things to you today. You should have them by tomorrow afternoon."

"If I haven't died of heat exhaustion by then," Ramsey muttered.

"Say, Ramsey, on a different subject, there's something up here with Rita. Have you talked to her recently?"

Ramsey shook her head. "Not for a couple of days. What do you mean, something's up?"

"Well, the rumor is that she's seeing someone."

Ramsey transferred the telephone receiver to her other ear. "What do you mean, seeing someone? Like a doctor? A therapist? A ghostly vision?"

"Come on, you know what I mean. She's seeing someone, seeing someone. As in a romantic interest."

"Are you sure?"

"That's the rumor."

"Well, if all it is is a rumor..."

"Oh, no! It's more than that. We've even seen her."

"Who?"

"The woman Rita's been seeing. And is she hot! Wouldn't you say so?"

Ramsey wiped sweat from her upper lip. "How could I say so? I haven't seen her."

"I know you haven't. I was talking to Justine. She just walked into my office. What's that? Oh, really? Ramsey's gotta hear this. Ramsey?"

"Yes?" Ramsey replied in a voice filled with forced patience.

"Hold on a minute. Justine found out something else about Rita's mystery woman. Rather than have her tell me and then me tell you, I'm going to try to get us all on a conference call."

Ramsey sighed, reached into her pocket, and impatiently jiggled change. The phone clicked a few times — "Don't hang up on me, Bernice," she warned into the receiver when she heard the sounds — and then a faint hum came on the line.

"Ramsey?"

"Is that you, Justine?" Ramsey asked.

"Yes."

"Hi, Ramsey."

"Bernice?"

"Yes."

"Okay," Ramsey nodded to no one. "Hail, hail the gang's all here. Now will you guys please tell me what's going on. It's hotter than fucking hell standing here. I think my feet have melted into the asphalt."

"I wish we knew exactly what was going on, Ramsey," Justine began, "but we'll tell you what we know so far. There's a woman who's been showing up at the office for the past week or so, a woman who's as stylish, attractive, and, we think, as wealthy as Rita."

"Hmmm ... a carbon copy of Rita?" Ramsey asked. "What a vision! That'd certainly make me seriously consider a ménage à trois."

Justine sighed. "You still have your brains in your panties, don't you Ramsey?"

"Touché, Justine."

"Touché, yourself. Now if I may continue," Justine said.

"You may," Ramsey replied.

"Well, Chris always ushers this woman right into Rita's office, then guards the door and won't let anyone disturb them for as long as they're in there."

"Well, if I were in there with Rita, I wouldn't want anyone disturbing me, either," Ramsey replied.

"Ramsey!" Bernice cried out. "Would you just let her finish?"

"Fine."

"Go ahead, babe."

"Babe?" Ramsey asked. "Who are you calling babe, Bernice?"

"Uh ... well ... "

"She's calling me babe, Ramsey," Justine broke in.

"Oh," Ramsey replied. "Have you changed your name?"

"No. Bernice and I are seeing each other."

Ramsey let out a quick laugh. "Seeing each other? Do you mean in the visual sense or in the flesh-on-flesh sense?"

"We mean neither. How we're seeing each other falls into the category of a sense you've most likely never experienced before."

"Touché again, Justine."

"Enough of this dueling," Bernice broke in. "Can we continue with the Rita rumor?"

"By all means," Ramsey agreed. "I'm just shocked by all the goings-on at the formerly staid offices of *Woman to Woman*. First I hear about Rita rising above her genetic predisposition for life-long celibacy, and now I learn that you two have become an item. This phone call is certainly one for the gossip column."

"Ramsey, it's not common knowledge at this point," Justine stated.

"Oh? You mean the commitment ceremony invitations haven't been printed yet?"

"I told you she'd be a real ass about this if she ever found out," Bernice moaned to Justine.

Ramsey sighed. "You're right, Bernice. I am being an ass about this. I have no right to say anything to either one of you unless, of course, this seeing each other starts to affect your work."

"It won't," Justine replied cooly. "But the person whose work may soon be affected is Rita's. What I heard today might be a good indication that Rita has fallen for this woman big-time."

"What did you hear?" Ramsey asked.

"Well, a little while ago I was talking to Chris when Rita's door opened. Rita stood at the door with the mystery woman, smiled at her, and said, "'Just bring your stuff to my place this weekend. We'll settle then.'"

"Wow!" Bernice bellowed into the phone. "'We'll settle then.' That sounds serious. Like maybe she's going to move in with Rita."

"That's what I thought, too," Justine agreed. "So what do you think, Ramsey? Is that good enough to add to your gossip column?"

Ramsey stared out over the flat, dusty desert that surrounded the campground, then slowly hung up the phone.

Ramsey pulled her shirt out of her shorts and shook it repeatedly to let air flow underneath to dry the sweat on her stomach and back as she listened to the last touch-tone digit she had pressed connect her call.

On the first ring, a voice answered, "Shane Sterns."

"Shane? Ramsey."

"Hey, how ya doin', girl? Guess I'll be seeing you soon."

"Yeah. Say, Shane, is there anything going on at the office I should know about?"

"What do you mean?"

"Well ... uh is everything running smoothly?"

"Yeah."

"Has anyone left the job or have we hired anyone new?"

"Nope."

"Is there anyone I know that used to be single who's now maybe seeing someone?"

"Ramsey, you're amazing! But how did you know?"

Ramsey shrugged her shoulders. "I don't know. Lucky guess."

"Get out of here. You've got to be psychic."

Ramsey sighed and muttered, "Psychotic, maybe. So," she began in a louder voice, "Tell me about her. Is she attractive? Nice? Whatever?"

"She's wonderful," Shane gushed. "Tall. Athletic build. Long arms and legs. Beautiful brown eyes. Dimples. A very pretty smile. She's intelligent and extremely well-read. She teaches at Boston University — in the sociology department — a course in African-American Studies."

Ramsey shook her head. "I don't know, Shane. It seems this woman has more in common with you than with Rita."

"Well of course she has more in common with me. She's the woman I'm seeing."

"Oh. I didn't know you were seeing anyone."

"But when you called up, you asked me if — "

"I was asking about Rita," Ramsey cut in.

"Then, girl, why didn't you just ask, 'Is Rita seeing anyone?'"

"Okay. Is Rita seeing anyone?"

"I don't know."

"Well, Bernice and Justine told me — "

"Oh! Now *there's* two people who used to be single, but now are seeing each other," Shane interrupted her.

"I know, I know," Ramsey said impatiently.

"Well, excuse me. For someone who called up wanting to know

things, it seems you already know more than most of the people around here."

"I'm more interested in Rita."

"The entire office staff knows that," Shane pointed out.

"Shane! Just tell me, is Rita seeing some rich-looking, hot babe?"

"I honestly don't know. I have heard talk about some attractive woman who has had appointments with Rita recently, but — "

"Then she *is* seeing someone!"

"Why? Just because she has appointments with some woman?"

"Well, when that's combined with what Justine overheard today — "

"Which was ... ?" Shane prompted.

"Which was Justine heard Rita tell the woman to come to her house this weekend and settle in."

"Settle in?"

"Settle in."

"Oh, I think there must be some mix-up with what Justine — "

"Well, let me ask you, has Rita been acting any differently lately?"

"Differently?"

"Yeah. Like, is she coming into work late, then yawning the entire time she's at work?"

"You mean like how you used to act when you had a date the previous night?"

"Funny. But is she dressing any differently? Is she wearing a new perfume? Has she been receiving gifts of candy or flowers at the office?"

"As a matter of fact, she *has* been getting lots of packages lately."

"Oh. They're probably from *her*, Shane."

"Who?"

"The woman Rita's been seeing. The woman who's going to be moving in with Rita."

"You know, Ramsey, I'm not totally convinced that Rita's

interested in another woman."

"Then I need you to find out."

"Girl, I couldn't possibly find that out before I have to meet you in — "

"You're going to be meeting me in Healing Hills in three days, right?"

"Right. But — "

"Good. Then that gives you two days to find out what you can about Rita."

"Ramsey, I've got a pile of work to get through, at least three staff meetings, packing, and — "

"Great! I knew I could count on you, Shane. I'll see you soon."

Ramsey hung up before Shane could respond.

"Rita Hayes's office," Chris's voice came over the line.

"Put her on, would you Chris?" Ramsey asked. "It's Ramsey."

"I'm sorry, but she's not to be dist —"

"I don't give a shit, Chris, put her on the damn line."

"Ramsey, I can't. She —"

"Chris!"

"Ramsey, yelling at me won't help. She told me that she wasn't go —"

"Dammit, Chris! Just tell her who it is and then let me talk to her. Now!"

"Ramsey, I —"

Chris's voice became garbled for a moment. Then Rita's voice came over the line.

"What is it, Ramsey?" she snapped.

"Hi, boss. Just thought I'd call and check in."

"You could've done that with Chris, Ramsey. In fact, why don't you? I'm in the middle of an important meeting right now."

"I'll bet you are. With who?"

"Isn't it 'with whom'?"

"With whom, then. With whom are you in a meeting with, boss?"

"With someone you don't know."

"But is that going to change?"

"Is what going to change?"

"My knowing her?"

"Why are you asking me these questions?" Rita asked.

"Oh, I'm feeling lonely, here in the heart of Texas, and left out of the day-to-day operations. I just want to know every little thing that's going on for you. So tell me, boss, is this lady someone I'll eventually get to know?"

"You'll get to know her, Ramsey, and so will everyone else on the magazine," Rita whispered. "But I'm only telling you that because you're thousands of miles away and can't tell anyone here. You won't, will you? Mentioning anything about this too soon may mean I'll lose this. And I wouldn't want that to happen."

"Gee, boss. It's all so ... so ... secretive!"

"I have my reasons for that."

"I know, boss. You've got to uphold your image of being a mystery woman. So tell me, what's she like?"

"Who?"

"The woman *with whom* you've been meeting."

"She's extremely capable."

"She's what?"

"Extremely capable. And that's all I'm going to say, Ramsey. I've got to go now."

"But what's she extremely capable of, boss?"

"She's capable of providing what I need. Now I'm very busy and can't talk. Goodbye."

The hum of a disconnected line droned in Ramsey's ear.

"Shit!" she said out loud, then slammed the receiver down. Then she turned and leaned against the phone booth, dispassionately watching the sky turn majestic sunset shades. After several minutes she said out loud, "Hell, woman. If you'd only given me a chance, you might have found me extremely capable, too."

Woman *TO* Woman
M A G A Z I N E

August Issue

A Lesbian Movie Script Plot

Girl one meets girl two.

Girl one invites girl two to a party for their first date, but makes an ass out of herself at the party by drinking too much and insulting girl, thereby losing out on the possibility of a second date with girl two.

The next morning, girl one learns girl two met another woman at the party and has moved in with her.

Girl one swears off drinking and resolves to win back girl two through carefully calculated moves designed to impress girl two.

First, girl one dons an Indiana Jones hat and goes off in search of a famous lost treasure, finds it, returns home to a ticker tape parade in New York City, and is featured on the *Phil Donahue Show*.

Girl one writes to girl two, but receives the letter back, marked "Return to Sender. Address unknown. No such number. (bah-bah-bah-bah) No such zone."

Next, girl one signs on with the NASA First Lesbian in Space Shuttle Launch, is hurled successfully into space, returns to earth, writes a best-selling novel about her experience, and is featured on the *Oprah Winfrey Show* .

Girl one calls girl two, but has the phone slammed in her ear.

Girl one spends a dollar on a lottery ticket, is the sole winner of $25 million, and is featured on David Letterman's "Top Ten List of Out-of-the-Ordinary Millionaires."

Girl one shows up on girl two's doorstep, but has the door slammed in her face.

Girl one discovers girl two is on the same softball team.

Girl one tries to get girl two to notice her all season, but girl two refuses to even sit next to her on the bench. By the end of the season, girl one leads the league in batting average, runs batted in, putouts, and stolen bases, but during the final inning of the championship game, with two outs and the winning run on third, strikes out.

Girl one sits alone in the bleachers hours after the game is over, looking out over the darkened playing field, and is joined by girl two, who puts her arm around her and says, "I don't think I could love you any more than I do at this moment, because you've shown me that you're human."

Girl one doesn't know what to make of girl two's pronouncement, but feels the sympathy factor is working well for the time being and coaxes tears out of her eyes.

Girl one sniffs pathetically while girl two kisses her lightly on the cheek and says, "I want to make you happy for a long time."

Camera pans back slowly on two female figures who kiss in the glow of the full moon's light.

THE END.

From Ramsey Sear's column, August issue, *Woman to Woman.*

Chapter 2

"Shit!" Ramsey cursed as she flung her legs over the side of the small bed, ripped off her damp tank top, and used it to wipe trickles of perspiration from her face, arms, and stomach. "Now I know what it feels like to be a piece of meat cooking in an oven," she said as she glanced at her travel alarm clock and noted that it was one A.M. She got up, stumbled into the Wanderlust's small bathroom, and splashed water on her face, behind her neck, and under her arms. She flicked on the overhead light, squinted at her reflection in the mirror, commented, "God, I look like a greasy french fry!" then flicked the light off, stomped to the refrigerator, and drank a half a bottle of Gatorade. She took the bottle and stood in front of the screen door of the camper, sipping on the drink and hoping to catch a hint of a cool breeze, but no air stirred. "Who the fuck would want to live here year-round?" she asked. "Who the fuck *could* live here year-round?" she added. "This is hell. It's gotta be. I can't imagine anything hotter than this.

"When they say there are hot babes in Texas, now I know what that statement really means."

Four hours later, Ramsey was lying on her back on the small bed, staring at the ceiling, occasionally reaching over the side of the bed to take a facecloth out of a pan of tepid water, wring it out, and rub it over her body. The action provided only temporary relief from the heat.

Gradually, the interior of the camper grew brighter. Ramsey slowly raised her body from the bed to look out the camper windows.

"Oh, hurrah," she said sarcastically. "The sun's coming up. More heat. Yahoo. I guess I should make sure I'm cooked well on both sides." Ramsey rolled over onto her stomach, hung her arm over the side of the bed, collapsed into a restless sleep, and dreamed...

She was sitting in a metal folding chair on a well-manicured lawn in the backyard of a large mansion. Around her, neat rows of metal chairs were set up but unoccupied; ahead of her, a freestanding lectern was surrounded by massive and colorful floral arrangements.

"Are all the guests here?" Ramsey heard a voice say.

"Uh, yup. Ramsey's here. That's it," came a reply.

"Then we can begin."

A burst of organ music startled Ramsey, who suddenly noticed a black woman standing at the lectern. The woman had cropped hair and was wearing a white robe trimmed with an inch-wide purple band.

"Welcome," the woman said as she smiled and looked out over the chairs.

"Thank you," Ramsey responded.

The woman's smile disappeared as she looked directly at Ramsey. "Your participation is not necessary during this ceremony."

"Oh. Sorry."

"Don't apologize to me," the woman answered.

"Okay."

"And please don't say anything further."

"Okay."

"I asked you not to say anything more."

"I'm just letting you know that I heard you."

"Don't."

"Fine."

"Stop responding to me. You're ruining this service for every-one else."

"Everyone else?" Ramsey asked. "Who?" she queried as she turned in her seat and swept an arm around her to indicate the empty folding chairs.

"US!" a chorus of female voices suddenly shouted.

Ramsey twisted in her chair and saw Nan, Pam, Justine, Shane, Bernice, and Rita, along with two women Ramsey didn't recognize, standing in front of the woman at the lectern.

"Oh, hi!" Ramsey called out to her friends and coworkers.

"Shhh!" Pam hissed at her.

"But I — " Ramsey started to protest.

"Is every woman here ready?" the black woman called out.

"YES!" the women in front of her replied in unison.

"Can the audience withhold comment until the end of the ceremony?" she asked. Before Ramsey could open her mouth to reply, the woman said, "Wonderful! Then the commitment ceremony can begin."

The group of women shifted positions to form couples: Nan stood next to Pam, Justine put her arm around Bernice, Shane linked arms with a striking black woman Ramsey didn't recognize, and Rita held hands with a woman who looked like Meryl Streep and was dressed as if she had just completed a shopping spree through the pages of *Vogue* .

The woman at the lectern began to speak, but Ramsey couldn't make out what she was saying. More pairs of women materialized and stood before the lectern, filling, then gradually overflowing the available space, knocking over the empty folding chairs. As the rows of empty chairs were disrupted, Ramsey realized she'd better retreat from her seat or risk being overwhelmed by the sea of lesbian couples that was about to crash over her.

But the minute she stood up to leave, the sea of couples parted to reveal the black woman at the lectern, who raised an arm dramatically in the air and shouted to Ramsey, "Who are you with? Who will be your woman for years to come?"

"She has no one!" cried out a voice from the crowd.

The crowd gasped as one.

"A single woman!" shouted another.

"My God, don't look!" cried out another woman as she shielded her lover from the sight of Ramsey.

"Sin-gle! Sin-gle! Sin-gle!" the women began to chant.

"So?" Ramsey shot back at the crowd. "Coup-le! Coup-le! Coup-le!" she mimicked.

"But who do you sleep with every night?" a voice cried out.

"Anyone I want," Ramsey bragged.

"Not any one of us," a woman argued. "And look. There are more of us joining together. Soon there will be no one left for you."

Ramsey saw hundreds of couples walking hand-in-hand and arm-in-arm toward the group of women.

"Soon we will all be joined together as couples," someone shouted at Ramsey. "Every lesbian in America. Every lesbian in the world! Then where will you be?"

"Yeah? Where will you be?" another voice challenged her.

The women now surrounded Ramsey. There was nowhere to run from them, nowhere to hide from them, no escape. Ramsey began to feel panicked. Beads of sweat trickled down her face...

Ramsey woke from the dream with a stifled scream. Her skin was damp, her mouth dry, and her body cried out for water. She groaned and slowly arose from the bed.

"I think I could sell my body heat to an Eskimo right now," she muttered as she stumbled to the refrigerator and drank the rest of the Gatorade.

Then she pressed the cool bottle to her face and replayed the dream in her mind as waves of morning heat rose up from the ground and shimmered around the Wanderlust.

Ramsey turned off the faucet marked COLD, breathed a sigh of relief, and stepped out of the campground shower room. As she reached for her towel, she noticed an attractive woman with long black hair pinned on the top of her head watching her. There was no expression on her face.

Ramsey nodded at her.

"Y'all Rahmsey Sears?" she asked in a Texas drawl.

"That's me," Ramsey replied.

"Fer y'all," she said as she indicated the Fed Ex envelope she held in her hands.

"Thanks," Ramsey replied as she casually threw the towel over her arm and extended a hand to take the envelope.

But the woman walked towards her and stopped in front of her. She pointed to the return address on the oversized envelope.

"This where y'all from?" she asked, pointing to the state of origin.

"Yup. Massachusetts," Ramsey replied as she crossed her arms and assessed the woman's dark brown eyes and cream-'n-coffee complexion.

"Y'all think it's good?" the woman asked.

Ramsey smiled and cocked her head. "What?"

"Y'all's state. S'it hot?"

Ramsey shook her head. "Never like this. When it gets hot, there's always a thunderstorm to cool things off." As Ramsey spoke, she visualized lying on top of the woman, both of them naked, and imagined the woman's sexy Texas drawl moaning encouragement to Ramsey's lovemaking.

"Y'all have snow?"

"Yeah. Not lots of it, like Maine or Vermont, but we get our share of snow." In her mind, Ramsey posed the woman on a ski slope, booted into a pair of skis, but clad only in a wool hat and gloves.

"Y'all like the sea?"

Ramsey nodded. "Yup. Love it. Beautiful beaches. Lots of sand and cool water. In fact, I wouldn't mind dipping into the ocean right now. That shower provides only temporary relief from this heat." Ramsey saw herself with the woman at the beach near Race Point, just outside P-town, where the dress code was so casual that suntan oil was the only required apparel.

"S'it fahr?"

Ramsey dreamily stared at the woman. "Yeah. Right now it seems very, very far away."

"Thanks," the woman said as she handed Ramsey the Fed Ex envelope. Then she walked out of the shower room and into the heat of the day.

Ramsey stared after the woman, then looked down at her chest. For the first time since she had arrived, goosebumps played over her skin and sent a chill up her spine.

"Maybe Texas isn't so bad after all," she mused as she wrapped the towel around her body and headed back to the Wanderlust.

After she threw on a pair of shorts and a clean tank top, Ramsey sat at the Wanderlust's kitchen table, nibbled on a stale muffin, and sipped warm water as she opened the Fed Ex envelope and dumped the contents on the table. She tossed a few pieces of junk mail aside, then tore open a letter from Athena Broadcasting Network, a small cable channel that was giving the three major television networks major headaches because it had two hit shows that were trouncing them on Monday and Thursday nights.

Ramsey read the letter.

Dear Ramsey:

We were pleased to read your proposed script for "Kristen's Bay," an hour-long weekly romance/drama series that chronicles the lives of lesbian couples who have created a community of their own in the fictional Carolina seacoast resort town called Kristen's Bay. Although we had not been familiar with your work before, the writing samples you sent us, your listing of personal achievements and awards, and the letter of recommendation from your editor at Volpine Publishers convinces us that you can not only follow through on your proposal, but that you are also a powerful force who can make this series a success.

At this point, our network would be committed to producing a pilot show, two hours in length, and seven, hour-long shows to be included in our fall lineup for next year, beginning in September.

This means we would need to begin production of the pilot by August of this year. The scripts for the seven remaining shows would be needed by the fall-winter of this year.

Obviously we need to go to contract on this prior to first production, so please advise us as soon as possible of your interest in pursing this project. If we can sign an agreement by mid to late July, we should be on schedule.

Looking forward to hearing from you.

Sincerely yours,
Isabelle Larson
Executive Producer, Athena Broadcasting Network

"Wow!" Ramsey cried out as she stared at the letter. "This is unbelieveable! I've sold a series about lesbians to a television network. What a coup! What an opportunity, working for television! That could open up doors for a lot more projects for me. The show could be a hit. But even if it isn't, I could learn about the television industry. Maybe I could even write a made-for-TV movie. Hell, for that matter, I could write movie scripts for Hollywood. I could..." She stopped and thought for a moment.

"But that means I'll need to work full-time writing the pilot and scripts for 'Kristen's Bay,' starting as soon as I return from this cross-country trip. That means I'll either have to take a leave of absence from the magazine or quit."

Ramsey thought about the telephone conversations she had had yesterday, then shrugged her shoulders.

"Hell, maybe it's time for me to move on. I can finish this trip, just as I promised Rita I would, provide her with enough columns to hold her for awhile if she wants me to take a leave of absence, then start work on 'Kristen's Bay.' That way, I won't have to go into the office every day and I won't have to deal with Ms. Extremely Capable, or Bernice and Justine, or Shane and whomever, or any other stupid office romances."

Ramsey nodded at her decision, folded the letter, and put it aside.

Then she read the postmark on the last letter — "Marbleton, Pennsylvania! I wonder if — ," eagerly opened the envelope, and shuffled through the handwritten pages to the last sheet. "It is! It's from Nan and Pam!" she smiled as she returned to the first page of the letter and started reading.

Dear Ramsey:

We miss you! It was so nice to meet you and have such fun when you were here. We don't know where you are now or when you'll get this letter, but we have lots of news for you.

First, did you ever see the movie "Baby Boom?" Diane Keaton plays a woman who is this hotshot executive who's been left a baby through a will. She makes a choice to leave the lucrative job she has and go to Vermont to live with her child. While she's there, she sells some applesauce at a local store as gourmet baby food and taps into a market ready to buy her product in large quantities.

Well, enough of such a long-winded introduction!

It seems that Pammy and I may have had the same thing happen to us. We've been selling some of our surplus relishes, pickles, preserves, etc., to local markets for the past few years. The day after you left, a woman in town who's a baker saw our things and asked us if we would like to combine our products and sell them together. She came up with the idea of promoting our foods into product packages with themes. For example, a package called "Good Morning" will contain her breakfast muffins and our preserves to put on the muffins.

Another package called "Take a Break" will have two of her sweet breads and our "famous" strawberry honey. There's a package called "High Noon" (Pammy named it) with whole wheat bread and two of our homemade honey-mustard spreads. Finally, "Snack Time" has delicious chocolate chip cookies and Pammy's special hot fudge sauce.

Anyway, we approached the local markets with some samples, and they sold out right away! A large food chain in Philadelphia that we had mailed a brochure to contacted us and wanted to know if we could deliver some product packages to them. So we've hired two local high school girls to work in the fields during the summer, doing what Pammy and I would be doing — harvesting, weeding, etc. Pammy and I have been working straight out making products to keep up with the demand. We've even been experimenting with other ideas for a dinner package, a picnic package, a barbecue package, etc. It's great! We're turning our farm into a success, all because of this woman's marvelous idea.

Right now Bert is working with us, taking care of most of the deliveries in our truck. As soon as you're back at your home, we'll send you all of our samples. Maybe you can even feature us in your magazine! The publicity wouldn't hurt, your readers might find our story interesting, and it would be a good excuse for coming to visit us again.

What do you say?

Now onto other news. You might think that what we just told you was exciting, but what we have to tell you now is so exciting that you might even think it's shocking.

Ready?

Guess what couple is now an item?

Give up?

Bert and Tough Tina!

Can you believe it? We couldn't!

I guess Tough Tina's bike wouldn't start one night when we were all out at the bar.

Bert strode over to the bike, tinkered with it a bit, and got it going. Tough Tina and Bert then started talking to each other a bit (although we still don't understand how they could have carried on a conversation with the roar of the motorcycle in the background—we think, to them, it was like romantic music) and Tough Tina asked Bert to 'grab a brew' the following night (isn't that the greatest pickup line you've ever heard? "'Let's grab a brew?'").

They've been an item ever since.

We don't know what'll happen next year at the snowmobiling competition. Bert's thinking of retiring because she has what she wants—the "best damn snowmobile around" and "a babe." Get this—Bert told Tough Tina she has no problem with Tough Tina entering the competition and will even help her by being her manager. It's hard to believe that, since those two have been rivals for years. For the life of us, we never thought we'd see them become even semi-friendly with each other, let alone lovers!

Well, at any rate, that's all the news from here. Keep us posted on your whereabouts. And do drop in whenever you'd like. Our door is always open to you.

Love,
Nan

Ramsey reread the letter. She shook her head, laughed, then sighed. "I just don't get it. Now Bert and Tough Tina. Two more bite the dust. Maybe I *will* end up being the Last Living Single Lesbian on Earth." She folded the letter and slid it back in the envelope. "I thought Bert would never settle down with anyone, never mind that she's chosen to be with Tough Tina. Who knows what she sees in her? For that matter, who knows what any woman sees in another woman, to want to spend years just with her?" Ramsey thought back to the snowmobiling competition, at the moment when Tough Tina had revealed her tattooed chest to the crowd of women, then smiled.

"Well, in Bert's case, the attraction was probably based on

Tough Tina's tough titties."

Ramsey then recalled how mortified Shane had been to hear Bert's references to titties when Shane had joined her in Marbleton to cover the snowmobile competition. Ramsey smiled, thought about Shane, which then led to thoughts of Rita, which finally brought back the letter from Athena Broadcasting Network.

Ramsey lost her smile and suddenly felt the heat of the day press in on her.

"Time to stop thinking and time to move on," she declared as she got up from the table and readied the Wanderlust for the open road.

Ramsey parked the camper outside the front office of the campground, then walked in to pay her bill. The attractive woman who had delivered Ramsey's mail to her in the shower stood behind the counter.

"Y'all goin' now?" the woman asked her.

"Yeah," Ramsey replied.

"Y'all off to Massachusetts?"

"Uh, no. Not for awhile." Ramsey reached for her wallet and pulled out money to pay the bill.

"Y'all have family there? A lover perhaps?"

Ramsey laid two fives on the counter. "Nope. No family. No lover."

The woman sighed, then handed Ramsey a receipt. "Y'all sure do have the life. Me, ah've been settled with Molly now goin' on six years. She's mah first — we been high school friends; she mos' likely'll be mah last." She paused, furtively looked around her for a moment, then lowered her voice. "Sometimes ah must admit, ah've thought about being with another woman or pictured mahself jes drivin' away one night, not lookin' back once. Mind you, ah love Molly, that's fer sure. But sometimes ... sometimes I jes think."

Ramsey nodded. "I understand."

"Ah imagine you do."

"Well, thanks," Ramsey said as she turned and walked to the door.

"Say — " the woman then called out.

"What?" Ramsey asked as she paused at the door.

"Ah jes want ta say y'all have quite a nice birthday suit. Might'a thought ah didn't notice in the shower, but ah did."

Ramsey gave the woman a slow grin. "I'm glad you noticed."

"Ah did. Well, have a good trip," the woman said.

Ramsey opened the door, stepped out into the blazing Texas heat, and whistled as she walked to the Wanderlust.

Woman *TO* Woman
M A G A Z I N E
February Issue

If I was meant to be in a couple, I'd have a bicycle built for two ... and other justifications for being a single lesbian

The Great L.G. (Lesbian Goddess) didn't intend for *every* lesbian to be in a relationship, to be considered as one person who is also "a couple." (Which doesn't make any sense anyway.)

The Great L.G. *blesses* single lesbians; after all, if She didn't want some lesbians to remain single, then why would She have created —

— vibrators and other sex toys. Come on, do you really believe all those toys are solely for couples to increase their sexual pleasure?

— microwave meals-for-one. Although couples often buy these meals and stockpile them for future arguments that may occur during mealtime, meals-for-one validate that it's okay to eat alone.

— Walkmans. There's no way two women can enjoy one of these at the same time.

— bars. Most lesbians often mistakenly assume that bars are places for single lesbians to meet other single lesbians for the purpose of forming couples. Not so. The purpose of bars is simple: to drink, to dance, and to discover the pleasures of *any number* of women.

— motorcycles. These vehicles are designed with the single lesbian in mind because they really only have enough room for one lesbian and all her stuff.

— team sports. Two of the most popular lesbian team sports — softball and basketball — are specifically for singles, a fact that's supported by the odd (not even) number of players required on each team. The most successful lesbian teams are composed entirely of single women, for any team that has even one couple on its roster runs the risk of being subjected to embarrassing and distracting domestic arguments both on the sidelines and during play.

— role models. The most revered lesbian role models are committed to single-mindedness. Martina competes in tennis singles; Rita Mae Brown is aways pictured holding her cat (not another woman) in her arms; and Madonna dumped Sean so she could be with anyone she wants, without ever having to justify her love!

From Ramsey Sear's column, February issue, *Woman to Woman.*

Chapter 3

Ramsey traveled Route 10 at a steady pace.

"On the road again!" she sang at the top of her lungs, then repeated the line several times because she didn't know the words to the rest of the song. That done, she popped open a plastic jug of water, tipped it to her mouth, and took several swallows. Then she wiped her mouth with the back of her hand, recapped the jug, and resumed her driving stance.

"Yup. This is the life," Ramsey proclaimed. "I have the freedom to do whatever I want, to go where ever I want, just like the woman at the campground said. And I go at my pace. There's no one to slow me down, to say, 'Ramsey, let's stop here,' or 'Ramsey, I have to go to the bathroom.' I don't have to worry about anybody but myself. I can stop whenever I want, pee whenever I want, eat whenever I want, sleep whenever I want. I'm free to do whatever I damn well please, when I want to. It's *my* party, and I'll cry if I want to," Ramsey grinned, then switched lanes to pass a pickup.

"I make my own choices," she continued. "I answer to myself. No one tells me what to do, when to do it, or how to do it. I'm on my own, with nothing and nobody to tie me down. And that's the way I like it," Ramsey nodded her head. "I truly believe relationships are the worst form of human bondage. They tie you down and take away your freedom. There's no way I'd want what Justine or Bernice or Shane or Nan or Pam or Bert or Tina have right now. NO WAY!" Ramsey sped past the pickup.

"After all, I'm not meant to be tied down. I like it best when it's just me, myself, and I. Maybe that's because I spent far too many years taking care of Mom after Dad left. I washed the dishes and mopped the floors and used the money I earned to buy our food. I took out the trash and made us sandwiches for dinner and got Mom to bed when she passed out from her booze. I cleaned up her puke and pulled her out of bars and — shit — I did all that from the age of five. What a pain in the ass. I discovered early on what a chore taking care of someone else is. Who wants the burden of worrying about someone else? That's all a relationship is anyway — taking care of someone else. Mom took up all my time until she died. Then, when she did, it was like a breath of fresh air. I couldn't believe how many hours were left in the day, just for me, or how much cheaper it was to take care of one person's needs. When I didn't have to constantly think about her anymore, I just worried about me. Then I realized how much easier it was to live every day without having a burden on me." Ramsey wiped sweat from her brow and stepped on the gas.

"Now I find out that everyone, including Rita, is wrapped up with love interests. So? I had a taste of what a relationship is all about when I was with Sheila, and there's no way I'm going to go through that again. Sheila didn't mean that much to me. Sure, I loved her. But she was *in love* with me — that head over heels bullshit — for the duration of our two-year relationship. And she wanted me to care for her like she cared for me. I couldn't. But that didn't change her feelings for me. I'll admit that sometimes it was nice, knowing how much she cared. Sometimes it was nice she'd call me every day when I was at work, 'Just to check in,' she used to say. But I rarely had anything to say to her in those conversations. Heck, sometimes I'd even ask her, 'Sheila, why do you waste our time with these silly phone calls? I said 'Goodbye and have a nice day' to you two hours ago. There's not much more I can add to that.' But she'd reply, 'Oh, I just wanted to hear your voice, to tell you that I'm thinking about you, and that I love you.'" Ramsey shook her head. "What a funny woman."

"Sometimes it was nice to have someone to come home to, someone who was waiting for me with dinner on the table. It mattered to Sheila whether I was home on time or not and that we sat down at the dining room table and had dinner together. 'Isn't this cozy?' she'd ask as she'd light the dinner candles. Then she'd sit down, pull her chair closer to the table, take her napkin in her hand, lay it on her lap, and ask me, 'How was your day, dear?' with such an earnest expression on her face that I wanted to burst into laughter. What she was doing felt so staged, so 'Ozzie and Harriet.' Dinner — what I ate, when I ate it, and where I ate it — didn't matter to me. After all, I was raised on meat-scrap sandwiches I used to make for my mother and me, which we'd eat whenever I finished sweeping the floors at the grocery store and I had collected whatever scraps of meat I could from under the meat slicer at the deli counter." Ramsey steered the Wanderlust into the middle lane of traffic and switched off the turn indicator. "I mean, dinner's dinner, right? What's the difference whether I grab a pizza and work late at the office, go out for burgers with my buddies, or sit across the table from someone who's talking to me like we're in a TV sitcom?" Ramsey shrugged her shoulders.

"Sheila certainly had a funny way about her. She'd worry if I wasn't home on time. She'd get herself all worked up, imagining that I had become a highway statistic. She'd do crazy things, too, like the time when I got the flu and was so sick I couldn't get out of bed. She called in sick the next day and stayed home from work to make sure my fever didn't run high." Ramsey slapped the palms of her hands against the steering wheel. "Isn't that just the craziest thing? I mean, what was the point of her missing work? I was sick. She wasn't. It was up to me to take care of myself, not her. My Mom never took care of me when I was sick, so why should Sheila? I kept telling her to go to work that day, but she wouldn't." Ramsey expelled a breath of air. "And there were so many other kooky things she'd do. I remember I told her once, after she was pissed off at me for eating dinner out and not calling her to tell her so, that it was ridiculous to care about someone that much, to dedicate that much energy to what another person was doing. I told her there was no point to it. 'Live your own life,' I told her. Heck, I learned that after years of taking care of my mother, when I finally discovered that I didn't have a life of my own until my mother was no longer in my life. But Sheila totally missed the point. Instead she shouted at me, 'This isn't about caring too much or devoting too much energy to another person or living your own life. It's about common courtesy towards another human being. People in a couple tell each other what they're doing. They do things like have dinner together. They learn that the other person is equally important.'" Ramsey glanced in the side mirror to take in the road behind her, then shrugged her shoulders. "Hey, it wasn't *my* fault that the relationship ended. I was tired of Sheila being so wrapped up in me and in putting pressure on me to give to her, to devote myself to her, in the same way she was giving to me and devoting herself to me. Sheila made a mistake. I told her it wasn't a good idea to care about someone like that. That it was more important to hold onto yourself and what you've got and not to get so involved with another person. But did she listen to me? Nooo! So I told her to get out of my life. Wait. Excuse me. I believe the correct wording I used at the time was, 'Get the fuck out of my life.'" Ramsey rapped the steering wheel with the knuckles on her right hand. "I did the right thing. I know I did. Breaking up with Sheila was for the best. She was just too involved with me. And that kind of involvement is scary. Frightening. Not right. I mean, not only did she have this crazy idea about how we should be together, but she also had this thing about us — how did she phrase it? — oh yes, 'creating our own family of friends.' She wasn't close to her family and I didn't have one, so she was always inviting our friends, particularly Rita and Shane, to our place for special dinners. She'd arrange tree-trimming parties and Valentine's Day get-togethers and would cook enormous Thanksgiving dinners for them. She told me once that she considered them to be our family. Our family — what a ridiculous idea!"

Ramsey paused to swallow water from the jug, then continued her monologue. "I remember one time, around Christmas, when Shane had just gotten out of the hospital. Why had she been in there? Oh! There was some biopsy she had to have, which later turned out to be nothing to worry about. But Sheila had been frantic with worry. She had invited Shane and Rita over to our house for dinner and had gone out of her way to make it a festive and elaborate pre-Christmas feast. We had just sat down to eat when Sheila reached out, took one of my hands in her own and one of Shane's in her other hand, and said, 'I don't know what Ramsey and I would do without you, Shane. You mean so much to us. You and Rita are our family, and we just hope everything turns out all right.' Sheila had gotten misty-eyed and that had started Shane crying. I remember I looked at Rita and started to laugh, thinking to myself, 'Oh, give me a break. Let's just dive into this food and get on with it.' But Rita reached out for Shane's hand and mine so we now formed a circle of hand-holding females around the table. I didn't know what to make of what was going on. I thought Shane and Rita were going to laugh at what Sheila had said, but they looked as serious as Sheila. I thought it was the stupidest thing in the world to do, to sit around a table of steaming food, holding hands and bawling, but no one else seemed to feel that way. I didn't understand what was going on. Then Rita replied, 'You're like family to me, too. My parents' idea of the Christmas spirit is to send me a few hundred shares of preferred stock. We've never once sat down to a meal together or let one another know that we cared. I've been brought up to think that money and material things matter, not people. I realize now that I'd have gone nowhere with the magazine, or even in my life, without Shane and Ramsey's help and support and your being there too, Sheila.' Rita grabbed my hand tighter in hers and smiled at me in a way she had never smiled at me before... . " The blare of a truck's horn startled Ramsey out of her reverie and into the realization that the Wanderlust had strayed outside the lane markers. Ramsey's heart thudded in her chest as she corrected Wanderlust's position, then sheepishly waved her hand as an apology to the truck.

"Okay," she said as she shifted position in the driver's seat. "Earth to Ramsey. Keep your eyes and your mind on the road and not on some stupid memory. Here you are, in the middle of Texas, getting moony over remembering things Rita did years ago. A touch of her hand in yours. A smile. Come on, Sears. Since when have you been so...so...mushy? Never! So get a grip." Then she signalled an exit off the highway and into a gas station to replenish the Wanderlust's depleted tank.

"So ever since Sheila left, it's been me, myself, and I," Ramsey said ten minutes later as she resumed her ride on Route 10. "And that suits me fine. I remember Rita and Shane came over the next Christmas, after Sheila had left. I think they thought I was lonely, but I wasn't. Maybe *they* were. But I would have preferred to be alone. Shane kept asking me if I missed Sheila, and I told her I wouldn't have asked Sheila to leave if I had thought I was going to miss her. Rita, for some strange reason, got the urge to make dinner and failed miserably. So we ended up ordering out from a Chinese restaurant and watching *It's a Wonderful Life* on the tube. The next Christmas Rita asked if the three of us could get together, but I said I was busy. I got drunk by myself and watched *It's a Wonderful Life* .

"You know, drunk or sober, I can't stand that movie."

"And as the sun set slowly in the west," Ramsey announced as she viewed a spectacular display of red-orange-purple hues from the front seat of Wanderlust, parked in the breakdown lane of the highway, with the lesbian guidebook held open on her lap, "the lone lesbian looked longingly ahead of her in search of other lone lesbians who might keep her company for the night." Ramsey smiled. "Perhaps that's the start of the Great American Lesbian Novel, the one that Paula wants me to write. Perhaps I should do some more research tonight into what happens to a lone lesbian, deep in the heart of hot, hot Texas, after the sun sets. Will she have another unbearably hot night in bed? I think she will if she stays in her camper alone. But she might have an even hotter night if she checks into an air-conditioned motel and entices a hot babe to join her. And the latter choice is exactly what she's going to do," Ramsey decided as she tapped an entry in the guidebook.

"The town of Fullton, according to this book, has a small women's bar and grill named Delila's and a group called the WILD Women. Fullton is about a half hour's drive from here. I suppose if I'm looking for a hot night, there's no more promising place to start than with a group that calls itself the WILD Women." She closed the guidebook, buckled her seat belt, and eased the Wanderlust onto the highway.

"Now *that's* something I don't mind dedicating a lot of energy to," she commented with a smile, "meeting new women, especially ones who call themselves WILD Women!"

MEMO

TO: Rita Hayes
FM: Ramsey Sears
RE: New column idea called "I'm Just Wondering ..."

"I'm Just Wondering ..."

Where the name 'dildo' came from.
If one could survive solely on a diet of edible underwear.
Why there are more shows where men dress as women than there are shows where women dress as men.
Why straight women can never, no matter how hard they try, look gay.
Why every feminist bookstore smells like incense and sells crystals.

(Rita — More to come... R.)

Chapter 4

An hour later, Ramsey stood in front of Delila's Bar and Grill and read the sign that was taped on the door:

WILD Women meet at Garcia School for pickup b-ball, 7 to 9 tonight. Directions below. $2 non-members. Bar opens at 9:30. All ball players, free admission.

"Basketball?" Ramsey said. "In this heat? I've just checked into a motel, showered, and am ready for dinner, a few beers, and some quiet conversation. Shit!" She read the directions to the school, noted that it wasn't far from the motel, and sighed. "The things a girl has to do for a plate of food and a cold draft," she muttered as she returned to the Wanderlust and drove back to the motel to change her clothes.

Ramsey drove into the Garcia School parking lot a half hour later and spied nine women dribbling basketballs and shooting baskets on an outdoor basketball court. "Well, at least we're not playing in a hot, airless gym," she said to herself. "I guess the WILD women aren't *that* wild," she added as she bent over and laced up the basketball sneakers she had decided to pack at the last minute. She exited from the camper and walked towards the group of women.

"How y'all doin'?," asked one woman in greeting as she turned and sank a three-pointer with an easy swish.

"Fine," Ramsey nodded and picked up a ball that had rolled in her direction. She looked for someone to pass it off to.

"Take it," a tall black woman told her.

Ramsey dribbled the ball onto the court between her legs a couple of times, then stopped and popped a shot. It hit the backboard and banked into the net.

"Nice shot," the black woman said. "Hey Dolores," she called out to a taller, muscular, olive-skinned woman with broad shoulders who was wearing a ripped white tank top and brilliant purple and black spandex shorts. "I got this new woman here on my team."

Dolores strode over to them as she placed a white bandana on her forehead and tied it around her head. Her dark, shoulder-length, curly hair was already wet with sweat. Dolores locked eyes with Ramsey. "Short, isn't she?" she commented without taking her eyes off Ramsey.

"No. The name's Ramsey," Ramsey replied as she met the woman's eyes.

Dolores ignored her, looked at the printing on Ramsey's navy tank top, which read Ball Busters, and asked, "Whose balls do you bust?"

Ramsey smirked. "Anyone who gets in my way on the court."

The start of a smile played around Dolores's full lips. "And what if *I* get in your way?" she asked as she put her hands on her hips and looked down at Ramsey's five feet five inches.

Ramsey smiled. "Then I bust your balls, woman."

Dolores's lips smiled at her. "I'm looking forward to it, Shortcakes."

Ramsey laughed. "Shortcakes?"

Dolores chuckled. "Yeah. Come meet the rest of the players, Shortcakes. Hey, everybody," she called out to the women. "Let's get going. Here are the teams. Me, Sharon, Bee-bee, Carla, and Bo against these guys."

The tall black woman tapped Ramsey on the shoulder. "I'm Leeanna. This is Lisa, Adrianne, and Christy," she said as she pointed respectively to the three other women on their team. Ramsey nodded at them and noted that all the members of her team had dark hair and wore dark shirts. "We have the ball first, Dolores," Leeanna said. "Ramsey, you play point guard. Take the ball down."

Dolores shot the ball quickly at Ramsey, who caught it instinctively before it hit her. "Let's see what you can do, Shortcakes," Dolores grinned as she jogged off with her team to take defense at the opposite end of the court.

Ramsey dribbled the ball down the court, stopped at the top of the key, and popped a pass off to her left. Her teammate took the pass and popped it quickly back to Ramsey. Ramsey passed the ball to a player on the right, then followed her pass. Her teammate turned to set a screen and tossed the ball back to Ramsey, who shot the ball for an easy two.

"Nice shot," her teammate said as she touched hands with her, then strode down the court. Ramsey backstepped with her. "I'm Lisa," the woman said.

"Ramsey," Ramsey replied. "Although it seems I'm also known as Shortcakes," she added as she looked at Dolores.

Dolores heard her and smiled.

"Good to meet'cha, Shortcakes," Lisa said as she raised her arms above her head and took a defensive position under the basket.

"Nice basket, Shortcakes," Dolores remarked as she ran toward Ramsey, stopped, then turned and pushed her back against Ramsey to set a position to take a pass from her point guard. Ramsey anticipated the pass and reached in front of Dolores, knocking the ball away from Dolores's hands. She beat Dolores to the loose ball, grabbed it, then looked down court to see Leeanna racing for the basket. Ramsey lobbed a long pass to Leeanna, who scooped it up and put in a lay-up.

"Nice pass," Leeanna called out as she pointed to Ramsey and ran back on defense.

"Good basket," Ramsey replied as she wiped sweat from her brow and settled into her position at the top of the key as the other team in-bounded the ball. Dolores stood next to her. "You trying to make me look bad, Shortcakes?" she teasingly asked under her breath as she positioned herself against Ramsey to set a pick for her point guard.

"I'd never make you look bad," Ramsey muttered in reply as she put her hands on Dolores's hips and pulled her out of the way. "I just like making *me* look good."

Ramsey went around Dolores and knocked the ball from the point guard's hands, dribbled the ball past her, then shot the ball to Leeanna, who was once again waiting under the basket.

"That's a big six-zero, Dolores," Leeanna grinned. "Are you guys gonna start playing pretty soon?"

Dolores smiled. "We're letting your team get a little overconfident, that's all," she called back to Leeanna. Then she turned to face Ramsey. She leaned the front of her body against Ramsey's as her team set up a play. Ramsey held her position and pushed her hips against Dolores's body. They breathed heavily into each other.

"You've got quick hands, Shortcakes," Dolores whispered as she held her arms out from her body and pushed her hips hard into Ramsey's stomach. Ramsey felt a surge of energy between her legs in reaction to the pressure of Dolores's body, then put her hands on Dolores's hips to pull her out of the way again. But Dolores held her ground and the two were locked in a sweaty, athletic embrace. Ramsey looked at Dolores's chest and noticed that the woman's nipples were erect. The point guard dribbled past them, then took a shot that went in.

"You don't know how quick these hands can be," Ramsey replied as she relaxed her body when the shot scored. She met the stare of Dolores's deep brown eyes. Dolores put her hands on Ramsey's shoulders and playfully pushed her away.

"Maybe you'll let me find out later," Dolores said as she smiled, then walked backwards to the other end of the court, never releasing Ramsey's eyes from her own.

"You never know," Ramsey muttered to herself as she took the in-bound pass from Leeanna, then dribbled down court. Leeanna caught up with Ramsey, then walked next to her for a moment. "I don't know what you're doing to Dolores, Shortcakes, but you seem to have broken her concentration. We almost never beat her at this game, so keep doing whatever it is you're doing. It's working."

Is it ever, Ramsey thought as she felt the mixture of sweat and the anticipation of sex soaking her underwear. She stopped at the top of the key and dribbled the ball as she waited for one of her teammates to break towards the basket.

She was aware of where Dolores was, her scent, and her touch the whole time.

An hour later, a majority of the sweating women agreed that Leeanna's team had won and the game was over. Ramsey high-fived with her teammates, then sat on a basketball as sweat dripped from her face and her breathing slowed to a deep, even rhythm. A pair of shoes stopped in front of her and she looked up to see Dolores, who offered her a drink from a jug of ice water.

"Thanks," Ramsey said as she reached for the water and, at the same time, noticed a damp stain on Dolores's shorts, between her legs. Ramsey tipped her head back and drank, then handed the jug back to Dolores.

"Where you from, Shortcakes?" Dolores asked.

"Massachusetts," Ramsey replied.

"That your camper?" Dolores nodded her head in the direction of the parking lot.

"Rented."

"It's nice."

"It's hot," Ramsey commented.

"So are you," Dolores dropped her voice in reply.

Ramsey grinned as she looked around her. "Looks like everyone is."

"Yeah," Dolores nodded. "But not like you, Shortcakes." They stared at each other for a moment, still breathing heavily from the exertion of the game. "Are you going to be staying in the area for awhile?" Dolores finally asked.

"No. I'm just passing through. I have to be in Healing Hills in a couple of days."

"You've got a bit of a ride left."

"I know."

"Well, you're staying tonight aren't you?"

"Yeah."

"Then how about joining me and the rest of the players later on at Delila's?"

"Sure. That's where I started from, as a matter of fact. A sign on the door led me here."

Dolores raised an eyebrow at Ramsey. "I'm glad it did."

Ramsey returned the raised eyebrow. "So am I."

"Good. I'll see you at Delila's, then?" Dolores asked as she extended a hand to Ramsey to help her up.

"Yeah."

"Great. See you in a little while, Shortcakes."

Ramsey walked into Delila's at 9:45 after a shower and quick change of clothes and was greeted by shouts of recognition from the basketball players, who sat at a table in the back of the small bar. Ramsey waved to them, then walked to the table.

"Grab a chair, Shortcakes," Dolores said as she smiled at Ramsey. Most of the players had come to the bar straight from the game and were still in their sweaty clothes, but Ramsey noticed that Dolores had changed into a clean pair of black kayaking shorts and a bright orange tank top that made her complexion and dark hair striking.

Orange is definitely one of your colors, woman, Ramsey thought as Leeanna handed her a chair. Ramsey positioned her chair directly across the table from Dolores.

"Punch?" Lisa asked Ramsey as she raised a pitcher of red-orange liquid to an empty glass and prepared to pour.

"Uh, sure," Ramsey replied.

"They do serve other drinks here," Leeanna cut in. "If you want a beer, Ramsey, just order it from the bar."

"We don't drink," the woman next to Ramsey said.

"On the wagon," another added.

"Punch is fine," Ramsey replied as she nodded to Lisa.

As she reached for her glass, one of the group called out, "Here's Bo!" Everyone raised their glasses in Bo's direction and shouted a greeting to her. Bo waved back to them, then took the hand of a woman who was obviously her lover and led her through the bar to join the boisterous group at the table.

Bo high-fived with a couple of her teammates, then grabbed two chairs and brought them to the table.

"Do you know what tonight is, ladies?" she asked as she sat down.

"What?" someone asked.

"Full moon."

"No shit!" Lisa said. "Then we should do it tonight!"

"Yeah, what do you think, Dolores?" Bo asked.

"I didn't know it was time for the full moon," Dolores replied.

"Well, it is," Bo answered. "A full fucking moon and a clear night — what're we waiting for?"

"Yeah," a few women chorused.

"Okay," Dolores nodded. "Okay. Tonight's the night, then."

"Great!" Leeanna replied.

"This is going to be excellent," the woman next to Ramsey commented.

"Oh?" Ramsey answered her.

"Shortcakes," Dolores broke in, "tonight you're going to have the thrill of your life."

Ramsey looked suspiciously at the group of women, who were grinning at her. "Oh?" Ramsey said again.

"The new person is the first," Lisa said with a smile.

"I don't know — " Ramsey started to say.

"Shortcakes comes with me," Dolores cut her off. "*And* she gets to go first."

"No fair!"

"No way!"

"Yes, fair and yes, way," Dolores said as she finished her punch with a swallow. "It was my idea to begin with, so I get to set the rules."

Napkins and straws were playfully thrown in Dolores's direction. She tossed them back, laughing, then got up from the table.

"Now let's go. Everyone get your stuff and meet me at the foot of the canyon at 10:30." She looked at Ramsey. "Come on, Shortcakes, you're coming with me."

Ramsey got up from the table to the teasing hoots of the other women. Gathering up her curiosity and anticipation, she swallowed the rest of her punch and followed Dolores out the door and into the night.

"Let me drive you back to your motel so you can change into clothes you don't mind getting wet," Dolores said as opened the passenger door of her pickup for Ramsey.

Ramsey paused before she stepped into the truck. "Would you just give me a hint about what I'm getting myself into?" she asked.

"You're going to be getting yourself into cold water," Dolores grinned at her.

"Doing what?"

"Tubing, Shortcakes."

"Tubing?"

"Yup. We're going to be tubing down the Rio Malaris. We can only do it when there's a full moon, so we can see the rocks."

"The rocks?"

"Yeah. But don't worry. The water is pretty high. I think we'll be able to avoid some of the bigger rocks."

"You *think*? Listen, I'm pretty tired. I've been on the road for —"

"Oh, don't chicken out on me, Shortcakes. It's a lot of fun."

"Fun? It's fun to just *think* you're going to miss some rocks on a river in the middle of the night? That's not very reassuring to me. And what happens if we *don't* miss some of the rocks?"

"Then we fall out of the tube, into the river. And I reach out," Dolores explained as she slid an arm around Ramsey's waist, "and pull you close to me in the cool waters and I take you safely to shore." She drew Ramsey close to her, then bent her head down to touch her lips to Ramsey's. Ramsey closed her eyes and thought, She's tall, dark, and handsome, as she met Dolores's lips. "So soft," Dolores murmured as she lifted her lips slightly from Ramsey's.

"You've tried soft. Now try this," Ramsey suggested as she pressed her lips hard against Dolores's. They kissed more passionately, then broke the kiss into shorter, harder explorations of their lips.

After a few moments, Dolores lifted her head away from Ramsey's mouth. "Oh, I won't let anything happen to you tonight on that river, Shortcakes. Not when you're such a good kisser."

Ramsey chuckled. "Well, it's good to know that my lips may save my ass tonight."

"No dear. *I* will save your ass."

"Then my body is in your hands," Ramsey grinned as she stepped into the truck.

"That's right where I want it to be," Dolores remarked as she watched Ramsey slide into the seat.

"Being a lesbian writer," Ramsey said aloud after Dolores had shut her door and walked around the back of the truck to the driver's side, "is not just a job. It's an adventure."

"So tell me about WILD Women," Ramsey said as she zipped her backpack closed and placed the pack underneath her feet in the truck.

"What do you want to know, Shortcakes?" Dolores asked as she steered the truck out of the motel parking lot.

"Why do you call yourself WILD Women?"

"We call ourselves WILD Women," Dolores began as she looked out of her window, then gunned the truck onto the road, "because of what it stands for."

"Which is...?" Ramsey prompted.

"'We're Into Living and Doing.'"

"Living and doing what?"

"Just living and doing, Shortcakes."

"I don't get it."

Dolores smiled at her, then rubbed a hand up and down Ramsey's leg as she drove. "Remember how someone said in the bar that we don't drink?"

"Yes."

"Well, that wasn't always the case. The group of us — there are others, too, who you haven't met — all have had drinking or drug problems. We did drugs or abused liquor to escape from living and doing. Each of us has her own story about how bad things got when she was drinking or drugging, but what all of us share is the reason we drank and drugged. We weren't living then. We were just surviving. There's a difference. When you're just surviving, you take what life throws your way and you try to deal with it, try to cope, in whatever way you can.   But when you're living, then you're in sync with life. You're in control of who you are and what you do. Life doesn't throw curve balls at you because you're not waiting for something to happen. When you're living, when you're doing, you're making something happen. Then you don't need drinks or drugs to escape. Then, you enjoy life and relish everything it offers."

Ramsey rested her arm on the open window and felt the night air wash over her as she listened to Dolores. "You said everyone in your group has her own story," she said after a moment. "So what's your story?"

Dolores squeezed her leg. "Cut right to the chase, hey Shortcakes?"

"Why not?"

"Okay. My story is that my father liked to have sex with me a lot more than he liked to have it with my mother. There wasn't a Saturday night that went by when I was young when he didn't fondle or rape me. Needless to say, I didn't cope with that very well. In fact, as soon as I found out how numb I could feel with alcohol, I tried to stay as drunk as I could until I was old enough to leave. But after I left, I still tried to stay numb. I graduated from high school by sheer luck, then learned how to build houses. During the day, I worked with wood. During the night, I worked with alcohol. Pretty soon I got that reversed. I was fired from my job, tried to kill myself, then met Leeanna, who's a nurse in Sealy Springs, about an hour from here, when she was pumping out my stomach. She became my first woman lover and helped me stop drinking."

"Whew!" Ramsey exclaimed. "And I thought I had it pretty tough."

"Why? What happened to you?"

"Very little, compared to your life."

"So tell me about it anyway."

"Not much to tell. My mother was a drunk. My father left when I was young. I took care of my mother. She died my junior year of high school. That's it."

"It must not have been easy for you, taking care of your mother while you were growing up."

"I think it was a lot easier for me growing up than it was you. I wasn't... well...it was easier for me."

They rode in silence for a few minutes. "Are you still with Leeanna?" Ramsey asked.

"Just friends. Good friends. Being lovers was pretty complicated for us because as I was getting sober, she was working off a cocaine addiction. We got clean and sober together, but as we did our relationship changed. Sometimes that happens. But it was okay."

Ramsey sat in silence for a moment. Then she chuckled.

"What're you laughing about, Shortcakes?"

Ramsey turned to her and smiled. "I guess I thought WILD

Women meant something different. Like you were *really* wild."

"Do you mean playing basketball in ninety degree heat and rafting down a raging river in the middle of the night aren't wild?" Dolores responded.

"Yeah, they're wild all right. But when I think of the word wild, it connotes something more along the lines of — "

"Sex."

"In my own rambling way, Dolores, I was getting to that word."

"You were taking too long."

"Very few women have ever said that to me."

"You *were* taking too long."

"Well, then, why don't we speed this up and skip the attempt to avoid rocks as we surge down a raging river?"

"Not a chance."

"Damn."

Ramsey, Dolores, and the rest of the women stood at the bank of the Rio Malaris under the moonlight and peered out at the raging river that cascaded over velvety black rocks.

"Doesn't it get any calmer than this?" Ramsey asked above the roar of the water.

"This *is* calm," Dolores shouted back. "That's why we start here. We'll end up at the foot of the canyon where we met everyone before we hiked up here."

"Oh, joy," Ramsey said sarcastically.

"It's great!" Lisa yelled. "Let's get going!"

"Yeah! Stop wasting time, Shortcakes! We can't go until you go," Bo shouted.

Ramsey turned to face the group of women. "Why do I get the feeling that I'm some sort of sacrificial lamb?"

"Baa!" Bo responded.

"Baa! Baa!" the rest of the group joined in.

"Great! I'm being encouraged to place my life on the line by a bunch of sheep comediennes," Ramsey retorted.

The group hissed.

"Let's send her down the river without a raft for that sheep pun!" Bo suggested.

"Come on, Shortcakes," Dolores said as she lifted the large rubber tube. "The crowd's growing restless."

"I'll say."

"Grab your side of the tube and let's get our feet wet."

Ramsey picked up the other side of the tube. "As long as that's all I'll get wet," she muttered as she followed Dolores into the river.

"Now I'm going to hold the tube steady while you get in," Dolores explained.

"Will you do that the whole time we're on the river?" Ramsey asked as she threw a leg over the side of the tube and into the inner circle.

Dolores smiled. "I'll try."

Ramsey grimaced. "You'll *try*. You *think*. Can't you be a little more definite about this?" Ramsey propped her shoulders against the back of the tube as she settled into a semiprone position on one side of the tube.

"Great, Shortcakes. You look like you were made for my tube."

"That's the nicest compliment I've ever received, Dolores," she responded. "And perhaps, when I die on this river, I'll come back in my next life as an inner tube you'll use to take on your next trip down this river. Then we'll see who has the last laugh."

Dolores vaulted onto the other side of the tube, sending Ramsey's body crashing into hers. Their faces were only an inch apart.

"Thank you, Dolores," Ramsey spluttered at her. "I feel much more relaxed after that graceful approach."

"Did you like that, Shortcakes?" Dolores smiled as she delivered a quick kiss on Ramsey's lips. "I thought I'd just give you a preview of what lies ahead."

"Get me out of here!" Ramsey yelled as Lisa pushed their tube out into the river.

"Oh, relax, Shortcakes. You'll have the time of your life," Dolores said as she put her arm around Ramsey.

"Maybe the *last* time of my life," Ramsey groaned as the tube spun around several times as it met the river's current. "Did I tell you that I throw up on carnival rides?" she yelled above the rush of the water.

"Well, just be sure to lean in the other direction when you lose your cookies," Dolores shouted back and whooped with delight as the tube rode on top of the fast-moving water and carried them downstream.

"I...don't...think...I...like...this!" Ramsey cried out as they hit a rock, spun around several times, then shot off in a different direction.

"Shortcakes," Dolores shouted into her ear as she pulled Ramsey towards her. "Relax. Look up at the sky."

Ramsey looked up at the full white moon.

"Look at that, Shortcakes. Isn't that beautiful? Listen to the river. Feel the cool waters. Smell the air, how fresh and clean it is. This is living, Shortcakes! You're alive! Enjoy it!"

"I will!" Ramsey shouted back as they ricocheted off another rock. "Just as soon as you get me off of this tube!"

Dolores leaned over Ramsey. The added weight on Ramsey's side of the tube caused it to dip and sent waves of river water over Ramsey. "What are you doing?" she screamed at Dolores and clutched her left arm over the edge of the tube and her right arm around Dolores's neck.

Dolores grinned down at her. "I want to kiss you, Shortcakes."

"I'm not in the mood right —" Ramsey began to say, but Dolores planted her lips on Ramsey's, then used her tongue to pry Ramsey's clenched lips apart. Ramsey groaned in protest at first, then relaxed her jaw and let Dolores's tongue fill her mouth. Slowly, Ramsey responded to Dolores, losing herself in the kiss, feeling dizzy and giddy, weightless and powerless, and overwhelmed with both fear and passion. With her lips firmly planted on Ramsey's, Dolores used her free hand to pull Ramsey's soaked tank top up from her skin, slipped her hand underneath, and cupped Ramsey's left breast and began to play with it. At that moment, the tube hit a rock and Dolores's fingers squeezed tightly around Ramsey's hardened nipple. They hit another rock, and the pressure Dolores had on Ramsey's nipple increased.

I can't believe I'm doing this, Ramsey thought. I should be seeing my life flash before my eyes as we rush down this roller coaster river, but I'm letting a beautiful woman start to make love to me. I guess if I die on this river tonight, there may be those who say at my funeral that the circumstances of my demise were quite fitting.

"You...feel...so...good," Dolores moaned as she held Ramsey's lower lip between her teeth and rubbed her tongue on the soft flesh.

Please let's not hit a rock, Ramsey thought. I like my lower lip. I don't want to lose my lower lip.

"I want...you..." Dolores panted as she moved her mouth to Ramsey's neck.

Ramsey groaned and raised her hips in the air, seeking Dolores's body. Dolores locked her lips on Ramsey's neck and sucked hard as she moved her hand from Ramsey's breast and slipped it under the elastic waistband of Ramsey's shorts. She burrowed her hand under the soaked shorts, down into Ramsey's underwear, and between Ramsey's legs. Dolores let her middle finger dance up and down between Ramsey's legs until her finger met with warm, dense liquid. Then she plunged a finger into Ramsey at the same time that the tube bounced off a rock, which sent Dolores's finger deep within Ramsey. Ramsey grabbed Dolores's shoulder and tried to spread her legs farther apart in her awkward position on the tube, but she couldn't. So she began to rotate her hips and push her clitoris against Dolores's wrist to create friction on the sensitive, but now throbbing nodule. Spasms of erotic delight shook through Ramsey. As the tube swept down the river, each movement amplified Dolores's own motions and added a new dimension to the pressure Ramsey was feeling between her legs, both inside and out. Dolores released her lips from Ramsey's neck and settled her head on Ramsey's chest. As her inner spasms increased, Ramsey thrust her hips in the air in a rapid, rhythmic motion that lifted her body higher, then higher off the tube until her body was arched above it.

Nearly exhausted as she tried to maintain her precarious position and still satisfy Ramsey, Dolores summoned up a final burst of energy and pushed as hard as she could into Ramsey, timing the thrusts of her hand to meet the push of Ramsey's hips.

Ramsey gasped and threw her head back as she lost herself in the intensity of physical spasms deep within her. She came with a vocal release that reverberated off the canyon walls and with a physical shudder and tightness that pulled Dolores's finger even deeper into her, held it there, then caressed it with soft spasms of inner waning delight.

Ramsey opened her eyes, saw Dolores's deep brown eyes looking down at her, and felt the tube gently nudge them against the bank at the foot of the canyon. The shouts of the tubers that followed them were muffled in the distance.

"A hell of a ride," Ramsey replied as she yawned in response to the double release of fear and sexual tension.

Dolores looked down at her. "You're yawning, Shortcakes. Were you a little bored with the ride?"

Ramsey nodded. "Just a bit. I mean, wasn't it supposed to be exciting?"

Dolores smiled. "So it wasn't good for you?"

"Nah. I don't even want a cigarette."

Dolores laughed. "You're pretty funny, Shortcakes."

"Thanks," Ramsey replied. "Now, Dolores."

"Yes?"

"If I'm going to reciprocate the same pleasure to you," Ramsey sighed as she stretched her legs and arms and tried to sit up, "do we have to start at the top again?"

"No, Shortcakes. You can just ask me back to your motel room. I'd ask you to my place, but my roommates are home and we wouldn't have any privacy."

"Then privacy you will have, woman. Dolores?"

"Yes?"

"Would you like to spend the night with me in my motel room?"

"Shortcakes, nothing would please me more than to spend the night with you."

"Dolores, *I* will please you more. I guarantee you that."

Woman TO Woman
M A G A Z I N E

April Issue

A conversation with Clara Commitment, 2,000-year-old lesbian therapist, about one-night stands

Hi, Clara.

Hello again, Ramsey.

I'm glad you consented to speak with me today about one-night stands.

Well, I don't know what I can tell you about furniture, but I'll do my best.

Furniture?

Yes. You want to know about a nightstand, don't you? Although I have no idea why someone would want to buy only *one*. Don't they usually come in twos, for either side of the bed?

Clara, those are nightstands.

Yes, I know dear.

I'm asking you about one-night stands. You know, having sex with someone for just one night, then never seeing that person again.

Ah. Sex. Let me think for a moment what that is. It has been several hundred years since I've had a sexual experience.

Well?

I'm thinking, dear. Don't rush me. You young lesbians are always in such a hurry to do things. You race off to your bars and your marches and your rallies. You want things to happen in the space of a few hours or a few days. In my day, those things used to take a long time. Why, when I met an attractive lady, we'd spend time together over several months getting to know each other. We would plant the seeds of our attraction and watch them blossom, over time, into exquisite, beautiful flowers. You young ones today are ready to hop into bed with the first lady who turns your head without so much as a nod in her direction.

Well, that's what one-night stands are all about, Clara.

No, I don't think they're about that at all.

You don't?

No.

Then what are one-night stands all about?

Well, one-night stands are a bit like an elaborate meal.

Here we go again with your food analogies.

Well, food is oral and so is sex, isn't it? Just stay with me on this one, dear.

Okay, Clara. Tell me how one-night stands are like an elaborate meal.

With an elaborate meal, you spend hours selecting the foods you're going to serve, setting the table, and preparing the food. You might be nervous as you hope that everything turns out all right. As you wait for the food to cook, you smell the enticing aromas and your mouth waters in anticipation. Finally, the moment arrives when the meal is ready to be served. You dish out the food, sit down, and then, in a matter of minutes, eat your fill. After all that beautiful build up, what you've got left to show for it is some rather improper belching, a bellyache, and the strong desire to take a nap.

So that's what a one-night stand is?

Right. A whole lot of preparation for something you wish didn't have to be over so quickly.

But that can be satisfying to some people.

Certainly it can. But how often do you want to stuff yourself with a grand meal and then have to wait for who knows how long for another wonderful meal? Wouldn't it be better to nibble on small snacks over a long period of time than to grab every bit of food you can during only a few minutes?

It depends on whether you're starving.

Dear, with small snacks you never starve. You always want more. But when you've stuffed yourself with a big meal, do you want to see food after that?

I guess not.

So instead of looking for a one-night stand, dear, I think it's always best to look for someone with whom you can share the little meals of life. A lunch. A picnic. A brunch.

Or maybe even a nice breakfast in bed?

Of course. You can prepare a lovely tray of enticing, mouth-watering delectibles, then set the tray on your one nightstand.

Thank you, Clara, for this food for thought.

You're welcome, dear.

From Ramsey Sear's column, April issue, *Woman to Woman*.

Chapter 5

Ramsey leaned against the headboard of the bed in the motel room and bent to kiss Dolores on the top of the head. She breathed in the scent of Dolores's hair, a scent that was a mixture of shampoo, ambergris oil, the outdoors, and sex. Dolores sighed with pleasure in response to Ramsey's kiss and gripped Ramsey's arms more tightly to her chest as she nestled between Ramsey's legs, with her back against Ramsey's stomach and Ramsey's arms wrapped around her.

"It's very comfortable being with you, Shortcakes," Dolores murmured as she snuggled closer.

"I feel the same way."

"You're a great lover. Very satisfying."

Ramsey smiled, leaned her head back, and closed her eyes. "Thanks. So are you."

They listened to the hum of the air conditioner for a few moments. "It's late," Dolores remarked as she broke their silence. "Or early, depending on how you want to look at it."

"What time is it?"

"Almost three a.m."

"That's early."

"You mean the night is still young, Shortcakes?"

Ramsey chuckled. "I wish. This is one of those times when I'd love to turn the clock back and do everything all over again, just the way it happened."

Dolores nodded. "That would be nice, to have an instant replay. The time has certainly flown by."

"But think of all we've done," Ramsey commented with a smile. "I satisfied you, you satisfied me, then I satisfied you again, then you satisfied me—"

"We should be pretty damn satisfied, shouldn't we?"

"*I* certainly am."

"So am I."

"Are you tired? Do you feel like getting some sleep?"

Dolores thought for a moment. "When are you leaving?"

Ramsey considered the miles ahead of her and her scheduled meeting with Shane at Healing Hills. "I should probably leave soon."

"What's soon?"

"Well, later on today."

"Can't you stay another night?"

Ramsey shook her head.

"Even if I promise there'll be no basketball games and no rides down the Rio Malaris?"

Ramsey smiled and hugged Dolores to her. "Enticing as your offer is, I can't. I have to rendezvous with my photographer, and we both have reservations that can't be changed."

"Okay."

"I wish I could."

"It's okay, Shortcakes," Dolores said with a sigh. "I knew you'd have to leave. And so do I." She lifted her body and separated herself from Ramsey.

"Where are you going?" Ramsey asked.

"I should get my things together so you can get ready to leave."

"At three a.m.? That's not my usual drive time, Dolores."

"Well, I just thought — "

"I'm not going anywhere yet," Ramsey stated as she pulled Dolores back against her body and wrapped her arms around her. "So there's no need for you to rush off now. We still have time together. It's early. Remember?"

Dolores relaxed her body between Ramsey's legs. She raised one of Ramsey's hands to her mouth and kissed it. "How about a little nap, Shortcakes, just like this, with you holding me in your arms?"

"That sounds great," Ramsey smiled, then sighed and closed her eyes.

Dolores gently rubbed her head back and forth across Ramsey's chest, feeling the soft curves of Ramsey's breasts and the hollow between them.

"What're you doing, Dolores?" Ramsey asked sleepily.

"Just feeling you."

"Do you like what you feel?"

"Mmmm. Very much."

Ramsey slid her hands to cup each of Dolores's breasts in her hands and gently massaged them.

"What're you doing, Shortcakes?"

"Just feeling you."

"Are you trying to start something?"

"Maybe," Ramsey smiled as her fingers gently rubbed Dolores's nipples. She felt them harden at her touch.

"Shortcakes, you're turning me on."

"That's the idea, Dolores."

"Then don't stop."

"I don't intend to."

"Shall we postpone our nap for a little while?"

"Fine with me."

"Good," Dolores said as she turned over to lie on top of Ramsey.

Ramsey lay on her back. Dolores's head rested on Ramsey's shoulder; one leg and an arm were draped across Ramsey's body.

"Comfortable?" Ramsey mumbled as she slowly drifted awake from a light sleep.

"Very," Dolores murmured.

"It's getting light out."

"Mm. I noticed."

"I'm going to have to leave in a little while," Ramsey pointed out, then yawned.

"I know."

"It's been nice."

"I agree."

Ramsey closed her eyes and fell back to sleep.

"Shortcakes?"

"Um?" Ramsey responded as she drifted into consciousness at the sound of Dolores's voice.

"I don't usually do this. I want you to know that. I haven't been to bed with someone in a while. It's not like I haven't been attracted to other women. But I haven't acted on it. Until you."

Ramsey yawned, then rubbed her eyes. "Okay."

"What about you?"

"What do you mean?"

"Well," she hesitated as she gently ran a finger up and down Ramsey's breastbone. "Do you go to bed with women a lot? Is this something that you usually do?"

Ramsey smiled. "There are people who know me — well, there are people who *think* they know me — who would say that that's all I want from *every* woman, to go to bed with her. I think I acquired that reputation when I broke up with a woman I had been with for two years. I was so happy being out of that constricting relationship that I slept around with every woman I met, whether I was attracted to her or not, for a few months. I guess I was acting out my newfound freedom."

"So what happened after you slept around for a few months?"

"Well, I stopped going to bed with women for awhile, but those few months of promiscuity apparently lived on in people's minds. I acquired a reputation of being a lesbian Don Juan — a Donna Juanita, so to speak."

Dolores chuckled. "You mean you're *not* a Donna Juanita? And here I thought I was going to bed with the best!"

"Oh, you can still hold that thought, Dolores. I won't be upset if you'd like to think I'm the best."

"You are," she murmured as she kissed Ramsey's neck. "So have you met other women on this trip who think you're the best, too?"

"Do you mean, have I been to bed with anyone else?"

"Yes. Anyone else recently, that is. Do you mind my asking?"

Ramsey shrugged her shoulders. "No, I don't mind. But I can't see where this conversation is leading or why you're so interested."

"Oh, I'm just being silly, I guess. It's just that, well ..." Dolores placed her hand in the soft valley between Ramsey's breasts. "You know, Shortcakes, I think, if you were going to stay here for awhile, that I could easily fall for you."

"Fall? As in trip over your shoelaces?" Ramsey asked.

Dolores chuckled. "There's that humor of yours again."

"Yup. It keeps cropping up at the strangest times."

"Usually when you're nervous, Shortcakes."

"I'm not nervous."

"Is that what you think?"

"No. It's what I *know* ."

"Okay. I won't argue with you."

"Good. I hate arguing with someone I've just slept with."

"You know, you're a very interesting person, Shortcakes. I think that's why I could fall for you."

"Interesting, huh?" Ramsey asked as she stretched her body. She wrapped her arms around Dolores and pressed her tightly to her. "Verrry interesting? Or just merely interesting?"

"Somewhere in between the two." Dolores propped herself up on an elbow and looked down at Ramsey with a grin on her face. "And one more thing I want you to know, Shortcakes. I've *never* made love to anyone while floating down the Rio Malaris. I probably never will again. I can't believe I did it. Do you realize how dangerous that was?"

"Believe me, Dolores, I was well aware of the danger from the moment you mentioned rocks," Ramsey replied. "And I, too, can honestly say that I have never been made love to while tubing down a wild river. That alone was a once-in-a-lifetime experience for me that

I'm glad I survived."

"Oh, you did more than survive it, Shortcakes."

"I did?"

"Yeah. You lived it and you did it. And you know what that qualifies you as?"

"No, what?"

"That qualifies you as an honorary WILD Woman. You, Shortcakes, are a WILD Woman."

"And don't you forget it," Ramsey growled as she rolled on top of Dolores and nibbled her neck.

Two hours later, the sun fought its way through the drawn curtains of the motel room.

"Do you have someone special, Shortcakes?" Dolores asked as she and Ramsey lay awake in bed.

"Nope. I don't want to, either. The Lesbian Surgeon General has issued a warning that falling in love can be extremely hazardous to your health."

Dolores rolled onto her stomach, leaned up on both elbows, and looked at Ramsey. "Well, that's a crummy attitude, Shortcakes. Falling in love is the most exhilarating feeling ever. I like being in love. I *love* being in love. It makes me feel connected and complete."

"That's how being alone makes me feel," Ramsey commented as she crossed her arms behind her head.

Dolores smiled. "I used to feel the same way. I never wanted anybody. I just wanted to be left alone — just me and my bottle."

"So you gave up your bottle, but you still had yourself," Ramsey said.

"When I gave up my bottle, I realized how empty I felt inside. I had used the liquor to fill me up, to take away the sadness and the loneliness and the pain."

"And that's what people do."

"That's what I found out, Shortcakes. I realized that people help take away the sadness and the loneliness — "

Ramsey touched Dolores's shoulder. "No, that's not what I was saying. People don't take those things away. They *bring* them."

Dolores reached out and laid a finger gently on Ramsey's cheek and slowly stroked it. "You need someone, Shortcakes."

Ramsey laughed. "I don't need anybody."

"Everybody needs somebody."

"Shall I sing Dean Martin's song, 'Everybody Loves Somebody,' right now?"

"I'm serious, Shortcakes. You need to love someone and to be loved. Then you'll see that people don't cause pain. They can help take it away."

"*I* don't cause myself pain. So I'm hanging out with me."

"Shortcakes, you can't be alone for the rest of your life."

"Says who?"

Dolores smiled. "Says me."

"Yeah? What do you know? You don't have somebody now."

"No, not now. But I want to share my life with someone. To go to bed each night with the person I love, to wake up every morning with her, to build a house together, to share a lifetime together."

"That's too much together for me," Ramsey commented.

"Okay. But you don't have to physically be with someone you love all the time in order to feel an emotional connection."

Ramsey laughed. "An emotional connection? What's that? An umbilical cord between two lovers? I don't need an emotional connection with anyone."

Dolores frowned. "Yes, you do, Shortcakes. I don't know you very well, but you seem so...so...I don't know, self-contained. It's like you're in this little box and you keep the lid tightly closed."

"Maybe I'm a present," Ramsey teased.

"Oh, you're a wonderful present, Shortcakes. But presents are meant to be given away, not kept hidden and closed."

"My goodness, Dolores, you're getting awfully deep after only a few hours sleep."

"Shortcakes, you're teasing me. I'm trying to be serious."

Ramsey sighed. "I don't want to be serious."

"Why?"

"What's the point?"

"The point is that you can't keep yourself closed off from people, from love, forever."

"I can't? Says who."

"You can't because how can you ever be happy?"

"Who says I can't be happy being with myself?"

"Are you happy?"

"Of course I'm happy," Ramsey smiled, raised her head, and delivered a quick kiss to Dolores's mouth.

"I don't believe you," Dolores responded.

"Well, believe me. I've got a hot babe who I beat in basketball, who then mercifully spared my life on the Rio Malaris, and who has been great in bed. I couldn't be happier."

"But over the long term, Shortcakes, don't you want someone for more than just a night or two?"

"Only if the sex is as good as it is with you."

Dolores shook her head. "You're always making jokes, Shortcakes."

"That's because I don't want to talk about this. How did we get onto this subject anyway?"

"I brought it up. But I won't say anything more."

"Good."

"— except one last thing."

Ramsey groaned "What?"

"Someday, Shortcakes, someone is going to mean more to you than anyone ever has. And that woman will probably be able to make you happier than you've ever been in your life. Don't let her get away. Do everything you can to hold onto her. Because if you let her go or if you keep her out of your life because you think you don't need her, then you're going to be miserable for a long time. And you'll always regret never giving love a chance to grow."

Ramsey groaned. "I feel like some schmaltzy music should start playing in the background now."

"Go ahead. Keep making fun of the things I'm saying. But someday, Shortcakes, you'll remember my words."

Ramsey rolled her eyes. "When I do, I'll call you up and say, 'Dolores?'" Ramsey began as she held an imaginary phone receiver next to her ear. "'It's me, Ramsey. Say, remember those things you told me in the motel room? Well, darned if what you said didn't cross my mind today!'"

Dolores raised her eyebrows at Ramsey and tipped her head to one side. "Sometimes, Shortcakes, you're very witty."

"And other times I'm a pain in the ass, right?"

"No, sometimes you won't admit how much you hurt inside."

Ramsey expelled a loud burst of air. "Oh, God! From a lecture on love to a psychoanalysis. Spare me. I do not, repeat, do not hurt inside."

"But you do. Your words have a sharp edge to them. I think deep down you feel — "

Ramsey put a hand over Dolores's mouth. "Please, Dolores, no therapy session. Especially not in bed. Can't we just end this conversation and talk about something else?"

Dolores removed Ramsey's hand from her mouth. "What are you afraid of?"

Ramsey shook her head. "I'm not afraid of anything. I'm just tired of talking about this."

"Okay."

"Okay?"

"I won't say anything more."

"Good."

"That's it."

"Good. Then I have something I want to say to you," Ramsey said as she suddenly flipped Dolores over onto her back, pinned her arms above her head, used her legs to force Dolores's legs apart, then moved to lie on top of Dolores.

"I'm listening," Dolores smiled as she wrapped her legs around Ramsey's hips and lifted her chest up to bring her breasts closer to Ramsey's open mouth.

While Dolores was taking a shower, Ramsey called Shane at the office.

"Shane? Ramsey. What have you found out about — "

"I'm glad you called, Ramsey," Shane interrupted her. "I wanted to ask you about the accommodations at Healing Hills."

"They're accommodating. Now about Rita — "

"I haven't seen her."

"But what did you find out about her and that woman."

"I found out the woman's name is Melissa."

"Melissa?" Ramsey sniffed. "What kind of name is that?"

"It's a common, ordinary name. What difference does it make?"

"Don't you think it's a stupid name, Shane?"

"No, I don't. Now can we get back to talking about Healing Hills. I don't know what to — "

"I mean, what does Rita call the woman when she's with her? Melissa? Mel? Missy? Melissy?"

"Ramsey, I don't care what Rita calls Melissa when they're together."

"And another thing, Shane. Rita and Melissa just doesn't work as a name combo. It's, I don't know, awkward sounding, don't you think?"

"No."

"What's your woman's name?"

"Jackie."

"See? There you go! Shane and Jackie. That works for me."

"It works for me, too, Ramsey, but if Jackie's name had been Tugooboogle, I still would be with her. I don't think someone's name should be a determination as to whether or not a relationship will last."

"So you think it's a relationship, then?"

"Well, I'm serious about her and she's — "

"Not you, Shane! I mean Rita. Rita and Sissy, or whatever her name is."

"Ramsey, does Bernice have a brochure for Healing Hills in her files?"

"Sure she does. Why?"

"Because I'll go talk to her and find out what I should pack. I'm going to hang up now."

"But wait, Shane, you haven't told me anything."

"Neither have you, Ramsey. Goodbye!"

Ramsey held the phone out from her ear and stared at it. "Geez! I was only asking a simple question."

"Thanks again," Dolores said as she and Ramsey walked out into the parking lot of a steakhouse where they had eaten their first meal of the day, an early dinner.

Ramsey leaned into Dolores and playfully shoved her. "Will you stop saying that? That's the fifth time you thanked me. And *you* paid for dinner."

Dolores shoved her back. "Watch it, Shortcakes. This kind of body contact on the basketball court was what got us started."

"Yeah. And I loved it. You know, I think I liked stealing the ball out of your hands the best."

"Well, what I liked the best was seeing your expression when you first saw the Rio Malaris."

They stopped as they reached the Wanderlust.

"I'll tell you what I liked the best," Ramsey said as she reached her arms out and pulled Dolores to her. She put her face close to Dolores's ear and whispered, "I loved it when I was making love to you and you'd tell me, 'Just like that, Shortcakes, just like that.'"

"Yeah," Dolores sighed as she slowly drew her arms across Ramsey's shoulders and looked down at her. "You felt so good, Shortcakes. I never wanted you to stop."

They held each other for a long minute, then slowly separated their sweating bodies.

"Texas heat does have a way of spoiling these spontaneous moments," Ramsey commented as she waved a hand in front of her face like a fan.

"True," Dolores grinned. "But Texas heat can also make you want to run to the nearest air-conditioned motel room and get better acquainted."

"Which we did."

"Yes. Quite well, as I recall."

"So," Ramsey said as she stuck out her hand, "should old acquaintance be forgot — "

"Not you," Dolores said as she grasped Ramsey's hand in hers and held onto it. "I won't forget you, Shortcakes."

Ramsey squeezed Dolores's hand, then smiled.

"Gotta go."

"I know."

"Thanks."

"Thank *you*."

"Stop saying that."

"Okay."

"Good. I like a woman who follows orders."

Dolores playfully saluted Ramsey and watched her open the door to the Wanderlust.

"Oh, Shortcakes?"

"Yeah."

"The next time you see a full moon, think about me, okay? I'll be on the Rio Malaris, remembering the time we had together."

"I'll do that," Ramsey smiled, then closed the door.

Dear Dolores:

I'm writing you this postcard from the parking lot of a gas station / convenience store, about two hours from you.

I just wanted to tell you one thing.

Now I know what Tina Turner was singing about in "Proud Mary." You know — rolling, rolling, rolling on a river!

Thanks for a great time, both on and off the river.

Shortcakes

Chapter 6

"Not now, Missy. Behave yourself, Melissa. Mel, I'm just not in the mood tonight." Ramsey grinned. *"Those are the types of statements you should be saying to this Melissa bimbo, Rita, not 'Let's move in together.'"* Ramsey shook her head as she guided the Wanderlust west on Route 10, heading away from the last big city she had passed through — Fort Stockton — and towards the Barilla Mountains and more rugged Texas terrain.

"I can't imagine you with someone named Melissa, Rita. Hell, I can't imagine you with any woman — except for me, that is, and that's because I'm not just *any* woman. But come to think of it, I don't know if I've ever known you to be with anybody. You haven't been in a relationship since I first met you, have you? Wait. I may be wrong about that. Hadn't you just ended a relationship with someone in New York when I first started working for you? Yes, you had. You said you had been with someone named...hmmm...Donna? No. Debbie? No. The name began with a D, though, I'm sure of that. I've got it — Deena! Deena. You had been with her for almost four years. But why did you two break up? You know, I don't think you ever told either me or Shane anything more than you had been with this Deena person for almost four years, but it didn't work out. Yup. Those were your exact words. 'It didn't work out.' So you moved to Fairfield and hired Shane and me to help you start *Woman to Woman*. But why didn't it work out, Rita? How could anyone *not* work out with you?" Ramsey switched on the radio and idly began turning the dial through AM stations.

"Didn't you date someone once? Oh, yeah. Sheila fixed you up with a college friend of hers. What was her name? Susan! That's right. You and Susan had drinks at our place first so, as Sheila put it, you 'could break the ice.' Break the ice — ha! — I don't think you two even put a chip in the ice. Neither of you said more than three words to the other for an hour while Sheila and I stumbled over one another trying to converse about topics that we thought might spark some common point of interest between you. We failed miserably. Then Sheila and I sent you off to have dinner together—I wondered if one of you would volunteer to speak to the waitperson, or if you'd both just mime your order so you wouldn't have to. We watched you drive away into the night, feeling like worried parents watching their teenage daughters leave on their first dates. Sheila was worried that you two wouldn't hit it off at all. I was worried that you would. I remember wondering to myself at the time what it would be like to have a romantic dinner with you, one where we'd be together and get dressed up and look into each other's eyes and converse in soft tones as we sat across from one another — not like the business dinners you, Shane, and I usually had together, where we'd push food dishes and salt and pepper shakers out of the way so we could spread our work out in front of us and occasionally shovel bites of lukewarm food into our mouths." Ramsey paused for a moment.

"Rita, I promise you this," she then resumed. "If I ever take you out on a dinner date, we'll go to an intimate Italian restaurant I know on Newbury Street in Boston, where the owner has original Milton Greene photographs of a sexy Marilyn Monroe adorning the walls and the chef adds a spice to the marinara sauce that can heat you up from head to toe." Ramsey breathed deeply, inhaling her memory of the aroma of the sauce as she envisioned what Rita's face would look like lit only by soft candlelight.

"Yeah, well, anyway," Ramsey broke into her vision, "as it turned out that night, Susan came home two hours later and told us that you two didn't hit it off, but thanked us anyway for the opportunity to meet Rita. 'She's a babe,' Susan had concluded, then said goodnight and went into the guest room.

"I don't think you've gone on another date since," Ramsey concluded as she finally locked into a radio station that was playing oldies. "Name that tune," Ramsey challenged herself. "It's 'The Boy from New York City,'" she pronounced. "Or, as we lesbians would rather say, 'The *Girl* from New York City.'" Ramsey hummed along with the tune, then sang out, 'And *she's* cute in *her* mohair suit'" as she and the Wanderlust traveled through the hilly Texas countryside.

"So what's gotten into you all of a sudden that you want to settle down with some woman you hardly know?" Ramsey asked a half-hour later as she picked up the one-sided conversation she had been having with Rita. "I haven't been out of the office for even a month, and suddenly you're ready to select a silver pattern with this Schmellissa. That's so unlike you, Rita, to jump at something — or someone — that quickly. That's my style, remember? I'm the one who has no problem going to bed with someone I hardly know. You're the one who once told Shane and me that if you ever settled down again, it was going to be after long and careful consideration and deliberation and, even after such intensive soul-searching, you probably wouldn't end up with anyone but would grow old alone. Do you remember that conversation? Probably not. You become a different person after you've had champagne, and that night the three of us were at the office after hours and were sharing a few bottles of Dom Perignon to celebrate the first year *Woman to Woman* had operated in the black. Shane asked why you refused to see a woman who was putting the moves on you, and who was really nice.

"'I just don't know if I like her,' you told her.

"'But you don't know unless you get to know her.'

"'I know. But it's more than that. I have these incredibly high standards that few women can meet.'

"'Like what?' I asked.

"You shrugged your shoulders. 'I don't know if I know what they are, but I have them.'

"'Then how can you know if someone fulfills them?' Shane pursued.

"You drained your fifth glass of champagne and replied, 'I

won't. But it doesn't matter. I don't think I'll ever find a woman I want to have a long relationship with. I'm just not meant to be with anyone.'

"'That's ridiculous,' Shane responded.

"'It sure is,' I agreed.

"'No, it's not,' you sighed as you poured yourself another glass of the bubbly. 'It's because of the Big C that I'll never settle down.'

"'The Big C?' Shane asked.

"'I can relate to that,' I replied as I toasted your full glass of champagne. 'That's why I'm not with anyone now, either. Commitment scares me, too.'

"'Oh, it's not commitment I'm afraid of,' you answered. 'It's the fact that my career is more important to me than anything or anybody could ever be. I don't think many women understand that or accept it.'

"'*That's* your Big C?' I asked.

"'Yup,' you hiccuped. 'I'm a career woman. And that takes priority over everything and everybody.'

"'Well, you're probably right, Rita,' Shane grinned. 'Most lesbians can understand softball as a priority, but few can accept a career.'"

"Do you remember the last time we had champagne together?" Ramsey asked the invisible Rita after she steered the Wanderlust out of the parking lot of a roadside diner she had stopped at for a snack. "You were at my place for my going-away party. It was late. Everyone else had left, and you were sprawled on my couch, working your way through the last remaining bottle of champagne. I still don't understand what you were trying to say to me at the time with your words — you were babbling about the trip and making no sense to me — but I understood what your body was telling me. Do you remember kissing me? Letting me push my tongue in your mouth and taste you? Do you remember my hands on your breasts — your velvety smooth, firm and full breasts that responded to me with their hard nipples?

Your body was telling me you had a sexual interest and response to what I was doing. But was it towards me, or was it a result of celibacy, of not having had a lover for so long? Is that why you're with this Melissa babe now? Is that what you meant when you told me the other day that she's extremely capable — do you mean that she fulfills you sexually? Did you finally discover that being satisfied by another woman can be as important to you as your career?" Ramsey stared out of the windshield at the road ahead of her.

"Do you know why I'm asking you all these questions?" she asked after a few moments, then drove in silence for a couple of hours.

Ramsey pulled off the highway into a roadside rest area at ten P.M., parked the camper, shut off the engine, then closed her eyes and rubbed them.

"My eyes are too bleary to drive the two hours left to Healing Hills, and I don't trust you to handle the driving alone, Wanderlust," she explained. "So why don't you and I settle in for the night?" Ramsey walked back into the kitchen area of the camper, opened the refrigerator, and took out a cold soda. Then she stepped out of the camper into the mild night air, tipped her head back to taste the soda, then stopped with the can on her mouth as she noticed the cloudless sky.

"Look at those stars!" she cried out. "And the moon! It's so bright and clear. What a gorgeous night!" Ramsey looked around her at the expanse of desert-like land broken by rocky shapes in the distance. "Tonight is one of those rare times when I wish someone was here with me, seeing what I'm seeing now," she sighed as she took in the beauty and solitude around her. "But I wouldn't want Sheila or Paula or Janna or even Dolores. No. I'd want someone — Oh, for crying out loud, Ramsey, stop being such a romantic drip. Anyway, you're not here alone, and you've probably hurt her feelings. Have I, Wanderlust? I don't mean to ignore you. Not after all the time we've spent together." Ramsey raised the can in the air and tipped it towards the Wanderlust. "To us, Wanderlust" she toasted. "To us and our trip from Massachusetts to Texas, without a mishap. To you, who have guided me safely upon the highways of life. To you, who have provided me with shelter. To you, my four-wheeled friend."

Ramsey tipped her head back and downed the rest of the can of soda, then tossed it over her shoulder directly into a metal trash receptacle.

"Did you see that, Wanderlust? Incredible! She scores!" Ramsey shouted in amazement as she jumped around the empty rest area. "The crowd goes wild! That shot just clinched the NBA Championship! Ramsey Sears banked that one home, folks!" Ramsey raced back and forth in the front of the Wanderlust, her hands stretched above her head. "Her teammates congratulate her! Photographers' flashes strobe on her. It's absolute pandemonium here! Ramsey Sears has won the game!

"Let's talk with her now if we can. Ramsey, tell me," Ramsey said as she closed her hand into a fist, shoved an imaginary microphone under her mouth, and imitated Boston Celtics announcer Tommy Heinsohn, "what were your thoughts when you knew there were only seconds left on the clock and your team was a point behind the Bad Boys, the Detroit Pistons?"

"Well, I knew my shot had to go in," Ramsey responded in an out-of-breath voice. "I gave a head fake that cleared Isiah Thomas back for a few seconds. That was all I needed. Coach screamed 'Shoot,' and I did. The moment I released the ball, I knew it would drop in. Isiah knew it, too. He stood next to me, and patted my ass when the shot scored. I said to him, 'Don't ever touch me there again, pal,' and raced off the court."

"Outstanding game, Ramsey Sears."

"Thanks."

"And there you have it, folks. In the closing seconds of a game that was a basket-for-basket, do-or-die match-up, Ramsey Sears displayed the cool calm under pressure she's known for in this league and scored the shot that we'll look at for a long time to come."

Ramsey released the imaginary mike, laughed, and slapped one of the Wanderlust's headlights. "What a kick, hey Wanderlust? What fun we've had together. Maybe we should think about commitment at some point, huh? You 'n me — metal and macha — what a pair!"

PART II.

HEALING HILLS

MEMO

TO: Rita Hayes

FM: Ramsey Sears

RE: Additional entries, new column idea called "I'm Just Wondering ..."

"I'm Just Wondering ..."

Why all women's music sounds like Chris Williamson's "Changer and the Changed" album.

If Amelia Earhart came back in her next life as Jimmy Hoffa.

Why little boys, when they need to use a restroom, are taken into the ladies' room.

If Nancy Reagan read her horoscope today.

Why women aren't concerned about the size of their breasts the way men are concerned about the size of their penises.

What children created by alternative insemination will tell their children about the birds and the bees.

Why politically concerned women, who have changed the spelling of everything from herstory to wimmim/womyn in order to eliminate male pronouns, haven't thought up an appropriate alternative spelling for menstruation and menopause.

Rita:

Let me know if you like this column idea.

Chapter 7

"You're early," Annharriet Lakota, the founder of Healing Hills informed Ramsey as she opened the screen door of the porch of the building marked OFFICE — ANNHARRIET LAKOTA, DIREC-TOR. "Our arrivals for a new week don't usually get here until noon. And since this is the beginning of a new month, our monthly participants won't be here until late afternoon. You're lucky I didn't go into town this morning, or no one would have been here to greet you. The staff doesn't have to report back to work for another hour. The grounds must seem pretty deserted to you right now, but in a few hours there'll be so much activity you'll wonder if you're in the same place."

Ramsey wiped her sweaty palms on the back of her shorts and decided to jump into the coversation as Annharriet paused. "I thought I was in the wrong place for a minute. The dirt road after the sign for Healing Hills seemed to go on for an eternity. This place must be ten miles from the main road."

"Yup. We're pretty far back, pretty removed from civilization."

"Well, I spent the night just a couple of hours from here, so that explains my early arrival. If it's more convenient for you to have me come back later, I can."

Annharriet threw a muscular, tanned arm around Ramsey's shoulders and pulled her through the doorway.

"Nonsense. You're the reporter from the magazine, right?"

"Right. But how — ?"

" — did I know? Because you're inquisitive, not curious. Most everyone who comes here for the first time is curious, wondering what to expect, and they're a little anxious, a little hesitant, as if they're waiting to be acted upon. But you're inquisitive, ready to investigate, not at all anxious or hesitant, like you're ready to take the bull by the horns."

"Well, I don't know about the bull part, but you're right about the fact that I'm the reporter. From *Woman to Woman*. My name is Ramsey Sears."

"Glad to meet you, Ramsey," Annharriet answered. "I'm Annharriet Lakota. I started this place in 1968 and have enjoyed watching it flourish and grow for over twenty years. We've had our ups and downs, but the past five years have been spectacular for us."

"Why is that?"

"Oh, it's the health and fitness craze. It's the stressful lifestyles people are coping with. It's the desire to feel better, not just physically, but emotionally and spiritually as well."

"And what impact has the lesbian community had on your success over the past five years?"

"Well, now, that's hard to say," she responded as she gestured Ramsey to one of the wicker rocking chairs in the waiting area in front of the massive oak check-in desk. Annharriet sat in a chair facing Ramsey. "I don't require women who come here to identify themselves as lesbians. I only ask the men to do that."

"To identify themselves as lesbians?"

Annharriet looked blankly at Ramsey for a moment, then smiled and chuckled. "No. I meant that I only require the men who wish to come here to identify themselves as gay."

"I didn't realize that men were allowed here, too."

"Yes, but not at the same time as the women. I set aside nine weeks of the year for gay men only, and seven additional weeks for gay male couples. No heterosexual or bisexual men are allowed, unless the bisexual men are currently in gay relationships. The remaining weeks of the year are reserved for women only. Every woman who comes here understands that women of all lifestyles are welcome — lesbian, bisexual, and heterosexual. Sometimes we may offer a special week that might focus on issues significant to a mixed group of women; for example, recovery from incest, where the population will include lesbians, bisexuals, and heterosexuals. Other times we may run a week-long program that's more exclusionary; for example, intimacy issues in lesbian couples. I open my doors to all groups except heterosexual men, and that's not because I have issues with straight men or am sexist, but because I feel that there are so many clubs, organizations, and resources that already exist for heterosexual men. I wanted to create a place where only women and gay men could go, because the options they have are not as numerous."

"So is that why you started Healing Hills in 1968, with the goal of creating a place for gay men and all women?"

"Actually, no. Patricia, my lover and partner, originally bought these thirty acres with me so we could have a space for ourselves and women like us, far away from civilization. You have to remember the year we're talking about now — 1968. To use the terminology from that era, we wanted a space where we wouldn't be hassled, where we could love women and express this love freely, where we could grow our own food without chemicals and sprays, where we could cultivate a crop of pot and get high whenever we wanted to, and where we could welcome others who shared ideals similar to ours, ideals of peace, harmony, connection with the universe, sharing — "

"You started a commune!" Ramsey broke in.

Annharriet grinned at her, then raised a hand and created a v-shape with her index finger and middle finger. "Peace."

"Peace, love, and tie-dye shirts," Ramsey grinned back.

"Actually, it wasn't as hippie-dippie as you might think. The commune never really got off the ground. Communes were great to talk about, great to fantasize about, but, in actuality, trying to create a successful commune required so much cooperative energy that it was like trying to get a politically active group of lesbians to get along with S/M dykes."

"That's not easy."

"No, it's not. And it wasn't easy trying to pay off our debts, either. So, two years later, Patricia and I brainstormed ways we could make our land become fiscally productive and, at the same time, have some fun. Being around a bunch of women who are high all the time can be very depressing. It's like everything and everybody moves in slow motion, and no one has any energy to do anything. Patricia and I took a look around us one night, at about a dozen dirty, lazy, drugged-out women lounging around the common room, and we realized how turned off we were to the whole scene. So we decided to create a place where spaced-out, burned-out women could get their feet back on the ground again, without drugs, and develop a greater regard for how they treated their bodies and themselves."

Ramsey furrowed her eyebrows. "Are you describing a charter for a drug recovery program?"

Annharriet smiled. "Sort of. We destroyed our marijuana crop, searched the house and the residents for pills and powders and needles, and then agreed that the only drugs we would offer to help promote each woman's physical, emotional, and spiritual development and maintenance were medicinal herbs. We asked a woman who had studied acupuncture and herbs to work with us, along with a friend of Patricia's who was a phys. ed. teacher and another woman who taught a form of rhythmical dance movements with music."

Ramsey sat forward in her chair. "So let me get this right. In the early seventies, you created a place for women that was drug-free, that offered Eastern healing philosophies, that encouraged physical fitness, and that promoted aerobics? Annharriet, you were way ahead of your time!"

Annharriet closed her eyes, bowed her head, then opened her eyes. "Thank you. I like to think that we're still ahead of our time with what we offer at Healing Hills today."

"Which is?" Ramsey promoted her.

"A drug-and-alcohol-free space that promotes the Healing Hills philosophy, better known as the three R's,"

"I'm sure you're not talking about reading, 'riting, and 'rithmetic," Ramsey chuckled.

"No, I'm not. Our three R's are relaxation, renewal, and rejuvenation, accomplished through participation in a revitalizing daily regimen. I like to think of Healing Hills as a space that combines the best qualities of a therapeutic retreat, a cleansing spa, and a health and

fitness resort. I believe that what we offer here is at least equal to —
and sometimes better than — what one would find at all three of those
places. In fact, Patricia and I spent thousands of dollars exploring
health spas and holistic healing centers in America and Europe before
designing the Healing Hills facilities and hiring our staff. In our
planning, we tried to be as fluid and as adaptable to individual needs
as possible. For example, if a woman wants to come here to focus just
on her physical relaxation, renewal, and rejuvenation, then that's what
we give her. We don't push anything else on her, like recommending
that she also explore emotional or spiritual issues, as we noticed other
facilities did."

"So I don't have to explore my past lives or mother-daughter
issues in order to feel comfortable here?" Ramsey grinned.

"Exactly. But if, while you're here, you decide that those *are*
things you'd like to examine in greater detail, you may. The individual
makes the choice, not the staff."

"So I can do whatever I want to while I'm here?"

Annharriet rubbed her hands together before she spoke. "Well,
remember that you're sharing this space with thirty other women when
you're here. And each of you has her own needs, her own charter —
so to speak — for relaxation, renewal, rejuvenation. It would be
difficult for our staff to service everyone's needs separately, so some
structure is necessary to our program. Perhaps I should tell you what
a typical day here is like, so you can get a better idea of the balance
we've created between structure and choice."

"Okay."

"The morning gong sounds at five-thirty A.M."

"What if I like to sleep late?"

"Oh, the gong sounds again at six A.M."

"I'm sure night owls find that extra half hour necessary."

Annharriet smiled. "Some do. But we find that most enjoy the
early wake-up call, particularly when the day ahead of them is filled
with activities that are new, different, and challenging."

Ramsey nodded. "Okay. I'm up, and it's six o'clock."

"Now you have a choice of going on one of three, hour-long morning walks. There's one we call The Flat and Easy, for those who want a pleasantly paced stroll through the countryside. Then there's The Break a Sweat, a warming morning walk for those who want a moderate challenge. Finally, there's The Mountain Goat, a taxing climb on uneven terrain that requires great exertion and physical stamina."

"Well, I'm going to opt for The Mountain Goat."

Annharriet grinned. "I knew you would. You look like you're in great shape."

"I'm a runner. Play a lot of sports, too."

"It shows."

"Thanks. But now that I've gone on this challenging climb, I'm so hungry I could eat a goat."

"Well, that's too bad, because our dairy goats are used only for their milk and the yogurt and cheeses we make from their milk."

"You have goats here?"

"Actually, we have a barnyard of animals. Goats. Chickens. Ducks. Horses. But no animal is ever killed or consumed here, and we never serve meat products, although we do use chicken eggs solely for the baking that's done on the premises."

"I don't know, Annharriet. I've kind of always been a meat-and-potatoes gal. I don't know if I could last a week without a steak."

"I'm not surprised that you say that, particularly if you're physically active. You've been encouraged to eat red meat. But I think you'll find that your diet here, comprised of complex carbohydrates, fresh fruits and vegetables grown on Healing Hills land, and high-in-protein dairy goat products, will actually make you feel more energetic, more physically fit. Our breakfasts are quite substantial, with whole grain breads, honey and homemade jams, goat's cheeses and yogurt, fresh fruits and fresh-squeezed fruit and vegetable juices, granola cereals, and goat's milk."

"I guess I'd better start to like the taste of goat."

"You will. Our soft goat cheese tastes just like cream cheese, and we've created a cheddar and a gouda that taste terrific in sandwiches."

"I hope I don't start to have cravings to munch on tin cans after I leave here."

Annharriet grinned. "I doubt you will. Unless you already had those cravings before you came here."

Ramsey chuckled. "So what happens after breakfast?"

"Then a number of healing treatments are offered. We have certified massage therapists who work on particular muscle groups or give full-body massages. We have mud baths and herbal wraps."

"What are herbal wraps?"

"Oh, they're wonderful! They're relaxing and invigorating at the same time. Your body is covered with steaming, herb-soaked sheets — everything but your nose and mouth. It's like you're a living mummy, except you're not wrapped as tightly, or for as many centuries," Annharriet chuckled.

"I think I may pass on that one."

"Well, perhaps you'd like to try a mud bath."

"Is that what it sounds like?"

"How does it sound?"

"Dirty."

"No. It's just the opposite — very cleansing."

"Is it like those facial mud packs?"

"Similar, except your entire body is covered with mud. And then we also have Reiki healing treatments, where your chakras are massaged and opened to — "

"Chakras?"

"Energy centers. Finally, Seika, our Chinese healer who joined us in the early seventies, offers acupuncture treatments in conjunction with the burning of moxa, a medicinal herb that accelerates the healing process."

"There certainly are a lot of choices."

"Oh! I almost forgot. On our staff are two social workers who offer therapeutic sessions for individuals, couples, or groups."

"What happens if I don't want to participate in any of these healing procedures?"

"Then you can exercise at the gym or pool, play tennis, or just relax in the Jacuzzi until the late morning gong sounds."

"Another gong."

"Yes. This gong summons everyone to the gym for an hour of dance."

"Is this like a mixer?"

"A what?"

"A mixer. You know, a...uh...social. A girl-ask-girl-to-dance event."

"Oh. No. This is designed to enhance physical health and well-being."

"So is dancing with a woman, in my opinion," Ramsey joked.

Annharriet smiled. "Well, then, your physical health and well-being will be greatly enhanced because you'll be dancing with a lot of women at the same time."

"Hmmm. I've never tried that before."

"It's fun. According to Katrina, our dance and movement teacher, one of the best ways to keep healthy is to dance for approximately one hour, or to at least keep moving rhythmically for that time period. Participants move in whatever ways feel comfortable to them as Katrina plays a variety of music — jazz, swing, rhythm and blues, New Age, and cultural music."

"What? No disco? No Donna Summer, Sylvester, or Village People?"

Annharriet shook her head. "No. And, alas, no Jimi Hendrix, Janis Joplin, or Jefferson Airplane, even though I once asked Katrina why she didn't play more popular, more well-known music. She told me that since the purpose of rejuvenating dance is to learn to move your body to different rhythms, it's best to listen to music that's unfamiliar. That way, you become more aware of your body's interpretation of the rhythm of the unfamiliar music."

"Interesting. I'll look forward to that. But by now, isn't the morning over?"

"That's right. And it's time for lunch. Often we'll have home-made soups, fresh vegetables and salads, goat cheeses and yogurts, whole grain breads, and pastries baked in our kitchens. Lunch is the biggest meal of the day. It's also eaten during the hottest time of the day. Because of that, lunch is followed by a two-hour free period. We offer half-hour group meditations at various serene locations near our pastures and the lake. Some participants return to their accommodations after lunch and nap, read, write letters, socialize — whatever. Following this period, everyone is encouraged to join together on the playing field to participate in New Games."

"Games that have just been released?"

"No. New Games is the term used to describe playful, noncompetitive games in which a group of people, as a team, strives together to reach a goal. Everyone wins in New Games; no one loses."

Ramsey thought for a moment. "Sounds kind of like playing pickup basketball, without keeping score. I think that's the closest I've ever come to playing a game without the ultimate goal of winning over someone else or another team."

Annharriet smiled. "Then I think New Games will be a refreshing change for you."

"What happens after the New Games?"

"Then the afternoon gong summons everyone to the Non-cocktail Happy Hour by the pool, where a wonderful spread of low-calorie crudités, stuffed mushrooms, appetizing dips, and delicious frozen fruit drinks is set up. This is the ideal time for socializing. The dinner that follows is very light — perhaps a clear vegetable broth or a salad and whole grain breads, with homemade sherbet for dessert. Then, after dinner, we offer lectures on a wide array of subjects, from holistic topics, such as biofeedback, to traditional subjects, such as stress reduction. The day concludes with music and storytelling by firelight."

Annharriet and Ramsey sat in silence for a few moments.

"That's quite a full schedule," Ramsey finally spoke.

"Very. People are usually asleep soon after the storytelling."

"What time is that over?"

"Oh, nine, nine-thirty."

Ramsey sighed. "I suppose the early-to-bed principle works well here because it's followed by an early-to-rise wake-up call."

Annharriet smiled. "That's right. But do you see now how energized you might feel the next morning, even at that early hour?"

Ramsey nodded. "Sure. There are no stresses in any day. There are no phone calls to return, no schedules to keep, no deadlines to make, no rush-hour traffic, no — "

"Exactly. There are no obligations here, no commitments, no demands. Participants often are amazed at the freedom they're allowed to experience here." A car door slammed outside. Annharriet got up and glanced out through the screen door. "It's Patricia! Come on in, Sweetie! There's someone I'd like you to meet."

"Oh? Do we have company?" a lanky, white-haired woman stepped into the office, removed a cowboy hat from her head, and stood next to Annharriet.

"Patricia, this is Ramsey Sears, the reporter from the magazine that's going to feature Healing Hills."

"Pleased to meet you," Patricia smiled as she extended her hand to Ramsey.

Ramsey stood up and shook a hand that had a firm grasp and the feel of stiff leather.

"I imagine Annharriet's probably told you all you need to know about this place," Patricia stated. "She's the talker, more so than me."

"Now, you're not going to get out of helping me with this article that easily, Sweetie," Annharriet smiled at Patricia, then met Ramsey's eyes. "Ramsey, don't you believe for one minute that she's not a talker. If you want to ask her anything, feel free to do so. She just pretends she's shy. She's not really."

"No, I'm not shy," Patricia grinned, then held the cowboy hat in front of her face and leaned over to kiss Annharriet on the cheek. "Not shy at all," she said as she replaced the hat on her head.

Ramsey grinned.

"Now, not to be pushy, Love, but have you handled the reservations cards yet?" Patricia asked Annharriet. "It's getting close to check in time."

"Oh, my!" Annharriet cried out. "I haven't done a thing. I've been having such a good time talking with Ramsey — "

"See what I mean?" Patricia asked. "She's the talker. Definitely the talker."

"Then I should leave you to your work, Annharriet," Ramsey said as she walked towards the door.

"Now, don't go rushing off too fast, because you'll just have to come back in here and ask me where you're staying," Annharriet stated. "Let me see. I must have your card around here somewhere," she said as she rushed around the checkin desk, pulled out some papers, and rummaged through them.

"Ah. Here we are. You're in Sage House. You go down the main road — the one in front of this office — until you see the sign that says VILLAGE. You're in the fifth house on the left."

"Okay," Ramsey nodded. "Oh. The photographer for the magazine, Shane Sterns — "

"I have her in Sage with you, too," Annharriet answered her.

Ramsey nodded. "Good. I'll be going now."

Annharriet smiled. "You're free to do whatever you'd like until you hear the gong for lunch."

"I think I'll pass on lunch for today," Ramsey replied.

"Then around four, you'll hear another gong. That's for Happy Hour."

"Great," Ramsey said. "I'll entertain myself until then. Thanks for the time you've already given me."

"It was no problem. I'll talk to you again soon," Annharriet said, then watched Ramsey walk out the door.

When Ramsey had driven off, Annharriet shuffled through the

reservations cards for a few moments, then called out Patricia's name.

"What is it?" Patricia replied from the next room.

"Can you come out here for a minute? And bring the housing chart with you, too, Sweetie."

"Sure."

Patricia joined Annharriet at the desk a few minutes later.

"I want to do a little juggling," Annharriet informed her.

"Love, we worked on the rooming for hours last night. Why do you want to change things now?"

"It's just a gut feel I have," Annharriet replied as she tapped a pencil on the desk top. "But I think Ramsey might benefit by having a different roommate."

"Well, you can't move her coworker out."

"I don't intend to. But I can move the third roommate — Carrie, the lesbian stripper from San Francisco — out. I don't think Ramsey Sears will learn very much about this place if she's bedding down in the same house with a stripper."

Patricia sighed. "I can't see that that matters."

"Well, Sweetie, you didn't talk with her for as long as I did."

"You're right about that. Then we've got to find someone else to move into Sage House. With ten houses, thirty women, and thirty beds, we're booked solid."

"Ah!" Annharriet stated as she glanced over a reservation card. "I think I have just the person."

Patricia read the reservation card over Annharriet's shoulder. "Love, I recall this woman. We decided to room her with the two other women who are also here for intensive therapy. Remember? These three women have therapeutic issues they want to work on while they're here. I don't think moving one of them in with Ramsey will be such a good — "

"Do you know what it will be?" Annharriet interrupted her.

"A roommate-from-hell situation?" Patricia grinned at her.

Annharriet lowered the card and stared at Patricia. "You know, Sweetie, I'll always rue the decision I made to let you take your teenage nieces on a camping trip for a weekend. You came back from that trip with a thousand mosquito bites, a bad case of indigestion from eating three s'mores in less than an hour, and the necessity to add 'from hell' to almost every situation we talk about."

Patricia tried to extinguish her smile as she shrugged her shoulders. "I happen to think it's a funny description."

"Apparently."

"Anyway, Love," Patricia said as she looked down at the card Annharriet was holding in her hand, "tell me what you think moving this woman in with Ramsey and Shane will accomplish."

"I think it will be the perfect challenge for Ramsey Sears."

Patricia's eyes widened. "Challenge? But Ramsey isn't here for a challenge. She's just here to write an article about us."

"I know. But I feel like this is the right thing to do. Let's give it a try, okay? What's the worst thing that could happen?"

Patricia shrugged her shoulders. "I don't know, Love. I have no idea what Ramsey's coworker is like, but if it were just Ramsey and this woman alone together, I'd say we might have the perfect female version of Felix and Oscar."

"Felix and Oscar?"

"Yeah. The Odd Couple."

"So what's wrong with that?"

"Well, Love, do you know how many times Oscar threatened to kill Felix?"

Woman *TO* Woman
M A G A Z I N E

September Issue

So what's in a name?

Do you know what my name, Ramsey, means? It means I had a mother who absolutely loved ancient Egyptian lore but who, for the life of her, couldn't pronounce the name of her favorite ruler correctly.

So she named me Ramsey instead of Ramses, for which I am eternally grateful.

And I, in showing her my gratitude, always call her Mom instead of Mummy.

From Ramsey Sear's column, September issue, *Woman to Woman.*

Chapter 8

An hour later, Ramsey sat cross-legged on her bed in Sage House with a notebook on her lap and wrote to Rita:

Hey, boss!

To bring you up to date on my goings-on (not that you asked, but I'm certain you're wondering about me all the time), I'm at Healing Hills, waiting for Shane to arrive, in the cabin where we'll be staying for the week. Our place is called Sage House, one of ten cabins on the property. It's designed for three people and consists of three rooms. There's a large bedroom with three double beds and a nightstand next to each bed, three chests of drawers, and track lighting above the beds for reading. There's a common area furnished with a sofa, coffee table, and upholstered chairs. There's also a large bathroom with both a shower stall and a bathtub, and there are two sinks with a wide counter between them in front of an oversize mirror. In addition, there are three ample closets, each containing a one-size-fits-all, colorful kimono — I guess for wearing when hanging out around the house.

When I first discovered that the house wasn't air conditioned, I thought it would be stifling inside. But the houses are nestled together in village-style and are surrounded by trees that shade the houses and protect them from the heat. In addition, there are windows in every room of the house and overhead fans to circulate the air. I've been in the house for awhile now, and I'm pretty comfortable.

Although I'm impressed by the health club facilities and the workout equipment I saw when I took myself on a quick tour earlier today, I'm not sold on the spiritual, therapeutic, or earthy crunchy aspects of this place. But I'm trying to keep an open mind; after all, the magazine's paying me to boldly go where not every lesbian has gone before.

But, Rita, is this place ever earthy crunchy! I can't have eggs and bacon for breakfast, but I can have goat yogurt. For lunch, I can't have a grilled cheese sandwich, unless it's made with goat cheese. For dinner, it's a cold fruit and vegetable salad plate with — you guessed it — goat yoghurt dressing. I may end up settling down with a goat after this is over! Well, I've always wanted a full-time nanny ...

Apparently no living creature is ever consumed here, but let me play devil's advocate for a moment. Aren't vegetables and fruits alive? I mean, has anyone ever asked a head of lettuce how it feels to have its roots pulled out of the ground and its leaves peeled off, or what it's like to be rudely tossed in the air or drowned in dressing? After this trip is over, boss, I'm seriously considering starting a new rights group: People for the Ethical Treatment of Fruits and Veggies. The charter of the group will be to protect the rights of fruits and vegetables everywhere. Our brochure will show gruesome pictures of broccoli being steamed to death, tons of tomatoes being led to slaughter in the spaghetti sauce vats at Ragu plants, and bushels of cabbages being shredded beyond recognition, all in the pursuit of making the perfect slaw or the tastiest 'kraut.

However, I guess I can give this place a week — or for as long as I can ration the stockpile of junkfood in the Wanderlust's kitchen-ette.

Anyway, I'll call you sometime soon so I can waste more of the magazine's money. Will I get to hear your melodious voice on the other end of the line? Perhaps so, unless you're tied up with Melissa (or, if you're _that_ kind of girl, _by_ Melissa).

R.

"Wah-wheeee! Wah-wheeee! Wah-wheeee!"

Ramsey slowly lifted an arm that she had flung over her eyes while she had napped in her bed, opened her eyes, and cautiously glanced around the bedroom in Sage House to discover the source of the strange noise that had awakened her.

"Wah-wheeee! Wah-wheeee! Wah-wheeee!"

Ramsey turned her body towards the sound, propped herself up on an elbow, and stared at a woman who sat cross-legged in the bed across from her. The petite, pale, plain-looking young woman, whose lifeless, shoulder-length hair hung limply around her face, had her eyes closed and was creating the strange sound by breathing in deeply through her nose, then blowing the air slowly out through pursed lips.

"Excuse me — " Ramsey began.

"PAHHHH!" the woman cried out suddenly as she abruptly thrust her hands out from her body.

Ramsey rolled her eyes to the ceiling and shook her head. "Let's hope *you're* in the wrong house," she muttered to the woman.

"PAHHHH!" the woman exclaimed again as she flung her hands out from her body.

"One more time?" Ramsey asked as she sat up and threw her legs over the side of the bed.

"PAHHHH!" the woman shouted.

"Thank you," Ramsey stated, then stood and leaned over the woman. "Excuse me?" she asked as she tapped the woman on the shoulder.

The woman jumped and gasped at Ramsey's touch. "My goodness, but you startled me!" she said as she drew back from Ramsey.

"My goodness, but you startled *me*!" Ramsey retorted.

"I thought you were asleep," the woman explained.

"You thought correctly," Ramsey replied. "I *was*."

"And I woke you, didn't I?" the woman sighed as she pulled her knees to her chest and hung her head.

"Yeah. But not right away. I think by the second pah, I was wide awake."

The woman looked up at her. "I'm so sorry. I really am. But, you see, I have asthma. Breathing exercises help me open up my breathing passages. My chest was very tight when I came in here. There must be something I'm allergic to in this house that triggered my attack."

"Possibly you're allergic to people who are napping."

"No, I don't think so."

"That was meant to be funny."

"Well, I'm sorry, but I don't find my allergies funny."

"Neither do I. Do your attacks occur during normal waking hours, or only when people are asleep?"

"Listen, I said I was sorry. But I felt like I couldn't breath. Breathing is fundamental, you know."

"I thought that was reading," Ramsey retorted.

"Huh?"

Ramsey shook her head. "Never mind." Then she crossed her arms over her chest. "I'm almost afraid to ask, but is this where you'll be staying for the week?"

"Sage House is where I've been assigned."

"Then I guess we'll have to make the most of being housemates. I'm Ramsey Sears."

"And I'm Katy Sunshine."

Ramsey placed her hands on her hips. "Listen, I'm trying to be friendly, okay?"

Katy peered up at Ramsey with a puzzled expression on her face. "So am I."

"Then what's your name?"

"My name is Katy Sunshine. And I'll thank you not to make any wisecracks about it."

Ramsey stared at Katy. "Your name is really Katy Sunshine?"

"Yes," Katy said sharply. "And you don't need to make any comments like, 'Gee, you must have a sunny disposition,' or 'Where were you yesterday when I wanted to go on a picnic?' or 'Why didn't your mother name you Lots-a?'"

Ramsey burst into laughter. "That last one's pretty funny. Lots-a Sunshine."

Katy sniffed. "*I* never thought it was funny."

Ramsey's smile faded as she noticed Katy's face. "No, I imagine you never have. I guess you wouldn't think being given the first name Sunny would be very funny either, would you?"

Katy stared at her. "Sunny Sunshine? Oh. That's a new one. How clever you are. I'm amazed no one has ever thought of that before."

Ramsey threw Katy a half-grin. "It appears you've mastered sarcasm pretty well."

Katy sighed. "Thank you. But when you've gone through as many years as I have enduring the comments and ridicule about my last name — "

"Oh, woman, give me a break!" Ramsey interrupted her. "Did you happen to catch my name? Ramsey. Sounds pretty close to the name of a species of mountain goat, doesn't it?" Ramsey paused for a moment. "I wonder if that's why I'm here," she muttered.

"Excuse me?"

Ramsey shook her head. "Nothing."

Katy pushed her lifeless hair away from her face, where it stayed for two seconds before it fell back. "Yeah-but, at least you could have been nicknamed Rambo."

"Not when I was growing up. Sylvester Stallone was probably just signing up for his first porn flick then. No, the kids in my school loved to call me Ram-a-Lamb and would make bleating noises whenever they saw me."

Katy reached a hand out to Ramsey. "Oh, you poor thing. That must have been so hard for you to endure. At least no one ever made sounds when they saw me."

Ramsey glared at Katy's hand. "Hard for me? Bullshit! Those were the kids I'd peg with water balloons. Even when I was young, I had a hell of an arm. I could toss a water balloon clear across a crowded school yard into a group of kids, and score a direct hit on the one kid I wanted to drench. Kids soon learned that if they wanted to bleat at me, then they'd have to deal with a wet head of hair for the rest of the day."

Katy scratched her cheek. "When I was young, kids'd put sunglasses on when they walked past me. That really hurt, you know."

"Why?" Ramsey said as she flopped back onto her bed. "They were only having fun with you."

"It's not nice to make fun of people. It hurts."

"Oh, for crying out loud, they were just kids. Hell, with my last name, Sears as in the department store — kids used to make fun of me all the time. You have to laugh along with them, ignore them, or retaliate. I chose to retaliate. That shut them up pretty quickly."

Katy's chin began to quiver. "I'd cry."

"That wasn't on my list of options."

"Well, that was *my* option."

"Why?"

Katy shrugged her shoulders. "I don't know. I guess because I cry whenever I feel hurt."

"Then you let some stupid kids get the better of you. You're not supposed to show people that they hurt you."

"Why not?"

Ramsey propped a pillow against the headboard of her bed and leaned back. "Because once they know how to get to you — like how to make you cry or how to make you angry — then they'll keep doing it again and again."

"They did," Katy responded. "The kids I went to school with never stopping making fun of me."

"See? You know, there's always one kid in school who gets picked on more than anyone else because that kid doesn't fight back, doesn't ignore the taunts and the laughter, or doesn't laugh along with the crowd."

"That was me," Katy said softly.

"Then you set yourself up, kid, and you kept yourself set up whenever you let them see you cry."

"But I didn't know what else to do!" Katy protested.

Ramsey sighed, tucked her arms behind her head, and closed her eyes. "What does it matter now? You're not a school kid anymore."

"Yeah-but, things like people making fun of my name still bother me."

Ramsey yawned. "Don't let it."

"But how do I — "

"Just don't let it." Ramsey yawned again. "Listen, I'm going to close my eyes for about a half hour. I'm still pretty tired."

"Oh. Okay."

Ramsey closed her eyes and sighed.

"Ramsey?"

"Umm?"

"Do you mind if I unpack while you sleep? If it'll bother you, I won't. But I think I can do it without being too noisy. If that's — "

"Katy," Ramsey broke in.

"What?"

"You're too noisy now. Just unpack and let me sleep."

"Ramsey? Ramsey?"

Ramsey felt a hand shake her shoulder, then drifted back to sleep.

"Ramsey?"

"What?" Ramsey muttered.

"It's been a half hour. Can we talk now?"

Ramsey forced her eyes open and was greeted by the sight of Katy's face. Ramsey groaned and asked in a gruff voice, "What do you want?"

"Can I talk to you?"

"I'm not awake yet."

"It's important."

Ramsey sighed, rolled onto her back, and slowly stretched her arms above her head.

"If you don't want to do this now, I'll understand," Katy stated.

Ramsey opened her eyes. "You just woke me up and told me you have to talk to me about something important. I'm awake. What do you want?"

"Could you come into the bathroom?"

"Why?"

"Well, I have to show you what I'm talking about in there."

Ramsey groaned again, then arose from the bed and stumbled behind Katy into the bathroom.

Katy flicked the overhead light on, throwing the room into a brilliant glare.

"Ugh!" Ramsey complained as she squinted her eyes.

"This is what I want to show you," Katy stated.

"What? That the lights in here are brighter than in the bedroom?"

"No. I wanted to show you the arrangement of my toiletries and medications."

"Why? Is this some sort of Sage House competitive event — toiletry and medication arrangements?"

"Ramsey, I feel that you're angry at me right now."

"Katy, I feel that you're being obscure right now. Can you please get to the point of why you had to wake me and why we're in the bathroom together?"

"Okay. It's very simple, really. I wanted you to recognize the difference between my toiletries and my medications in case I have an asthma attack in the middle of the night and I need your help to get my medicine for me."

"Katy, if you already know that you might have an attack in the middle of the night, then why don't you keep your medicine on your nightstand?"

"Because it needs to be in the bathroom."

"Why?"

"Because some medications need to be taken with water."

"Then why don't you keep a glass of water next to your bed?"

"Because I'm allergic to mold and dust, which often collect in the glass over the course of the night, creating a film on top of — "

"All right, all right," Ramsey cut into Katy's explanation, then glanced at the counter between the two sinks, half of which was cluttered with bottles, jars, vials, and plastic containers of varying sizes. Ramsey nodded her head in the direction of the counter. "I assume those with the prescription labels on them are medications. Could I possibly be right?"

"Yes."

"Good," Ramsey stated as she turned to walk out of the bathroom. "Now I hope you're reassured that I won't bring you a bottle of shampoo and a glass of water in the middle of the night."

"Wait! I need to tell you about each of the different medications —"

Ramsey whirled to face Katy. "No, you don't. I'm not here to be your nurse. I'm a reporter who decided to cover this ridiculous place, who is stuck here for a week, who hates health food, who thinks most everything here — aside from the workout equipment — is a waste of time, who has a roommate who — forgive me for saying this — seems to be a wee tad off the wall because she feels it's *my* responsibility to schlepp into the bathroom in the middle of the night to retrieve her pills — "

"Not just pills," Katy interrupted her. "I have inhalers and sprays, too."

Ramsey threw her hands in the air. "Of course you do."

"That's why I wanted to show them to you now so you — "

"Katy, if you're so debilitated from an asthma attack that you can't tell me whether to get you an inhaler or a spray or a bottle of pills, then you probably need an ambulance."

"Oh, God," Katy gasped as her eyes widened and she grabbed the edge of the counter with one of her hands. "An ambulance!"

Ramsey rolled her eyes. "For God's sake, woman, don't be so dramatic. Relax. No wonder you have asthma. You're too tense.

Look," Ramsey pointed to the counter. "You have your medications. The bathroom is no more than a dozen steps from your bed — "

"Actually, that's something else I need to talk to you about," Katy stated as she clasped her hands in front of her and rubbed them together.

Ramsey sighed. "What?"

"Well, your bed is closer to the bathroom than mine is, and I was wondering if you would — "

"You want me to move?"

"If it's not too much of — "

"I'll move! Anything else?"

"Well...uh...when are you going to put your toiletries out?"

Ramsey stared at Katy. "I don't put what you call *my toiletries out*. I've been living in a camper for weeks. I store my bathroom things — *my toiletries* — in a paper bag. So, don't worry, I won't hog more than my allotted counter space and my things — *my toiletries* — won't get mixed up with yours."

"Actually, those aren't my concerns. I need to know what products you use."

Ramsey sighed. "Katy, my bag is at the foot of my bed. Excuse me. *Your* bed. If you want to use anything, help yourself."

"That's not why I want to find out — "

"Then what is it, woman?" Ramsey exploded. "Why in hell does it take you so long to get to the point?"

"Okay. Okay," Katy said as she shifted nervously from one foot to the other. "Being asthmatic as I am — "

"Which has been hammered into my head until it's been indelibly printed on my brain," Ramsey broke in impatiently.

Katy clenched her fists by her sides. "That's why I can't say what I want! You keep interrupting me and making fun of me and getting me flustered. You know, I'm a very sensitive person, and I don't think you respect that."

Ramsey closed her eyes for a few moments, then opened them. "Katy, we're going to be spending seven days and six nights in this house together, which is not a terribly long period of time. If conversations like this continue — "

"Ramsey?" a voice called into Sage House at that moment.

Ramsey stopped talking, poked her head around the bathroom doorway, then cried out, "Shane!"

"Hey, girl!" Shane waved as she stepped through the doorway of the house with a broad smile.

Ramsey strode to the doorway, slapped Shane playfully on the arm, then stepped back from her tall colleague and asked, "What the hell are you wearing, woman? The latest in bondage fashion?"

Shane glanced down at her outfit. "What's wrong with what I'm wearing?"

"Your clothes are fine. But all these straps," Ramsey commented as she tugged on a strap, "just don't work."

Shane grinned. "Well, speaking of work, this *is* a working week, isn't it? So I have my a camera bag," she explained as she peeled one strap off a shoulder and dropped a black leather bag on the floor, "all my film containers and lenses," she said as she dropped a red vinyl pack next to her, "my flashes, light meters, and filters," she said as she shrugged a thick strap from her other shoulder, "and last, but not least," she proclaimed as she tipped her body forward, lifted a strap over her head, and grabbed hold of a long, tubular case, "my tripod!"

"Plan on taking some photos?" Ramsey joked.

"One or two," Shane smiled, then looked over Ramsey's shoulder and spied Katy, who was standing shyly in the bathroom doorway. Shane locked eyes with Ramsey. "I see you've wasted no time since you arrived."

Ramsey glanced over her shoulder, then emitted a short bark of laughter. "Believe me, Shane, it's not what you think."

"Isn't that what you always say?"

"Yes. But this time, it's the truth. This is our roommate, Shane. Her name is Katy Sunshine." Ramsey watched for Shane's reaction as a smile played on her lips.

Shane stepped past Ramsey and walked over to Katy. "What a

beautiful name. My name is Shane Sterns," Shane said as she extended her hand to Katy. "I'm the photographer for *Woman to Woman* magazine. I imagine Ramsey has already told you that we work together."

"Actually, Shane, my conversation with Katy never touched on such a mundane subject as work."

"Well, then, we'll all have lots to talk about," Shane responded. "Now, where do I sleep?"

Ramsey pointed to the bed in the middle of the room. "How about this one? Katy's in the bed near the bathroom, and I'm going to grab the bed next to the window."

"Fine with me," Shane agreed, then moved her bags out of the doorway and next to her bed. "Oh! Did you two hear a gong a few minutes ago? I heard it when I drove up."

"That must be the gong for the Happy Hour," Ramsey explained. "Appetizers and non-alcoholic beverages are served by the pool about this time every day."

"Then let's go!" Shane urged them. "I'm starved!"

"You may feel that way for rest of this week," Ramsey replied as she followed Shane to the door of the house.

Shane stopped at the doorstep. "Are you coming?" she asked Katy.

Katy pushed her hands deep into the pockets of her shorts and looked around the bedroom. "I think I'll stay and organize things a bit."

"Oh, leave it," Shane replied. "Come on with us."

"Maybe some other — "

"Come on, girl," Shane urged her.

"Well, if you don't mind — "

"For God's sake, just come on!" Ramsey snapped.

Shane turned and frowned at Ramsey. "Too much sex, Sears, or not enough?" she asked.

Ramsey inhaled deeply, then sighed. "A little bit of both, I guess," she muttered.

Shane shook her head, then turned her attention to Katy. "Come on, Katy. Let's go to Happy Hour. And you can ignore Ramsey if you'd like. I don't know if you've discovered it yet, but her bark is always worse than her bite ..."

ꙮ

As Ramsey waited for her Virgin Mary to be mixed at the poolside bar and half-listened to the conversation between two women who were standing next to her, her interest was suddenly aroused by their discussion about their roommate.

"I mean, what's the thrill of taking off your clothes in front of a bunch of women?" one of them was saying.

"Do you think she's going to subject us to her routine tonight when *we're* getting ready for bed?" the other asked. "Because if she does, I'm going to scream real loud. There's no way I want a woman like that in my house. Not that I'm prejudiced, mind you, but *she* goes overboard."

"I know," her companion agreed. "I can't imagine why they stuck her with us. We're here to work on some real serious issues. And there are other lezzies here for her to room with. Why us?"

"Look! She just took off her kimono. What a skimpy bikini she's wearing. That woman's an exhibitionist, that's for sure."

"Of course she is. She's got to be the center of attention wherever she goes. That's the stripper mentality. Remember the clothes we saw her unpack? Even *they* were flamboyant. A woman like her has got to make a statement all the time."

"I know. Oh! Look at her now! She's jumping up and down on the diving board so everyone can see how big her boobs are, so everyone can see them bounce!"

"I don't know if I can stand rooming with her for more than a day. How do you feel about asking the director if we can switch roommates?"

Ramsey stepped away from the bar to watch the woman on the

diving board stretch her arms back and then over her head, revealing the biggest set of breasts Ramsey had ever laid eyes on — outside of *Playboy* centerfolds. As the woman executed a perfect jackknife into the pool, Ramsey began to move towards the pool to watch the woman surface from her dive.

"Ramsey! Good to see you again!" Annharriet Lakota stepped in front of Ramsey and stopped her advance towards the pool.

"Oh, hi," Ramsey responded as she peered around Annharriet in an effort to catch a glimpse of the buxom diver.

"Ramsey, I'm glad you're here, because I wanted to speak with you about something," Annharriet said as she took Ramsey's elbow and guided her away from the pool to a deserted spot in a corner of the pool area.

Ramsey glanced over her shoulder as she was led away, lost sight of the pool, then turned to face Annharriet. "What do you want to talk to me about?"

"It's about a favor I need from you."

"Which is ... ?"

Annharriet scratched an eyebrow, then crossed her arms on her chest. "First, I have a confession to make. The woman in the pool right now — the one you were so taken with — is a stripper in a club in San Francisco. A lesbian club. Originally she was to room with you and Shane — "

"Then move her back!" Ramsey immediately responded.

"No. I moved her out for a reason."

"I sure hope it's a good one."

"It is, both for Carrie's sake and, I hope, for Katy's sake. That's the favor — "

Ramsey interrupted her. "About Katy, Annharriet — "

Annharriet cut Ramsey off. "Go easy on Katy, Ramsey. She's a fragile, needy woman who would benefit from your attention and support."

"I think she'd benefit from a lot more than that."

"Ramsey, I'd like to tell you a little bit about Katy so you might understand where she's coming from. Is that okay?"

Ramsey shrugged her shoulders.

"Good. As a baby she was placed for adoption, but had to be removed from her adoptive home because she was abused. She then spent years in numerous foster homes, some nice, but most not so nice, until she was seventeen. Then the state ended its obligation to her care. No foster home wanted to adopt her, so Katy became part of adult society at the age of seventeen, with no family and no financial support."

Ramsey listened to Annharriet, then asked, "So?"

Annharriet sighed. "Katy's here because she's trying to learn how to live instead of how to survive. Believe it or not, her meek exterior belies the strength she has inside. She needs to find out that she has that strength. Our staff will do all it can to help her in that process. But you, Ramsey, are the type of person Katy admires, the type of person Katy would like to be — independent, assertive, and successful. She could learn a great deal from you, if you let her, if you helped her. That's the favor I ask of you, that you — "

"No." Ramsey shook her head. "Annharriet, I can't help the woman. She drives me nuts. She's your reponsibility anyway, not mine."

Annharriet smiled at Ramsey. "I thought you'd say that."

"Then why did you bother going through this whole explanation?"

Annharriet sighed. "I had to try. For Katy's sake."

Ramsey rolled her eyes. "If you'll excuse me, I think I have a drink waiting for me at the bar. If you don't mind ...?"

Annharriet smiled and shook her head. "Not at all."

"Good." Ramsey walked away from Annharriet towards the pool, her eyes scanning the crowd.

Woman *TO* Woman
M A G A Z I N E

May Issue

The Lesbian Therapy Report
by A. Freuda Yerdreams

Imagine this scene. You're in a therapist's office, clutching a mug of coffee in one hand, balancing an ash tray on one knee while you light a fresh cigarette from your last, and running the sweaty palm of your free hand nervously up and down your jeans as you gradually sink lower and lower into the overstuffed couch across from the cool, detached, scarf-bedecked therapist, who has a pad of paper on her crossed legs and has just asked, "So ... why are you here?"

Sound familiar?

Most lesbians who go to therapy (and most lesbians do go to therapy) often have considerable difficulty identifying the issues that actually brought them into the offices of a therapist. To help these lesbians, a recent article in *The Field and Stream of Psychology Journal* reported that music can assist in the process of therapeutic issues identification because individuals most usually like particular songs not because the songs have a good beat and are easy to dance to, but because the message of the song taps into deep-rooted issues with which individuals are attempting to come to terms.

This phenomenon of the association between music and mental health is called Music Identification Field Therapy, or MIFT. MIFT has an eighty-nine percent success rate in issues identification; individuals who have identified a therapeutic issue because of a favorite song often comment, "Shit! So *that's* why I liked that song!"

To help those who are stumped when the therapist asks why fifty minutes of *her* time are being taken up, the article recommends that clients think of a song that's particularly appealing to them and ask, "What meaning does this song have for me in my life?"

The following list of well-known songs and their therapeutic messages are provided as catalysts for Music Identification Field Therapy, so you can get MIFTed the next time you're in your therapist's office!

— "Standing in the Shadows of Love" (fear of intimacy)

— "19th Nervous Breakdown" (coming out to the family issues)

— "Bette Davis Eyes" (mother issues)

— "Papa Don't Preach" (father issues)

— "You Can Call Me Al" (gender identification issues)

— "If I Could Turn Back Time" (childhood issues)

— "Don't Stop 'Til You Get Enough" (sex/love addiction issues)

— "Suspicious Minds" (trust issues)

— "Only You Know and I Know" (fear of outing issues)

— "Hurts So Good" (S/M issues)

— "50 Ways to Leave Your Lover" (fear of commitment issues)

—"It's the Same Old Song" (issues about repeating patterns of behavior)

— "Ball of Confusion" (bisexuality issues)

From Ramsey Sear's column, May issue, *Woman to Woman.*

Chapter 9

"Arrggghhh!" Ramsey screamed from the bathroom in Sage House two nights later. "I çan't stand my hair! That's it, I'm cutting it myself. No, wait. I'll do better than that. I'll shave it all off. Yeah. That way, it'll never get in my eyes again. A shaved head — that's not a bad concept. I can start a whole new trend, gather an entire following of lesbians who choose to have no hair. Bald lesbians, by choice. Sure. I can see it now. I, and other bald lesbians, will become part of a much larger group of bald gay men and women, a group of hairless homosexuals. We'll march in gay pride parades across the country, sporting political slogans atop our heads and tipping our heads at the most opportune times to reveal our sentiments. We'll — " Ramsey stopped in mid-monologue as she spied Shane and Katy's reflection in the mirror. The two stood side by side in the bathroom doorway, arms crossed, dressed in pajamas, watching Ramsey.

"Girl, what *is* your problem?" Shane demanded. "I was almost asleep, until I heard you shrieking."

"I was in the middle of my breathing exercises," Katy added.

"Sorry to interrupt such full lives, guys, but look at my hair," Ramsey moaned as she lifted handfuls of hair from both sides of her face, then let it drop. "See how it flops over my face? That's what it does — only ten times worse — when I'm running, when I'm working out on the exercise machines, when I'm — "

"Ramsey, we get the point," Shane broke in. "We both know what you've been doing for the past two days. All you've talked about, both day and night, is what a great running course you found, what your running time is, how many things you did on the health club stuff — "

"Repetitions," Ramsey cut in. "How many repetitions I did on the health club *machines*, not — "

"Who cares?" Shane threw her hands in the hair. "Katy and I both know what you've been doing, for how long you've been doing it, how great it feels — ad nauseam."

"So what are you trying to tell me, Shane?" Ramsey asked.

"Girl, even if you weren't bending our ears every time we run into you, we would be well aware of your workout schedule merely from the pile of laundry next to your bed. It's becoming a mountain and it smells like a gymnasium."

"Don't you love that smell?" Ramsey asked as she closed her eyes and took a deep breath.

"No," Shane replied.

"Ramsey, I think there's mold growing on some of your socks," Katy pointed out. "As you know, mold is one of the things that I'm aller — "

Ramsey opened her eyes and took a step towards Katy. "Don't say it! I told you not to say that word or the other word in my presence."

Katy's lips tightened, then she flung her hands on her hips and shouted, "Allergies! Asthma! Allergies! Asthma!"

Shane burst into laughter. "Atta girl, Katy! That's telling her."

"A fine friend you turned out to be," Ramsey muttered to Shane.

"A fine roommate you turned out to be," Shane imitated Ramsey's mutter back to her.

"What's wrong with me as a roommate?" Ramsey asked.

"What's wrong with you as a roommate is that you're *not* a roommate. You're only in the house to shower, change your clothes, or sleep. I haven't spent any time with you at all since I arrived, and the three of us haven't done one thing together here."

"Wait a minute!" Ramsey protested. "I've done a lot of things with you and Katy. I get up early every morning with you two."

"That's hardly a memorable time, Ramsey," Shane argued. "We're all just barely conscious then."

"Well, we go off on our walks together," Ramsey continued.

"No, Ramsey. *You* go off on your Mountain Goat walk while Katy and I go on The Break a Sweat."

"So?" Ramsey shrugged her shoulders. "You guys said The Mountain Goat was too strenuous."

"I know we did," Shane agreed. "But can't *you* go on a less strenuous walk so we can all go together?"

"No. I want something more challenging."

"Well, you could go on our walk with us, only you could walk backwards," Katy suggested.

Shane grinned. "There you go, Ramsey. A compromise so you still get a great workout and we get to spend time together as roommates."

"Wait a minute. I know what we do together. We eat breakfast together," Ramsey offered, ignoring the suggestion.

Shane nodded. "In principle, Ramsey, you do eat breakfast with us, which means you sit at our table and shovel food into your face. But your mind isn't with us. It's pondering ways to get Carrie the Stripper to eat breakfast with you."

"Preferably in bed," Ramsey grinned. "But anyway," she continued, losing her grin, "What's wrong with meeting new people while we're here? Don't you want to meet new people? I already know you, Shane. And Katy, well, I think we've taken our friendship as far as it'll go. So why shouldn't I meet new faces, have conversations with new people? I'm willing to bet Carrie would be a great person to talk to."

"As long as your topic is body talk," Katy quipped.

Ramsey stared at Katy. "That's the third quick retort from you in less than ten minutes. Who *are* you?"

Shane threw at arm across Katy's shoulders. "Ramsey, I'd like you to meet, Katy. Katy's your roommate."

"Yeah. I met a woman who called herself Katy when I first arrived. But this woman isn't her. I'm sure of it. That woman was timid and depressed and — "

"And she still is," Katy cut in. "But she — *I* — have been trying to have a better attitude. A more positive one." Katy paused. "I've been learning a lot about myself, Ramsey. I know I don't have much confidence in myself, so I'm trying to work on that. And I'm getting

up the courage to look things I've needed to look at for years, things
that — "

"Don't interest me," Ramsey broke in.

"Oh, cold, cold, cold," Shane muttered. "You are bitterly,
bitterly cold, Ramsey."

"Well, I'm sorry Shane, but — "

"No, you aren't! If you were sorry, you wouldn't make an
insensitive comment like that to Katy — "

"I didn't think it was insensitive," Ramsey shot back. "I was just
being honest."

"Didn't you ever take Tact 101 when you were in college,
Ramsey?" Shane asked.

Ramsey glared at Shane. "No. I took Advanced Honesty. Got
a problem with that?"

"I sure do. For one — "

"Hey, hey, you guys," Katy broke in. "What's going on? Why
are you so angry at each other?"

"I'm not angry!" Ramsey shouted.

"Neither am I!" Shane bellowed.

Katy shrugged her shoulders. "Okay. So maybe you're not
angry. You're pretty vocal, though. Why don't you both just say what
you have to say to each other in more civil tones? This shouting is
making me — "

"Don't say it," Ramsey quickly warned Katy.

"Don't say what?" Katy asked.

"Don't say that the shouting is making you asthmatic."

"Oh, for Pete's sake, Ramsey,   I was going to say that your
shouting is making me have a headache — is giving me an Excedrin
headache."

"Me, too," Shane agreed.

"Well," Ramsey said as she folded her arms across her chest, "if
it's any consolation, *I* have a headache, too. There. Does that make you
feel better about me as a roommate, Shane, that I can share a headache
with you and Katy?"

"Girl, what *is* your problem?"

"What is *your* problem?" Ramsey retorted.

"My problem," Shane began, "is that I've traveled halfway across the country, at your request, to come to this place to shoot the pix for the piece we're doing, and you haven't spent more than five minutes with me discussing what you want me to do. All you've said is, 'Take a ton of pictures.' Fine. I can do that. But I'm your friend, too, Ramsey, or at least I thought I was. You haven't seemed to want to spend any time with me, just talking or hanging out."

"That was good, Shane," Katy commented. "Very clear. Now, Ramsey, what do you have to say to what Shane just said?"

Ramsey stared at Katy. "Are you asking me to *share* ?" she mocked. "Gee, I'm a little rusty at this, but let's see what I can do, okay? Let me tell you, then, how I *feel*. My hair is really bugging me, big-time. We've already gone over that. I'm pretty bored with the whole atmosphere here because I basically don't believe in fifteen-sixteenths of the things that everyone else here is doing. I don't want needles stuck in me, I don't want to talk about my childhood, I don't want to chant at the moon, and I feel no desire to be embalmed like a mummy in sheets that smell like the inside of a van at Woodstock in the late sixties. I want to indulge myself in foods Healing Hills forbids and — "

"Ramsey," Shane cut in, "how in hell do you think you're going to write an article about this place if you don't experience at least some of what it has to offer?"

"Shane, I decided two hours after I arrived here that I wasn't going to write the article. I can't. I can't be objective. I want to ridicule everything here, from gorp to group meditation."

"Then why do you need me to — "

"Oh, the article will still be written. In between my workouts, I've been interviewing staff members and participants on tape. I sent the tapes to Bernice today. She and Justine will write a features article on Healing Hills — a cover-story article — and will use the pictures you've been taking."

"Oh," Shane replied.

"You know, in my opinion the only saving grace to this place is being able to work out. I can't stand this place. I really can't," Ramsey said as she lowered the toilet seat cover and sat down. "You guys have to understand that for weeks, I've been doing whatever I want to do, going wherever I want to go, eating whenever and whatever I want, and not worrying about money because the magazine's been covering all my expenses. What an arrangement, huh? I've had so much freedom that this place feels like a jail. I'm told when to get up, where to walk, what to eat and when to eat, when to go here, when to go there, what time to go to bed, etcetera, etcetera. Hell, I'm just waiting to be told when I can fart."

"When you're not in this house," Katy immediately suggested.

Ramsey looked at Katy, then grinned. "Believe me, woman, with the amount of beans I've eaten in the past two days, if I ever did let one rip in this house, no one would be able to light a match for hours."

Shane laughed. "Girl, I let one go last night when you and Katy were asleep that I thought burned a hole in my sheets!"

Ramsey caught Katy's eye and winked at her. "What do you mean, Shane, when Katy and I were asleep? *I* was awake. I heard that bean bomb you blasted in your bed. I thought we were under attack."

"I was awake, too," Katy admitted as she returned Ramsey's wink and looked at Shane with a serious expression on her face.

Shane groaned and slumped against the bathroom wall. "You heard it, too?"

Katy scratched her head. "Well, actually, I heard the first ten seconds or so of your symphony in F sharp."

"Very sharp," Ramsey added.

Katy nodded. "Then my ears started ringing and an oxygen mask dropped down over my bed — "

Ramsey slapped her legs and roared.

"Oh, shut up, you two!" Shane protested with a smile as she playfully pushed Katy's shoulder. "You did not hear me!"

"We didn't have to *hear* it," Ramsey gleefully explained. "But the minute you lifted your bedsheets — ow, woman! And you think *my* clothes smell like a gymnasium. I won't even tell you what your fart — "

"Okay, okay!" Shane cut her off. "I'm sorry I even mentioned it."

"I'm not," Katy replied. "Now Ramsey knows it wasn't me that laid the big one."

Ramsey tipped her head to Katy. "And Katy knows that I couldn't possibly smell any worse than a moldy pair of running socks."

"Next time Shane cuts one, Ramsey, I might ask you to toss me over one of those green socks of yours so I can block out the smell," Katy giggled.

"Will you guys knock it off!" Shane yelled.

Ramsey shrugged her shoulders. "Geez, Shane, I wish you'd make up your mind. Don't you want me to share roommate things with my roommates? I'm sharing the experience of your fart right now with my roommates, and you're getting mad at me."

"Girl, how did this whole discussion ever get started?"

"Ramsey started it," Katy pointed out. "She came into the bathroom and began screaming about her hair — "

"Which is still bugging me," Ramsey stated. "I don't know what to do. This cross-country trip happened so quickly that I missed my haircut appointment. My hair hasn't been this long in years. Look at it. I want to cut it all off."

Shane stepped across the bathroom, stood in front of Ramsey, and stared at her hair for a few moments.

"What?" Ramsey asked. "Do you think you can cut it?"

Shane shook her head. "I don't want to. And I don't think you should either. Grow it out for a little while. Pretty soon you'll be able to tie it back when you work out or go for a run."

"Pretty soon? Like in six months? Uh-uh," Ramsey protested. "Until then, I'm stuck with hair in my face."

"Not if you let me braid the sides," Shane suggested as she

grasped handfuls of hair on either side of Ramsey's face and pulled it back. "What do you think of that look, Katy?" Shane asked.

Katy walked over, stood next to Shane, and peered at Ramsey. "Very attractive, very soft around her face, and —"

Ramsey rolled her eyes skyward and stuck out her tongue.

"And particularly nice with that look," Katy finished.

"I don't know if I want braids," Ramsey stated. "Aren't they a little earthy crunchy?"

"Only if you stick a feather in them, walk around barefoot, and sing Bob Dylan songs," Shane grinned. "I'm giving you a variation of the tight braids you see a lot of black people wearing. I'll put a couple of beads in each to hold them together so they don't friz while you're on a run."

"Black people's braids, huh? So if I have these braids, will I start to like repeats of *Sanford and Son* and understand why Flip Wilson liked dressing up as a woman?" Ramsey asked.

Shane smiled. "Girl, black people have never understood Flip Wilson's fetish for female clothing."

"Who's Flip Wilson?" Katy asked.

Ramsey looked at Katy. "You don't know who Flip Wilson is?"

"Generation gap," Shane pointed out to Ramsey as she began separating the hair on one side of Ramsey's head into three strands. "Remember, girl, she's only twenty-three."

"Right," Ramsey replied. "A little older than a dyketeen."

Katy looked at Shane, then at Ramsey. "So?"

"So what?" Ramsey asked.

"So who was Flip Wilson?"

"You're too young," Ramsey stated.

"I'll tell you," Shane offered as she fussed over Ramsey's hair. "Flip Wilson is a black comedian who was popular in the seventies. He liked to dress up in drag to create a character he called Geraldine."

"Was he gay?" Katy asked.

"One wonders," Ramsey mused.

Katy watched Shane braid Ramsey's hair. "I wonder if braids

would look good on me," Katy said aloud.

Shane stopped working on Ramsey's hair and turned to look at Katy's hair. She tipped her head to one side, then said, "Sure they would. You have more hair to work with, too, which means I could put more beads in. I think braids on you would look very pretty."

"Could you do me next?" Katy asked.

Shane sighed. "I don't know about tonight, Katy. Ramsey's hair is going to take awhile, and it's late already."

Katy frowned for a second, then smiled. "What if you did Ramsey's and, at the same time, Ramsey did mine?"

"Ouch!" Ramsey cried out. "Do you have to pull so much, Shane? Or is torture a normal part of braiding?"

"Just trying to make 'em tight, girl, so they won't fall apart on you as you run." Shane twirled Ramsey's braid in her fingers, then asked, "Katy, would you hand me that bobby pin on the bathroom counter?"

Katy located the pin for Shane, who then pinned Ramsey's braid in place.

"Done?" Ramsey smiled.

"Not even half done," Shane answered.

"Oh."

"But Katy just came up with a great idea so all of us can be braided tonight. Come on," Shane said as she grabbed Ramsey's arm and Katy's arm and pulled them both into the bedroom. "Ramsey, I want you to sit on the bed first. I'll sit next to you. Katy, grab a chair and sit in front of us." Katy pulled a chair over to the bed, then sat down. "Good. Now, Ramsey, watch me make a braid on this side of Katy's head. See how I have one...two...three bunches of hair? Watch me weave them together. Now I want you to make a similar braid on the other side of Katy's head. You and I will do Katy's two braids, then Katy and I will do your two braids. Katy, you saw me doing Ramsey's braid in the bathroom. I want you to make a braid on this side of my head. I only have one braid."

"Why do we have two braids and you only have one?" Ramsey asked.

"Because I'm black and you're both white," Shane explained.

"But that doesn't tell us why we can't decide to have only one braid," Katy persisted.

"Oh, you can decide to have only one braid if you want," Shane stated. "But white women *always* have two braids. Black women either have one braid or a hundred braids. Never two."

"Well, how do you think I'd look with just one braid?" Katy asked Shane.

"You'd look like most white women who have only one braid," Shane responded. "You'd look like you were trying to be black."

"Well, I've always wanted to sing like Janet Jackson," Katy said.

"So has Michael," Ramsey quipped. "But I think you should stick with two braids, Katy. That way, you can maintain your wholesome image as an Anne of Green Gables lookalike."

"Anne of Green Gables?" Katy wrinkled her nose. "Ugh!"

Shane laughed. "You know, Katy, you *do* look like Anne of Green Gables. Whereas I, on the other hand, look like Tina Turner."

Katy stared at Shane. "You kinda do look like Tina."

Shane thrust an elbow into Ramsey's ribs and said, "See? I told you so."

"*That* was the wrong thing to say, Katy," Ramsey commented. "The staff at *Woman to Woman* has been trying for years to convince Shane that she doesn't even remotely resemble Tina."

"But she does!" Katy protested. "She has high cheekbones, like Tina, and the same length hair, and she's got long legs, like Tina — "

"And she's pushing forty and has a big mouth," Ramsey cut in.

"Okay, wiseguy," Shane said as she stopped braiding Katy's hair and turned to face Ramsey. "If Katy is going for the Anne of Green Gables look and I'm hopelessly striving for the Tina Turner look, what look could you possibly be trying to achieve?"

Ramsey beamed. "The best look of all, the look I do the best, the look that's the envy of every lesbian, the look — "

"The look that takes the longest time to describe," Shane interrupted her. "Just get to the point, will you?"

"The look I am trying to achieve, the look that I *will* achieve, is the look to end all looks. And this look, ladies, is the often copied, often envied, greatest look of all!"

"What is it?" Katy and Shane shouted in unison.

"Why, it's the Ramsey Sears look!"

Woman *TO* Woman
M A G A Z I N E

January Issue

Quote of the Week

(Heard at an under-25 rap group, in response to the discussion topic, "Dating a Bisexual Woman")

"I mean, you know, like, it's, I mean — REALLY — it's just all *too* too, if you know what I mean. I mean, I've gotta do what's right for me and she's gotta do what's right for her, but I mean, it's like, so confusing and like, then you don't know what to do or say and it's like, I've gotta ask myself, where's it goin' and what does it mean? I mean, that's the key. What does it mean? *What does it mean ?*

From Ramsey Sear's column, January issue, *Woman to Woman.*

Chapter 10

The next morning, Ramsey, Shane, and Katy jostled shoulder to shoulder to shoulder in front of the bathroom mirror after they had leaped out of their beds at the sound of the second morning gong, which signaled that they had less than five minutes to get ready for their morning walks.

"Say," Katy interrupted brushing her teeth as she looked at their reflections in the bathroom mirror. "With all of us in braids, we could easily be sisters."

Ramsey spit a mouthful of white foam into one of the sinks. "Of course, that would mean that you and I were adopted, right Katy?"

"Katy was adopted," Shane commented as she washed her face. "*You*, however, were created in a laboratory, somehow crawled out of your breaker, oozed out the laboratory door and into society, where my family rescued you from an uncertain future as a circus freak."

Ramsey rubbed her tongue across her teeth. "You just never let me forget my humble origins, do you, sister? Well, just remember this. You were probably an 'oops' to our mother and father while I, on the other hand, was carefully planned out and created."

Katy shrugged her shoulders. "Hell. Our being sisters was just a thought."

"Katy, I've decided to go on The Flat and Easy today," Shane announced as she shut the door to Sage House after Ramsey and Katy had walked out ahead of her. "I'm too pooped to break a sweat or even to politely perspire."

"Wimp," Ramsey commented.

"That's okay," Katy answered Shane. "I was thinking of doing The Mountain Goat with Ramsey anyway."

"You were?" Ramsey asked. "I don't know, Katy. The course is a little rough and — "

"I'm in good shape, Ramsey," Katy defended herself.

"I'm not saying you're not," Ramsey replied. "But I just don't want to be held back. See, I usually walk ahead of everyone else so I can go at my own pace."

"I'm not asking you to walk with me," Katy stated. "I'm just telling you that I'm going on the same walk you are. I know a couple of other people who are going on The Mountain Goat, so I'll hang out with them." Katy paused. "That is, if *you* don't mind."

"No," Ramsey replied. "Not at all."

"Say, where does that path go?" Ramsey asked Krista, the trail guide, as they stopped midway through the morning hike to allow the rest of the hikers to catch up to them. Krista shaded her eyes from the bright morning sun and peered down the path Ramsey was pointing to.

"That path loops about a half mile on a combination of sloped and descending terrain off this main path," Krista explained, "and then rejoins this one about a quarter mile beyond here. We were originally going to include that path when we were creating The Mountain Goat course, but discovered after a short time that it wasn't a stable hiking trail."

"Stable? What do you mean by that?" Ramsey asked.

"Well," Krista began as she wiped her brow with a scarlet bandana, "the path is greatly affected by changes in temperature and weather. If it rains, some of the path washes away. If it's dry for too long, the rocks and dirt tend to loosen up and the footing is unreliable. When we did include that path on the course for a short time, a few people took spills. Got their legs and arms scraped up pretty badly, sprained their wrists, or twisted ankles. We decided the extra challenge provided by the path wasn't worth the high risk of injury." Krista looked behind her on the main path and noticed that the majority of the group had nearly reached the stopping point. "Ready, then? Let's get going."

"Be right with you," Ramsey nodded as she stepped back off the path to allow hikers to pass her as she kneeled and laced her hiking boots. Ramsey stayed in a crouched position as the group of twenty women surged past her.

"Are you okay?" Ramsey heard Katy ask.

Ramsey looked up at her. "Huh? Yeah. Fine, fine. Listen, Katy, why don't you get going? You've got to help bring up the rear."

"I will. I just wanted to make sure you're okay."

"I'm okay. Get going."

"I will," Katy answered. "But why do you keep tying and untying your shoelaces?"

"Because I either tie them too tight or too loose. Now take off."

"Ramsey, why do you want to get rid of me? It's as if—" Katy's eyes suddenly widened as she spied the path next to Ramsey. "Ah-ha!" she exclaimed.

"Ah-ha what?" Ramsey asked.

"You're going down that path, aren't you?" Katy asked.

"What path?"

"You know what path I mean. The path next to you. The one that looks like the last living creature that ever walked safely on it *was* a mountain goat."

Ramsey stood and glanced over her shoulder. "Oh, that path. Yeah, well, I thought I might check it out."

"Ramsey!"

Ramsey quickly took a step towards Katy and lifted an index finger in the air. "Not a word, Katy. Not a word to anyone. Just catch up with the rest of the group. If anyone asks about me, just tell them I turned back because I felt light-headed."

"I will not!" Katy protested.

"Aw, come on. Why not?"

"Because I'm going on the path with you."

"No, you're not."

"Yes, I am."

"No, you're *not* ."

"Yes, I *am*. Ramsey, what if you hurt yourself?"

"Katy, *I* won't hurt myself. I'm an experienced hiker who's in four-star physical condition. If you come with me, well, you'll be the one to hurt yourself."

"I will not!" Katy protested.

"Katy, even if you don't hurt yourself, you won't be able to make the loop with your asthma. It's a half-mile long and rejoins this path only a quarter mile from here. That means you'd still have to complete the rest of the hike *I* can do it, Katy. You can't."

"I can too. I haven't had an attack since I started acupuncture. So if you don't let me go with you, I'm going to tell Krista."

Ramsey rolled her eyes. "God, you sound like a whiney kid sister. I knew we shouldn't have done these braids. This look-alike, sisterly stuff is making you act like you and I are members of some sort of braidy-bunch."

Katy folded her arms across her chest. "Either I go, or I tell. And that'll mean *you* can't go."

Ramsey glared at Katy. "Thank God I was an only child. Because if I had ever had a younger sister like you, I would've killed her."

Katy tapped her foot. "I go or I tell."

Ramsey threw her hands in the air. "Okay, okay. You win. Let's get a move on, though, before Krista misses us both."

"I told you it was too dangerous for you. I did. Didn't I say, the first time we had difficulty getting our footing, that you were going to get hurt? That this would be too much for you? Didn't I say that? Huh?"

"For God's sake, will you shut up!" Ramsey shouted at Katy, wincing in pain.

"And now you've sprained your ankle, you four-star, physical fitness, climb-every-mountain-ford-every-stream — "

"You know, Katy," Ramsey interrupted her, "I liked you much better when all you ever talked about was your asthma and your allergies. This therapy and no-preservative healing you've been doing —"

"It's holistic healing," Katy corrected her.

"Whatever. It's made you into Assertive-Woman-From-Hell."

"You know what your problem is, Ramsey? You don't like two things about this. First, you don't want to *admit* that you were wrong. Second, you don't like to be *told* that you were wrong."

"Are you finished with your psychoanalysis, Ms. Freud? Because at the rate my ankle is swelling, I'll need a shrink for my foot."

"Well, I told you not to take your shoe off."

"But I wanted to see what it looked like."

"So what does it look like?"

Ramsey shrugged her shoulders. "It looks like I twisted my ankle."

"Which is what I told you had probably happened before you insisted that your shoe had to come off. Now you won't be able to get it back on. And, with the heat and the injury, your ankle is going to keep swelling."

"Well, you're wrong about that," Ramsey insisted as she attempted to pull her hiking boot back on. After several attempts and with her eyes watering from pain, she stopped.

"Convinced?" Katy asked.

Ramsey didn't answer her.

"Fine. Sulk. But if you want my help, here's what I suggest we do. First, give me your bandana. I'd like to wrap it around your ankle like an Ace bandage."

Ramsey pulled a bandana out of her back pocket and handed it to Katy, who wrapped it tightly around Ramsey's ankle.

"Good," Katy nodded as she completed the job. "Now I'm going to wrap my sweatshirt around this thin piece of shale to hold it in place under your foot. That way, it'll function as the sole of a shoe so when you stand up, you won't place pressure right on your foot and won't feel the sharp stones and tree roots on the path when we start the hike back to camp."

Ramsey furrowed her brows. "You're not planning on going back to get help?"

Katy shook her head. "We can probably reach camp quicker together than if I went to get help and the help had to come back here. Also, Ramsey, the later it gets, the hotter you're going to get. You have no shelter from the sun and no water. You'll dehydrate or get sunstroke."

"But how will I walk? The path is too narrow for me to use you as a crutch."

"I know. I've thought of that already. I have a plan."

"I imagine you do," Ramsey mumbled.

"You know that viney shrub with all the trailing branches we've seen along the path? Well, those vines are as tough as twine. I thought I could cut a few. We could place them under your injured foot, then you could hold the ends like guide ropes. That way you could pull up on them and take some of the pressure off your injured foot when you walked."

"You mean use them like a kind of pulley system?" Ramsey asked.

Katy nodded her head. "Exactly. And we'll place some sticks between your foot and the vines to brace your foot. That will help cushion your foot when you pull up on the vines."

"Shit. That's pretty smart, Katy."

Katy shook her head. "I'll only be smart if it works. Let's try it first, okay?"

⊖⊖⊖

"So I said to Katy, you should have seen the mountain I climbed a couple of years back when — "

"Ramsey," Shane interrupted her. "I've heard that story a dozen times now."

"Oh. I guess the pain is radiating so badly to my head that it's impacting on my brain."

"Annharriet said it was only a sprain, my sure-footed friend," Shane declared with a grin.

"And with icing, elevation, and bedrest, like you're doing now, you'll probably be able to hobble around with only minimal pain and swelling in twenty-four hours. Isn't that great?"

"Great," Ramsey responded in a monotone.

"Girl, it could have been a lot worse."

"I know."

"It was your own damn fault for going on that trail."

"I know."

"If Katy hadn't insisted on going with you, things might have turned out very differently — and far worse."

"I know! I know!"

"Then why are you being such a grump?"

"Because."

"Care to elaborate?"

Ramsey frowned. "I was bored with this place before, but at least I had things I could do. Now I don't have anything to do for hours."

Shane patted Ramsey on the shoulder. "Well, maybe Katy and I can spend some time with you this afternoon instead of going to acupuncture and the yoga sessions we've signed up for."

Ramsey turned her head away from Shane. "No, that's okay. Go to your acupuncture and your yoga. They'll probably be a lot more exciting than spending time with your roommate, your roommate who is almost like a sister to you two ... "

An hour later, Ramsey was roused from a heated, fitful, pained sleep by a banging on the door of the house.

"Huh?" Ramsey pried her eyes open and lifted her head off the pillow. "Who's there?"

"Room service," Shane called out as she and Katy stumbled into the house, giggling, arms loaded with plain brown paper bags, and collapsed in Shane's bed.

"Room service?" Ramsey mumbled, then her eyes widened. "What's that smell?" she asked as she sniffed the air.

"Girl, I'm carrying a bag full of the greasiest fries and the rarest burgers, slathered in onions and cheese, this side of the Mississippi," Shane replied.

"You're kidding!" Ramsey exclaimed, then grabbed a bag Shane waved in front of her face. Ramsey ripped open the bag, stuck her face in, and breathed deeply. "What a smell!" She reached into the bag and pulled out some French fries. "For days, my body has been craving the four essential food groups — cooking oil, beef fat, melted cheese, and Coke syrup," she said, then stuffed the French fries in her mouth and moaned with pleasure.

"And," Katy announced as she tossed a bag onto Ramsey's lap, "we bought you a ton of candy, all carefully selected to remind you of the spiritual atmosphere here at Healing Hills. In that bag are Skybars, Mars, Milky Ways ... "

Ramsey laughed. "Look at all this food! I don't know where to begin. I could eat my fries. Or I could have my burger. Or I have my dessert first and — "

"Shut up and eat," Katy advised, "or Shane and I will eat it all up while you're trying to decide."

"Boy, does this ever remind me of when I was a kid," Ramsey said a half-hour later as she let a bite of chocolate melt in her mouth. She lay on her side, with her head propped on one hand.

"In what way?" Shane asked as she took a last swallow from a bottle of Coke, suppressed a belch, then leaned against a backpack she had propped against her bed as she sat on the floor.

"Well, sometimes I'd sneak a quarter from my Mom's purse and go to the corner drug store and buy five candy bars and eat them on my way to school," Ramsey explained. "Five candy bars for a quarter! Can you imagine that — only a nickel apiece. And they were even bigger than these. But if I couldn't sneak a quarter from my Mom, I'd go in the store anyway and rip off the candy bars."

"You'd shoplift?" Katy exclaimed as she sat cross-legged on Shane's bed. "Weren't you ever caught?"

Ramsey grinned. "Are you kidding? Never! The whole idea is to not get caught."

"I don't believe it," Katy stated as she shook her head. "I've been living in the same house with a juvenile delinquent."

"I stole something once," Shane spoke up.

"Not you, too," Katy moaned.

"Yeah? What?" Ramsey asked.

"A record album I wanted. I stuck it up under my shirt in the store, then walked out the door with it."

"You're kidding!" Katy exclaimed.

"What record was it?" Ramsey asked.

Shane shook her head. "I don't remember. I think it was some Supremes collection."

"I don't believe this!" Katy exclaimed. "And here I've respected you guys — "

"Put us up on a pedestal, huh, Katy?" Ramsey asked.

"Yeah. Kinda. But now — "

"Oh, for crying out loud, Katy, these things were no big deal," Ramsey cut her off. "We weren't criminals."

"Well, you stole candy and Shane stole an album. Stealing is criminal."

"We didn't knock off a bank," Shane clarified.

"No, but — "

"Come on, Katy, didn't you ever do anything like that when you were a kid?" Ramsey asked. "I know that was only a few years ago, but didn't you ever do something you shouldn't have? Something bad, Katy, *really bad*?"

"Never!"

"Never?" Shane asked.

"Never," Katy sniffed. "I was raised by lots of people, in lots of different homes, but I was always told not to take what wasn't mine and not to talk back to my elders and not to — "

"And not to have a good time," commented Ramsey. "Katy, no matter how or where you were raised, it sounds like you've been molded into the perfect child."

"I *was* the perfect child!" Katy said, a bit defensively. "I had to be!"

"You never smoked in the girls' room, did you, Katy?" Ramsey asked.

"I never smoked, period."

"And you never cut a class either?" Shane asked.

"I had perfect attendance. I even won an award for never missing a day of school."

"Now there's something you can put on your resume. Katy, don't you know that teachers like it when you miss school?" Ramsey asked.

"They do?"

"Of course they do. They get sick of seeing the same kids, day in and day out. When you're not there, they get a break."

"My teachers *loved* me," Katy proclaimed.

"I bet they did," Shane replied. "You probably washed the chalkboards and did all your homework on time — "

"And dotted all your 'i's and crossed your 't's," Ramsey continued.

"I had perfect penmanship," Katy stated.

"God, I hated classmates like you!" Ramsey exclaimed. "I bet you always had a hall pass in your hands whenever you walked the corridors, too."

"That was the rule," Katy emphasized. "And I didn't break the rules."

"Not even once?" Shane prodded her.

"Well...one time I got a...well...a detention," Katy almost whispered.

Ramsey's eyes widened. "Eewwww! Did you hear that, Shane? She got a detention!"

"It wasn't my fault!" Katy exclaimed defensively.

"Of course it wasn't. They never are," Ramsey laughed.

"But it wasn't!" Katy protested. "You see, I was in typing class my freshman year. I sat next to Maureen Beechy, the most popular girl in the senior class. She had the leads in all the school musicals. She could sing and dance better than anyone in the school."

"So what happened?" Shane asked.

"Well, we were learning the home-row keys. You know, a-s-d-f-g-h-j-k-l-semicolon."

"Huh?" Shane responded.

"That's typist's jargon, Shane. Kind of like what f-stops are to you," Ramsey replied.

"Oh."

"At any rate," Katy cut in, "Maureen started moving her feet in rhythm to her typing. I thought it was funny. So I started to laugh. The instructor looked in my direction and said, 'Miss Sunshine.' Which, of course, always made everyone burst into laughter. Then he said, 'Since you find the home row method so entertaining, I suggest that you stay after school today and practice it for another hour.'"

Ramsey shook her head. "Just think, Shane. We're living with a typing class rabble rouser!"

Shane and Ramsey burst into laughter.

"It's not funny!" Katy protested. "I was very, very upset over the whole thing. My foster parents grounded me for a whole week when they found out. And it wasn't even my fault."

Ramsey wiped the tears of laughter from her eyes. "Katy, if that's the only bad thing you've ever done in your life, then I wouldn't worry. You've obviously earned your angel wings. My wings, on the other hand, were clipped years ago."

Shane chuckled. "My older sister was the bad one in the family."

"What did she do?" Ramsey asked. "Fake taking a shower in gym class?"

Katy looked at Ramsey, her brow furrowed. "How do you do that?"

"You've never done that before?" Ramsey asked. "Hell, all you do is turn on the shower head, stick an arm under the water, then raise your arm above the shower stall when the teacher calls your name so she sees that you're wet."

"You're kidding!" Katy exclaimed. "No wonder everyone else was always done with their showers before I was."

Ramsey looked at Shane and rolled her eyes.

"So what about your bad sister?" Ramsey asked Shane.

Shane shrugged her shoulders. "She came home drunk one night."

"That was bad?" Ramsey asked. "If that was bad, then I was real, real, real, real bad. I got detentions, I cut classes, I got caught smoking in the girls' room umpteen times, and I was suspended from school for a week."

"How did they ever let you graduate?" Katy asked. "The administrators must have thought that you were not only a bad influence, but that there was no saving you at all."

Ramsey tipped her head to one side and grinned at Katy. "I was the most popular kid in my class. I graduated with honors. *And* I was voted the most likely to succeed."

"Oh," Katy replied.

"And just think, Katy," Shane grinned at her, "*you* got to save her life!"

Ramsey grinned at Katy. "And now we've corrupted you, too."

Katy narrowed her eyes at Ramsey. "What do you mean?"

"Who followed me onto a path where we weren't supposed to walk?"

"Yeah-but, that was be — "

"And who went off the grounds with me into town to purchase food that isn't allowed here?" Shane questioned her.

"Yeah-but, you said — "

"And who helped to eat the food that's forbidden to be consumed on these hallowed grounds?" Ramsey pursued.

"You can't prove that!" Katy protested.

"Oh, yes we can, can't we Ramsey?" Shane said, grinning at Ramsey.

Ramsey wiggled her eyebrows at Katy. "Ah, yes. Just a simple matter of tickling the poor woman for several minutes until her stomach heaves up its contents, at which point we'll be able to identify a large order of French fries, a burger — medium rare, no onions — two Skybars — oink, oink — "

Katy stood up from the bed and backed away from them. "Okay, okay. You've corrupted me. I'm no longer perfect Katy Sunshine."

Ramsey inhaled air loudly and placed a hand over her mouth. "Oh, horrors! What's that, you say? You're no longer Katy Without-a-Cloud-in-the-Sky? What does that mean?"

"That means she's Katy Partly Cloudy," Shane suggested with a grin.

"Uh-oh, Shane. She's getting mad. Looks like Katy Thundercloud's getting ready to burst."

"BOOM!" Katy yelled, then raced around the bedroom and leaped back and forth from her bed to Shane's, clapping her hands, and laughing as she cried out, "Katy Lightning! Katy Downpour! Katy Sleet! Katy Snow! Katy Blizzard! Katy Tornado! Katy Avalanche!" Then she fell back on her bed.

"Thank you for sharing that," Ramsey deadpanned as she stretched her arms above her head.

Katy sighed, then emitted a few weak chuckles as she rubbed

tears of laughter from the corners of her eyes.

"Hail, hail, to Katy, our all-weather friend," Shane said as she tossed a Mars bar onto Katy's bed.

"Katy Hailstone," Katy giggled as she unwrapped the candy bar and bit into it.

Katy:

Since you've never read my writing before (and hadn't even heard of me until Healing Hills — tch! tch! — post-teendykes such as yourself don't know what you've been missing by not knowing such an important lesbian role model as *moi*), here's an article I've written for you (and for the magazine), after you convinced me to participate this morning in an acupuncture session to alleviate the pain in my ankle.

For your information, my hurt ankle *does* feel better. But don't be too quick to say, "I told you so." My theory about acupuncture is this: *any* bodily part that has had needles jabbed into it for a half hour would speedily feel better once the needles were removed. So I guess you can't call me a "believer" yet!

—R.

A first hand report of a brief encounter with eastern medicine, or don't need to needle me no more

by
Rah-ja Ramsey

One of the forms of all natural, no-preservative healing that's quite popular is called acupuncture. Before undergoing my first acupuncture adventure, I had envisioned naked acupuncturees lying on uncomfortable boards, their bodies riddled with needles, similar in appearance to how a dog's face might look after it sniffed a porcupine.

I had also envisioned music playing in the background during this process. The melody would be reminiscent of the classic hit "Needles and Pins," but it would be performed with ancient chimes and flutes.

In a final vision, I imagined women dressed in flowing white robes singing or humming, in unison, a repetitious melody outside the acupuncture arena, something with long, drawn-out "ahs," "ha's," and "heys," which, if the women put them all together at a much quicker pace, might sound something like, "Ah-ha, hey-hey, let's all chant ... ah-ha, hey-hey, let's all chant ... "

But was I ever wrong!

First, relatively few needles are used; they're inserted very lightly on or just below the surface of the skin. The discomfort felt is minimal — akin to a mosquito's bite.

Second, the table where the acupunturee lies is padded and comfortable. Pillows are often placed under the head, behind the knees, or under other parts of the body that need cushioning and extra comfort.

Finally, the room is dimly lit or dark and is kept quiet and peaceful. Sometimes soothing music accompanies the acupuncture session. Or the medicinal herb moxa will be lit. Moxa burns with a heady smoke (which smells amazingly like pot) and creates a thick smoky atmosphere in the room.

Thus, in just one session, the preconceived ideas I had had about acupuncture were dispelled.

But when the acupuncturist asked me if I wanted to schedule another session, I declined. I told her that, contrary to my usual philosophy, once, in this case, *is* enough. And I left.

Why did I refuse? It's simple. During my acupuncture session, I lifted my head to see what I looked like with those needles in me.

I think I looked a bit like a giant who was felled by the swords from an army of tiny soldiers.

So will I ever do acupuncture again? Nope. You see, I'm the type of person who doesn't like to be pinned down — literally.

Chapter 11

"Don't you guys think you're pushing your luck?" Ramsey asked, limping behind Shane and followed by Katy, as the three women moved along a path edged with low brush that led to the secluded section of Healing Hills called The Mounds.

"What do you mean?" Shane asked.

"I mean, first you guys take advantage of me in a moment of weakness and get me to do an acupuncture session. Fine. Now you want me to get covered with mud — and not while wrestling some buxom babe — in a place called The Mounds, a name replete with sexual connotations."

"And, of course, you know them all," Shane cut in.

"Of course," Ramsey confirmed. "But the name also sounds suspiciously like a Peter Paul candy product. Which brings up the question: What if I don't like Mounds? What if I prefer Almond Joy? After all, sometimes you feel like a nut — "

"And sometimes you *are* a nut," Shane finished for her.

"I like Almond Joy," Katy stated.

"Well, there you go, Shane, two votes against Mounds," Ramsey said. "Let's turn back. I can go to the gym and lift weights or just sit in the whirlpool for awhile. I'm sure that'll be better for my ankle than this nature hike."

"I think we should keep going," Katy said. "After all, Ramsy, a mud bath will help bring down the swelling in your ankle."

"If that's the case, Dr. Sunshine," Ramsey called back over her shoulder, "then why can't I just give my foot a mud bath? The rest of my body isn't swollen."

"That's debatable," Shane cut in. "Some people think the appendage above your shoulders is."

"Very funny, Shane."

"Annharriet says a mud bath enhances your entire state of well-being," Katy stated. "She also says it'll hasten the healing process."

"Yeah, yeah," Ramsey grumbled, then bumped into Shane's back as Shane stopped walking on the path. "Don't you have brake lights, woman?" Ramsey complained as she grabbed Shane's arm to keep her balance.

"Sorry. But we're here," Shane whispered.

Ramsey rested her chin on Shane's shoulder. "Why are you whispering?"

"Because there's a woman in a full-length, flowing white robe standing in front of me who has a finger over her lips, like she's telling us to be quiet."

Ramsey looked over Shane's shoulder at the woman. "Maybe she's the Healing Hills librarian," Ramsey suggested to Shane.

"Karibu," the woman spoke in a soft, melodic voice.

"Kahreeboo?" Ramsey echoed, then howled in pain as Katy kicked her ankle.

"Sorry," Katy apologized as she threw Ramsey a weak smile. "I just wanted to get closer so I could see what's going on."

"At the moment, not much. Just a great deal of whispering," Ramsey explained.

"Hushhhh," the woman intoned.

"Sorry, but I just got my sore ankle kicked by Princess Grace here," Ramsey explained.

"Please keep your speaking to a minimum while you are in The Mounds," the woman smiled as she instructed Ramsey. "It helps to keep the atmosphere here pure."

Ramsey opened her mouth, then nodded at the woman and flashed her an okay sign created by a thumb and forefinger.

The woman nodded to Ramsey and Shane. "Karibu means welcome," the woman explained.

"Ah," Ramsey replied. "Then Karibu to you, too. Or thank you. Which is it?"

"Ramsey, shut up," Shane hissed at her.

The woman raised her arms and spread them out from her body. "Please move forward so you may all stand before me."

"Karibu," the woman repeated to Katy when Katy moved out from behind Ramsey and Shane and all three stood facing her. "I am Washita."

"Uh ... hi," Katy shyly replied.

"Well, now that we've been karibued," Ramsey said, "lead us to the mud, Washita."

Washita clapped her hands three times. A woman dressed in a sky-blue robe, carrying a pile of white cloth, suddenly appeared out of the middle of a clump of brush.

"Now that's a hell of a trick," Ramsey commented. "Where'd she come from?"

"Thank you, Marcia," Washita said as she took the pile of cloth from Marcia. Marcia bowed to Washita, then walked quickly back in to the brush, where she immediately disappeared.

Ramsey squinted her eyes. "I wonder if that's done with mirrors or something."

Washita smiled at Ramsey. "There is a simple explanation."

Ramsey stared at her, waiting for her to go on. "Which is?" Ramsey finally prompted her after several moments.

"It will be revealed to you soon."

Ramsey nodded. "Ah. A forthcoming revelation."

"Maybe she's not real," Katy whispered in Ramsey's ear.

"Who? Washita or Marcia?" Ramsey replied.

"Please," Washita interrupted Katy and Ramsey.

"Sorry," Katy apologized.

"These robes," Washita stated as she indicated the pile of cloth she held in her arms, "are for each of you to wear before your cleansing. You will put them on and then follow me," she instructed as she pointed to the area where Marcia had appeared and disappeared.

"And the three women were never seen again," Ramsey commented in a Boris Karloff imitation.

"Will you knock off the fun and games routine," Shane commented as she took one of the robes from Washita and began to put it on over her clothes.

"Naka!" Washita called out, shaking her head as she looked at Shane. "Please take off all your clothes. Then you may wear the robe. The robe is cleansed and may only come in contact with pure skin."

"Well, that eliminates you, Ramsey," Shane joked. "Your skin hasn't been pure in years."

Katy rewarded Shane's quip with a burst of giggles.

"Shane, will *you* knock off the fun and games routine!" Ramsey mimicked Shane, and then said, "You see, Washita, I'm here with a bunch of comediennes. Is there any chance that human sacrifices could be done while we're here? If so, I'd like to offer up these two," she nodded at Katy and Shane.

"Mesa, mesa," Washita replied.

"Does that mean yes?" Ramsey asked as she pulled her pants off.

"Naka. It means I have scolded you for making fun of ancient ways. Here it is not good to do so. Healing Hills is hallowed ground. The Spirits that reside here will be unhappy."

"Will you cool it?" Katy whispered frantically to Ramsey. "The last thing we need is an angry spirit."

"Oh, for crying out loud," Ramsey replied, then pulled her shirt over her head. "I've never heard of such a thing as an angry spirit, except one I've thrown up when I've had too much to drink." Ramsey donned her white robe, then stood facing Washita with her hands on her hips. "There. I'm pure."

"Danna," Washita pronounced as she looked at the three women standing before her in their white robes.

"Has she said anything yet in a language we've understood?" Ramsey muttered under her breath to Shane.

"Danna means good," Washita answered Ramsey.

"How'd you — ?" Ramsey began to say.

"I hear what you say, Woman Who Runs at the Mouth. My ears are sensitive," Washita explained.

Shane and Katy burst into laughter at Washita's nickname for Ramsey.

"Running Mouth," Katy giggled as she playfully punched Ramsey's arm. Ramsey opened her mouth to fire a comment at Katy, but Washita spoke.

"Now, let us go to The Mounds. Come." Washita beckoned to them, then turned and slowly walked towards a narrow path that sloped dramatically downhill from the grove where Marcia had appeared.

"So that's where that woman came from," Shane commented.

"Ah. The old trick-path routine. Fools 'em every time," Ramsey chuckled.

They followed Washita along the winding path edged by low bushes for several hundred yards and halted at an area where the bushes had been cleared. On the level ground, several small mounds of earth were piled next to long, narrow, shallow pools of muddy water.

"Hence, the name The Mounds," Shane nodded as she looked around her at the piles of earth.

"You are correct," Washita smiled at Shane. "Karibu to The Mounds, the site of cleansing mud baths, where you will receive physical purification and find the ultimate refreshment."

Ramsey hobbled up to one of the muddy, water-filled trenches and peered into it. "We're supposed to bathe in these?" she asked Washita.

"Not bathe in the sense that you know," Washita replied. "Here, you will *experience*."

Shane stepped closer to a trench. "I don't know. It looks pretty dirty to me."

Washita smiled. "It is pure soil," Washita replied. "The soil is clean. It has come from our planet. The water is pure spring water, taken from a mountain stream, the same mountain stream in which you will wash off the mud at the end of your purification."

"Well, soil is still dirt," Katy said as she wrinkled her nose.

Washita nodded. "Yes, soil is dirt. But here we prefer the word soil because soil is not necessarily dirty. That is how you are all viewing your upcoming baths. That will soon change. You see, you have been taught to think that dirt is unclean. You have been trained to wash this kind of dirt off. Yet you wear clothing made of synthetics and wash with cleansers created from chemical formulas. You believe that when you step out of a shower in the morning and put on your clothing, you are clean. But you are really unclean. To be truly clean, you must bathe in what the world was originally made of."

"And that's Grade A dirt — uh, soil — huh?" Ramsey asked.

"Well, I'm willing to give it a whirl," Shane piped up enthusiastically.

"Good for you, Shane," Ramsey replied. "Take my bath for me, too, will ya?"

"What do I do? Just step in here?" Shane asked as she wiggled a bare foot in one of the trenches of thick muddy water.

Washita placed her hands together in front of her in a prayer like pose, closed her eyes, and tipped her head to the sky.

"Uh-oh," Ramsey said. "That's not a good sign. Shane, step away from that water. If this woman has to pray before we get in these troughs, chances are we'll never get out alive."

Washita clapped her hands once. "You will please shed your robes, fold them neatly, and place them next to the Mound you select. Walk into the bath next to the Mound gently and carefully, then lie down full-length, with your head resting above the water on one end."

"Well I wouldn't put my head *below* the water," Ramsey muttered as she removed her robe, folded it, then stepped into a trench. The thick, liquid mud-water mixture made sucking sounds as she slowly tried to position herself in her trench.

"This feels weird," Ramsey commented.

"It's cool," Shane observed as she eased her way into her trench.

"This is the biggest mud pie I've ever played in," Katy giggled.

"Zutt! Zutt!" Washita called out sharply. "That means quiet. It is better not to talk. Quiet, inner contemplation aids the purification process."

"I think some of this mud is easing its way into inner comtemplation areas," Ramsey muttered.

"Zutt!"

"Sorry."

Washita clapped her hands together. "Now use your hands to pull the earth piled next to your trench into the water, to join with the mixture you lie in."

"Ah. Now we're going to bury ourselves alive," Ramsey observed. "Has Stephen King come by for any book ideas?"

Shane and Katy suppressed laughter as they scooped handfuls of soil into their trenches.

Washita raised her arms to the sky. "Now may the mountain waters and the healing earth remove from you the impurities of your lives. Lie in your trench until the sun shines brightly down upon you. Then remove yourself from your mud bath and lie down outside it while the sun bakes the mud to your skin. This ensures that the impurities of your life become part of the mud that surrounds your being."

Ramsey tilted her head back and looked up at the sky. "I don't see the sun yet."

"It'll probably be awhile," Shane answered her.

Washita spoke again. "Let your thoughts go where they will. Simply let yourself experience the peace and tranquility as you move towards a physically purer self." Then she clapped her hands twice and left The Mounds.

"Pssst! Ramsey!"

Ramsey opened her eyes, then closed them against the glare of the sun.

"Pssst! Shane!"

"Pssst! You sound like a flat tire, Katy," Ramsey mumbled as she spit muddy water out of her mouth. "I hate that when I sleep with my mouth open."

"You guys, look at the sun! We're supposed to get out now," Katy urged them.

"Okay, okay," Shane replied.

"Umphh!" Ramsey groaned as she struggled against the weight of the settled mud-water mixture. She gritted her teeth and pushed hard against the mud, exerting all her strength to free herself from the heavy liquid. Her success was accompanied by a loud, sucking sound. "Well, that sounded positively rude," Ramsey commented. "Is that what one of your bean blasts sounds like, Shane?"

Shane and Katy emerged from their trenches accompanied by similar sounds.

"And now, ladies and lesbians, The Fart Sisters!" Ramsey quipped.

Katy giggled and pointed to Ramsey. "You look like a swamp creature," she said to Ramsey.

"Why, thank you, Katy. It's not often that a girl gets such a nice compliment. And you look like an eclair with its insides squished out at the top."

Shane roared. "What do I look like, guys?" she asked.

Ramsey and Katy stared at Shane for a few moments.

"Well?" Shane asked.

"Are you thinking what I'm thinking?" Ramsey asked Katy.

"I don't know. What are you thinking?" Katy replied.

"Well, see how her braid is kind of sticking up at the top of her head? Like a swirly thing?"

Katy looked at Shane for a second, then smiled. "Oh, yeah. I do. That's cool. That makes her look just like a — "

Ramsey nodded her head. "I know. Just like a Hershey's kiss."

"Oh, I love to eat them!" Katy declared, then stared at Ramsey and Shane in confusion as the two women bent over with laughter. "What? What did I say?" Katy asked, then her eyes widened. "Ohhhh! I know what I ... but I didn't mean ... not that you're not ... oh, God! I'm so embarrassed!"

Ramsey and Shane continued to chuckle as the three women lay down on the ground in the sunshine as Washita had instructed them.

"You're pretty funny, Katy," Shane said.

"I agree," Ramsey said.

"I didn't mean what I said, you guys," Katy responded. "I mean, I meant what I said when I said that I liked to eat Hershey's kisses, because I do. I *really* like them. But I didn't mean ... well ... I *did* mean that Shane looked like a Hershey's kiss with all the mud on her, but I didn't mean that ... well ... that ...

"Katy, we know what you meant," Ramsey rescued her. "It's just that Shane and I are two dirty old ladies who — "

"Speak for yourself, Sears," Shane protested.

"I will Shane, but if you don't think you *are* a dirty old lady right now, covered with mud — "

"Okay, okay, I admit it," Shane muttered. "I'm dirty. I'm older than Katy."

"Everybody's older than Katy," Ramsey added.

"So, I'm a dirty old lady," Shane finished.

"See? That wasn't so hard, was it?" Ramsey declared.

"I guess not. But if *we're* dirty old ladies, Ramsey, then what is Katy?" Shane asked her.

"Katy is a dirty young letch," Ramsey grinned.

"A what?" Katy cried out.

"A dirty young letch," Ramsey repeated. "Of course, you didn't start out that way. Nope. It hasn't been easy, day after day, molding you, shaping you, influencing you, and exhorting you to change your ways — for the worse. But now, all that hard work has paid off. Your pseudo-innocent comment about eating a member of the female species makes me pleased to report that you're well on your way to becoming a dirty old lady just like Shane and myself."

"I had a different set of goals in mind before I came here," Katy commented.

"That was fairly obvious from the moment I met you," Ramsey retorted.

"You mean we've corrupted Katy?" Shane asked Ramsey.

"I'm afraid so."

"How terrible of us."

"Perhaps. But, you know, Shane, I like her a whole lot better this way," Ramsey declared. "She's more—I don't know —earthy, don't you think?"

"Yes, I do," Shane agreed. "But I think we're *all* pretty earthy right now."

"Earthy — and crunchy," Katy added as she waved her arms in the air above her, flinging chunks of dried mud off her body. "See?"

"Hey!" Ramsey protested as a chunk hit her leg.

"Sorry."

Ramsey quickly flung her arm in the air, in Katy's direction, loosening several chunks of mud in the process, which showered both Katy and Shane.

"Ramsey!" Shane yelled as she propped herself up on an elbow, ducking pellets of dried mud that Ramsey and Katy were flinging at each other. She pried a chunk of mud from her thigh, and cocked her arm to fire it at Ramsey.

"LA DA MIDI!" Washita's voice shouted as she clapped her hands several times in succession.

The three women stopped their mud flinging at the sound of Washita's voice, then squirmed uneasily as Washita stood for several moments and stared at them.

"You will arise and follow Marcia," Washita finally spoke in an even voice. "She will lead you to the cleasing waters, where you will wash. You will then return to your house. Washita does not want to see any of you in The Mounds again."

Ramsey, Shane, and Katy slowly arose to their feet, then followed Marcia to another clearing, where there was a clear pool of chilling, mountain spring water. They quickly rinsed the mud from their bodies, dressed in their clothes that Marcia had brought to them, and followed her as she led them to the path that returned them to the main grounds of Healing Hills.

Annharriet was standing on the porch of the office as they walked by. The three noticed her, then looked away and picked up their pace.

"Not so fast, ladies," Annharriet called out to them, stopping them in their tracks. "I'd like a word with you."

"Shit," Shane muttered under her breath.

"Oh, God, we're in trouble now," Katy whined as she slowly followed Ramsey and Shane to the steps of the office building.

"What's the worst she can do?" Ramsey whispered to Shane and Katy. "Kick us out? We leave tomorrow morning anyway."

"Ladies, I hear your time at The Mounds was a little different from what Washita had intended," Annharriet began as the three stood before her on the porch.

"News travels fast," Shane commented. "We just left Washita not three minutes ago. How do you know — ?"

"Washita probably teleported here ahead of us," Ramsey quipped. Annharriet laughed.

Ramsey furrowed her eyebrows and glanced at Annharriet. "You think that's funny?" Ramsey asked.

"Yes, I do. Even though Washita's the most earnest staff member I have, she can be far too serious, far too intense. She needs to lighten up a bit. I've been telling her that for months. But now, thanks to you folks, I think she has finally learned."

"What do you mean?" Shane asked.

Annharriet grinned. "Well, Washita just told me that it was all she could do not to burst into laughter at some of the lines you folks were throwing back and forth when she greeted you."

"Really?" Katy asked. "I thought she was mad at us. She kept telling us not to talk, but we went on talking anyway."

"And she didn't laugh once," Shane observed.

Annharriet shook her head. "Washita wouldn't. She has incredible self control."

"She also seems like she has a stick up her — " Ramsey began.

"Exactly," Annharriet agreed. "But she was so entertained by you three that after she got you settled into your mud baths, she parked herself behind some shrubbery and listened and watched. She told me she not only found your comments hilarious, but also liked the mud fight you had at the end. She came up with the idea of combining her mud baths with play therapy."

Ramsey grimaced. "Play therapy? Is that where you *have* to share your toys?"

Annharriet grinned. "Ramsey, you *are* a very entertaining woman."

"If you think my stand-up comedy is good, wait until you see my song and dance routine," Ramsey joked.

Shane rolled her eyes. "Annharriet, do you know why Ramsey is thousands of miles away from the office where she works? Because we don't think she's entertaining."

Annharriet shrugged her shoulders. "Perhaps if she was around me forty hours a week, forty-eight weeks a year, I might feel the same way. But I don't, nor does Washita."

"Nor do I," Katy commented. "You've been a neat roommate, Ramsey. So have you, Shane. I don't know how it worked out that all three of us got together, but I'm glad it did."

♡♡♡

"And you thought they'd be roommates from hell," Annharriet teased Patricia as they snuggled in bed late that night.

Patricia yawned. "Had all the makings of it, love."

"Well, it didn't happen, did it? And do you know that Carrie and her roommates have become best friends?"

Patricia shook her head. "I don't know how you do it, woman. You have this knack of bringing people together."

"Starting with you and me ... " Annharriet sighed as she nuzzled contentedly against Patricia's neck and fell asleep.

MEMO

TO: Rita Hayes
FM: Ramsey "Soybean" Sears
RE: A beginner's dictionary to all-natural foods, a new column
idea.

Alfalfa sprouts: Hairlike vegetable growths, used as sandwich and salad fillers, which *sprout* from the mouth when eaten, making one resemble a grazing cow.

All-natural: Containing no tasty chemicals, mouth-watering preservatives, or lip-smacking fillers.

Beans: Gas-producing protein tablets.

Bee pollen: Stuff collected by honeybees from every known allergy-producing weed.

Bran: Nature's laxative, in muffin form.

Carob: A pseudo-chocolate that looks like chocolate, smells like chocolate, but tastes like house dust.

Cucumber: A phallic vegetable with a nickname that not surprisingly rhymes with puke.

Fasting: Meditating on the idea of food.

Goat milk: A substitute for cow milk that tastes like water goats have bathed in.

Grains: Food for farm animals which, when consumed by humans, can result in such side effects as bleating, neighing, ground pawing, and a strong desire to graze.

Granola: Chopped pine tree parts.

Health food nut: A person who is totally unaware of the aphrodisiac qualities of chocolate, the healing powers of a bowl of Häagen Dazs ice cream, and the fact that things really do go better with Coke.

Hummus: A garlic and mashed bean dip that even a potato chip won't dive into.

Lentil: Barbara Streisand's favorite bean.

Macrobiotics: A strict, whole-grain diet designed and enforced by Catholic school nuns.

Mineral water: The soda pop for health food nuts.

Mushrooms: Tiny, dirty bits of rubber that grow in manure in dark places.

Oatmeal: The main component of kindergarten paste; with raisins added, it becomes edible kindergarten paste.

Okra: Sounds like the first name of the television talk show host, but not nearly as interesting.

Rice: A grain that resembles small, wingless parasites and sounds suspiciously like lice.

Shallot: An herb that sounds like a romantic heroine but is — alas — only an onion.

Soy milk: Liquid from squeezed soybeans that tastes like a street puddle.

Tabbouleh: A Middle Eastern appetizer, served by "I Dream of" Jeannie to her master, Major Anthony Nelson, his friend Roger Healey, and Dr. and Mrs. Bellows, before an evening of madcap adventures. 7:00 (R).

Tofu: What Little Miss Muffet left on her tuffet when the spider frightened her away.

Trail mix: A concoction of nuts, dates, carob chips, granola, and raisins, so named for the trail of crumbs it leaves behind after eating.

Vegetable: A term used to describe the catatonic state of those who subsist on a diet of plants.

Chapter 12

"Hey! Wake up in there! Long-distance call!" a woman's voice shouted through the screen door into the nighttime darkness of Sage House, followed by pounding on the door frame.

"All right, all right," Shane mumbled as she threw the sheet off her bed and stumbled to the door. "What's the matter?" she asked as she squinted at the woman on the other side of the screen.

"Is Ramsey Sears in there?" the woman asked.

"Asleep," Shane responded.

"Well, wake her up. She has a long-distance call. From someone named Rita."

Shane turned away from the door. "Yo! Ramsey. There's a call for — "

"I heard! I heard!" Ramsey interrupted her as she leaped out of bed, howled in pain as she put weight on her sore ankle — muttered, "Well, the mud bath obviously did my ankle a world of good" — then limped to the door. "Where's the phone?" she asked the woman.

"Office. Follow me."

Ramsey opened the screen door and fell in behind the woman. "What time is it?" she asked as she hobbled, barefoot, on the path to the office building.

"Past midnight."

"Rita's up late," Ramsey thought aloud as she followed the woman up the stairs and into the office.

"There," the woman pointed to the telephone receiver on the desk. "Just turn out the lights when you're done, okay?"

"Sure," Ramsey nodded as she picked up the phone and hoisted herself up on the bar-type stool behind the desk. "Boss?"

"Where the hell were you, Ramsey? I've been holding for an eternity."

"Boss, this isn't the Sheraton. We don't have in-room phones or room service or even those cute little bottles of shampoo and hair conditioner. I'm in the great outdoors here. It takes time to get from one place to another."

"Well, at least you could have jogged to the phone. You don't even sound out of breath."

"How's this?" Ramsey panted rapidly into the phone, then stopped and closed her eyes. "Whoa! I think I'm hyperventilating." Then she shook her head and opened her eyes. "There. Anyway, boss, I don't usually jog after midnight. That's what time it is here, you know. It's twelve-twenty, to be exact."

"Why, that's strange," Rita replied. "It's one-twenty here. Was there a spring forward, fall back thingy I forgot?"

Ramsey sighed. "Boss, Texas is in a different time zone."

"Just Texas?"

Ramsey raised her eyes to the ceiling. "No, Boss, not just Texas. All the central states are on the same — why are we talking about time zones at this hour of the night ... uh, morning?"

"I have no idea. Perhaps I should tell you why I called."

"Perhaps. Or we can play twenty questions. I can try to guess — "

"How quickly can you get to San Francisco?" Rita cut in.

"By driving?" Ramsey responded.

Rita sighed audibly. "What other way is there?" she replied tersely.

"My, aren't we snappy? And I'm the one who was woken up. I was asking because there's an airport a couple of hours from here. I can be in San Francisco in only a few hours if I fly. Driving will take a lot more time."

"How much more time?"

Ramsey expelled air. "Well, to get to California from here, I have to cross New Mexico and Arizona. Then I have to drive up from southern California, through Los Angeles, to San Francisco."

"How long will that take?" Rita pursued.

"That depends. If I make the stops I had planned for the maga — "

"No. I don't want you to stop," Rita cut in.

"But only two days ago I scheduled interviews with female strippers at a lesbian bar in Albuquerque called Top of the Bottom. And it took me hours to contact the manager of an S/M rock group called Nasty Girls that's gaining notoriety from the songs they write and perform about cruise bar bathroom liaisons, group sex, leath — "

"Getting to San Francisco is more important," Rita interrupted her.

"Why?"

"Because I need you to meet me there."

"Rita!" Ramsey feigned a romantic gasp. "You *need* me?"

"Just tell me how quickly you can get to San Francisco with only minimal stops," Rita ignored her.

"Do minimal stops include just gas, only meals and gas, or meals, gas and bathroom facilities? I'd prefer the third choice be — "

"Ramsey!" Rita shouted. "Will you stop being such a pain in the ass and just give me an answer?"

"Boss, I'm nowhere near your ass."

"Ramsey!"

"Okay, okay." Ramsey rubbed her forehead. "Now the question is, how long will it take me to drive to San Francisco from here? This is like that math problem that always used to stump me, the one about one train leaving the station at — "

"Do you have a map in front of you?" Rita broke in.

"No. Why would I take a map with me to answer the phone in the middle of the night? I'm trying to estimate the distances."

"Well, it's three hundred fifty miles across New Mexico and three hundred thirty-five across Arizona. The distance between Los Angeles and San Francisco is — "

"Rita, do you have a map in front of *you*?"

"Yes. A Rand McNally road atlas."

Ramsey sighed. "Then why are *you* asking me how long it'll take to drive to San Francisco? Why don't you *tell* me?"

"Because I don't know how many hours you want to drive in a

day."

"Neither do I. First tell me the total distance from here to San Francisco."

"About twelve hundred miles."

Ramsey whistled. "Give or take a few miles, huh?"

"I guess," Rita replied. "So how many hours do you think you can drive in a day?"

"Not more than six, because stops add another hour or so. That makes for a long day. Plus, you get a little loopy after staring at the road for too many hours."

"How fast do you drive?" Rita asked.

"The Wanderlust isn't like your Mercedes, Rita, which you drive at Mach three."

"I do not speed!"

"How many tickets have you gotten in the past two years, Boss?"

"They were out to get me."

"Of course they were. If you drive the same route at the same excessive speed every day at the same time, they *will* look for you. And they'll find you. I keep telling you to get a radar detector, since you insist on air drying your hair at ninety miles an hour."

"I only went ninety once."

"And ninety-one once, too, huh?"

"I never went over ninety-three."

"Well, let me inform you that Wanderlust hums along — and quite contentedly, I might add — at an even six-oh."

"Sixty? That's it?" Rita exclaimed.

"Rita, that's the legal speed limit."

"But they only say that to give you a rough idea. You've got some leeway with that."

Ramsey laughed. "Rita, you know those metal signs with a big fifty-five painted on them? Those weren't erected just to give motorists a rough idea. That *is* the idea — fifty-five. As it is, I'm going sixty."

"Whoa! Slow down! You're moving too fast for me," Rita protested sarcastically.

"I'll tell you what, Boss. For my next trip you can lend me your Mercedes and a video camera, and I'll film my cross-country travels from the driver's seat while I zip along at ninety miles an hour. It'll take me a week to go round-trip. But for right now, this trip is going to continue to proceed at an even six-oh. Anyway, driving over sixty in the camper burns up too much fuel, which means I would need more time for stops."

"Okay, okay," Rita agreed impatiently. "So if you drive six hours a day at sixty miles an hour, you can cross New Mexico and Arizona — each in a day — then take two days to travel through California. That means you'll arrive in San Francisco in four days. Great! That'll work out perfectly!"

Ramsey shook her head. "It'll be hell, but if you really want me to do it, I will. But why do you need me in San Francisco so quickly?"

"For business. It was either you or Shane."

"Why don't you send Shane? I'm putting her on a plane tomorrow ... uh, today. She can fly out and meet you."

"I won't be there for another few days. That's why it'll work out better if you come instead. Another consideration is, what would you do with the Wanderlust? And I need someone to run the office — Shane can handle that — because we'll be staying in San Francisco for at least a week."

"*We'll* be staying in San Francisco? Who's the we?"

"You and me and Melissa."

"Melissa? Why is she coming along?"

"Because she and I are making this trip together."

"Then, Rita, you don't need me. You and Melissa — "

"Ramsey, I think you have my relationship with Melissa all wrong."

"So set me right. Tell me what's going on. Is she moving in with you?"

"Is she what?" Rita exclaimed. "Where did you ever hear a silly thing like that?"

"From common, ordinary, office gossip, Rita. You might be

interested to know that I'm not the only one who's curious about you and Melissa."

"Well, it's not *me and Melissa*. It's not like that at all."

"Then what's it like?"

"I can't tell you anything about it yet."

Ramsey sighed. "Then the rumors about *you and Melissa* will persist. 'Are they an item?' people will continue to ask. 'Is Melissa moving in with Rita?' 'Why are Rita and Melissa going to San Francisco together for a week?' 'How long before — '"

"Well, I'd rather have harmless rumors like that than blow this deal."

"What deal?"

"Shit! I wasn't supposed to tell anybody anything."

"You haven't."

"Good."

"But why? Why can't you say anything to me about a deal?"

"Because Melissa said so."

"If Melissa told you to jump off a bridge right now, would you?"

Rita didn't respond.

"Would you?" Ramsey persisted.

"I was thinking."

"I can't believe you'd have to think — "

"Yes, Ramsey," Rita broke in. "I guess I might jump off a bridge right now if Melissa told me to. What she tells me is that important."

Ramsey sighed. "What *is* this woman to you, Rita?" she asked.

"You'll find out when you meet us in San Francisco. In four days, right?"

"Right," Ramsey responded in a monotone.

"Oh, and Ramsey?"

"Yeah?"

"I like the column idea, 'I'm Just Wondering.' How about sending me some more entries?"

"Yeah, okay." Ramsey lowered the receiver and placed it in its cradle. Then she stood up, stretched, and turned out the lights.

"I'm just wondering, Rita," she said as she walked towards the door, "what's going on between you and Melissa?"

"Is everything okay?" Shane whispered when she heard Ramsey tiptoe back into Sage House.

Ramsey sighed as she sat on the edge of her bed. "Yeah, I guess. I'm supposed to drive to San Francisco to meet Rita in four days."

"Four days? Isn't it over a thousand miles from here to there?"

"Twelve hundred."

"Then girl, you've got a hell of a lot of driving to do."

"Tell me about it. But you don't get off that easily either, Shane."

"What do you mean?"

"When you get back to the office, you'll be running the magazine as soon as Rita leaves — that's in four days — because she'll be in San Francisco for at least a week."

"At least a week? How'm I supposed to handle my own department, too?"

"Don't ask me. I'm only the hired help. The hired, soon to be quite tired help."

"And soon to be sick of driving," Shane pointed out. "Would you rather Katy and I took a taxi to the airport, instead of you driving us?"

"Nah. The airport's on my way."

"Are you sure?"

"Yeah."

"So what're you supposed to do with Rita in San Francisco?

"Correction. With Rita *and* Melissa."

"Melissa? Why?"

"Rita won't say, Shane. She won't tell me — A, why Melissa is going to San Francisco with her — B, what's going on between her and Melissa, like are they an item or what — C, why I'm meeting them in San Francisco — D, why I have to be there so soon — or E, what I'll be doing once I get there."

"Why won't she tell you anything?"

"Because Melissa told her not to."

Shane shook her head. "Girl, this makes no sense."

"I know. And listen to this. The one thing Rita was definite about in our conversation was that she would jump off a bridge if Melissa told her to."

"She didn't say that!" Shane exclaimed.

"Did too. Heard it with my own ears."

"Why would she say a thing like that? Rita is the most strong-willed, independent-minded — "

"Stubborn, pigheaded woman we know," Ramsey finished. "But it appears someone changed that." Ramsey sighed. "Shane, now do you believe me when I say Rita has fallen head over heels for this woman?"

Shane shook her head. "No, I won't."

"But I told you before what Justine and Bernice told me, about Melissa moving in with her. And I just told you that she and Melissa are going to San Francisco together for a week and that Rita said she'd jump off a bridge for — "

"Ramsey, I'll believe it when I hear Rita tell me Melissa's moving in with her and that her involvement with Melissa is romantic. Until then, I'm not going to jump to any conclusions. And neither should you. We're Rita's closest friends. When she has something to tell us, she will."

"Well, maybe *I* don't want to hear it when she finally does decide to tell us," Ramsey muttered as she lay back in bed.

"What about playing some games to pass the time?" Ramsey suggested after an hour of sporadic conversation with Shane and Katy.

"Sounds good to me," Shane responded from the passenger seat. "I'm a little more awake than I was when we left after breakfast.

"Me, too," Katy agreed as she edged forward on the kitchen

booth seat in the Wanderlust and leaned in between Ramsey and Shane. "I hate to fly, so I'd rather sleep on the plane than in here if I can. Playing games will keep me awake."

"What do you have in mind?" Shane asked Ramsey.

"Well, there's this word game I know called Last Letter," Ramsey stated. "What the first person does is say a word. Let's say the word is toad. The second person has to think of a word that begins with the last letter of the other person's word. The last letter in toad is 'd.' The second person might say the word danger. Then the third person uses the last letter of danger — the 'r' — to create a word."

"Sounds easy," Shane responded. "I'll go first. Sign."

"Okay," said Ramsey. "The last letter is 'n,' so my word is navy. Katy?"

"I use 'y,' right?"

"Right."

"Okay. My word is yellow."

"Shane?" Ramsey asked.

"Hmmm. 'W.' Worm."

"Merry," Ramsey said.

"A 'y' again," Katy stated. "Uh...yard."

"Door," answered Shane.

"Raspberry," said Ramsey as she tried to hide a grin.

Katy sighed. "'Y' again. Youth."

"Harp," Shane said.

"Pretty," smiled Ramsey.

Katy furrowed her eyebrows. "What is it with you and the letter 'y,' Ramsey?"

"Nothing."

"Well, having 'y' all the time makes this pretty hard. Let me think. Uh ... 'Y' — as in youngster."

"Rabbit," said Shane.

"Uh, tardy," Ramsey chuckled.

"Ramsey!" Katy exclaimed. "Uh ... Ha! Yummy! Now *you* have a 'y,' Shane."

"'Y,' huh? Let's see. Yam."

Katy immediately moved closer to Ramsey, formed the outline
of a gun with her right hand, and poked an index finger into Ramsey's
shoulder. "If you give me a word that ends in the letter 'y' one more
time, there'll be one less player in this game."

"That's telling her," Shane grinned.

Ramsey thought for a moment, then smiled. "Okay, Katy. I have
my word."

Katy pressed her finger into Ramsey's skin. "May I remind you
that this is loaded and I'm not afraid to use it."

"Don't worry, Katy. I won't give you a word that ends in 'y,'"
Ramsey reassured her.

"Good."

"My word is max. Now I could've said may," Ramsey quickly
explained. "But I know how much you don't like the letter 'y.' So I'll
give you an 'x.' How's that for being fair?"

Ramsey and Shane both burst into laughter.

"Sure, Shane, go ahead and laugh," Katy complained. "I'm so
glad I passed up a nap to play that game."

"Okay, okay," Ramsey conceded. "I guess you're wise to my
'y's, huh Katy?"

"Wise ass," Katy muttered.

"Ewww, Katy! Such a foul mouth," Ramsey declared. "Did you
hear that, Shane?"

"I sure did. I guess we've truly corrupted her."

"Now, we don't know that for a fact," Ramsey stated. "That one
swear word could be just a minor setback for her. But I have a way of
determining her true level of corruption."

"What's that?" Shane asked.

"Well, we have to play another game."

"I don't want to play any more games," Katy said.

"Oh, you'll like this one," Ramsey assured her.

"As much as I liked the last one?"

"More."

"Good. Because I didn't like the last one at all."

Ramsey smiled. "Then you'll at least be able to tolerate this game."

"What is it?" Katy asked with a sigh.

"It's called The Alphabet Game. What we do is go through the alphabet and name items in a category. Like fruits, for example. 'A' is for apple, 'b' is for blueberry, 'c' is for cantaloupe, and so on."

"That sounds like fun, doesn't it, Katy?" Shane asked.

"I guess," Katy replied as she shrugged her shoulders.

"But what category shall we do?" Ramsey asked as she drummed her fingers on the steering wheel.

"Not words beginning with the letter 'y,'" Katy declared.

Ramsey stopped drumming her fingers. "I've got it! How about things to do with a really funny category? Say, sex?"

"Oh, no," Katy quickly refused. "Not that. Romance, maybe. But not ... you know. You guys know I'm shy about... "

"You know," Shane finished for her.

"Yeah," Katy nodded in agreement.

"All right, then," Ramsey stated. "How about sex *and* romance?"

Shane and Katy nodded their heads.

"I'll go first," Shane offered. "Aphrodisiac."

"Buttocks," Ramsey stated.

"Cute," Katy said.

"Cute?" Shane protested. "What does that have to do with sex and romance?"

"Well, if you think someone's cute, then you might like to get to know her better," Katy defended herself.

"Why don't you just say the 'c' word?" Ramsey teased her.

Katy shook her head. "I'm not saying that word. I think it's ... uh ... disgusting."

"Do you think it's disgusting or the word's disgusting?"

"You know what I mean."

"Okay, okay," Shane interrupted them. "The letter is 'd,' and my word is dildo."

"Way to go, Shane," Ramsey commended her. "A woman who's unafraid to say what she really means. And my letter is 'e,' so I'll say ejaculation. Female, of course."

"Of course," Shane nodded.

"Katy?" Ramsey asked. "Your word has to begin with 'f.' Now think hard about this."

"Okay. My word is flirting."

"Ah," Ramsey nodded. "Which is what you want to do with someone who's cute."

"Yes."

"Of course you couldn't say the 'f' word, could you?"

"NO!"

"Shane, you're up," Ramsey said.

"'G,' huh? G-spot."

"A great choice," Ramsey nodded. "I think *you* really understand the game. And my word is harness. As in leather. Katy?"

"Interest."

Ramsey rolled her eyes. "Interest? That's what you get from a bank, Katy. Think sex, woman. Passion. Hot and heavy breathing."

"Interest-*ing*," she amended her word.

"I don't know about you, Katy," Ramsey commented. "Cute. Flirting. Interesting. You're going to have to wash your mouth out with soap with all this gutter language."

"Juices," Shane pronounced slowly and sexily.

"Kinky sex," Ramsey said.

"Love," Katy offered.

"For crying out loud!" Ramsey shouted. "What about lick? Or labia?"

"Love," Katy firmly stated, her cheeks flushed.

"MASTURBATE!" Shane shouted.

"NYMPHOMANIAC!" Ramsey cried out.

"OPENNESS!" Katy bellowed.

Ramsey groaned. "For God's sake, Katy, orgasm! ORGASM!"

Katy placed her hands over her ears and shook her head.

"PENETRATION! QUEER!" Shane screamed at the top of her lungs.

Katy began humming loudly.

"RUBBING! SUCKING! TITILLATION!" Ramsey shouted.

"UNDULATIONS! VAGINA! WHIPS! X-CSTACY!" Shane screeched.

"And Y," Ramsey broke in. "The letter that begins the word most often cried out by every babe who has been in my bed."

"And that word would be?" Shane prompted.

Ramsey wiggled her eyebrows. "The word is — yes, yes, YES!"

Katy shut her eyes and hummed louder.

"And ZIP-PE-DEE-DOO-DAH, I want every woman's body!" Ramsey exclaimed.

Shane and Ramsey grinned at each other, then turned their heads to look at Katy.

"What do you think of that game, Katy?" Shane asked.

"I CAN'T HEAR YOU! I CAN'T HEAR ANYBODY! I — "

"KATY!" Ramsey shouted. "THE GAME IS OVER! DONE! NO MORE SEX WORDS! I PROMISE!"

Katy stopped humming, then slowly slid her hands off her ears. "Sometimes you guys make me so mad," she declared as she repositioned herself back in the kitchen booth, folded her arms across her chest, and pouted.

Shane and Ramsey burst into laughter.

"Go ahead. Laugh. But I'm mad at you guys," Katy stated.

"We're mad about you, too," Ramsey said.

"I didn't say I was mad *about* you," Katy clarified. "I said I was mad *at* you. There's a difference, you know."

"And Ramsey said that we're mad *about* you, not *at* you," Shane reiterated. "There's a difference, you know." She reached a hand out to Katy's leg and patted it. "You know, Katy, you remind me of my kid sister Aleecia. Even if you do have two braids."

"And you remind me of my kid sister, too," Ramsey added.

"I thought you were an only child," Katy grumbled.

"I still am. But I think of you as the little sister I never got to torture, never got to torment, never got to tease, and never got to terrify."

"Oh, great," Katy muttered. "What a compliment."

"Well, look at it this way, Katy," Shane broke in. "You can think of Ramsey as your obnoxious big sister. So when you don't like anything she says to you, you can just tell her to fuck off and die. Sisters say that to each other all the time. That's Aleecia's favorite phrase, whenever she's upset with me."

Ramsey shook her head. "I don't think Katy knows how to say the f-word. She's such an innocent, pure, shy, reserved — "

"Fuck off and die, Ramsey," Katy spit out.

"Little asshole," Ramsey finished.

"Well, aren't we all companionable?" Shane commented. "Shall we sing together 'We Are Family?'"

Ramsey and Shane watched Katy's plane take off, then Ramsey accompanied Shane to the opposite end of the airport to the terminal for the eastbound flight to Boston.

They stopped in front of the metal detector and X-ray conveyer belt.

Ramsey gave her friend a quick hug. "Bye."

"Are you going to be all right, driving by yourself?"

"Oh, sure. Nothing to worry about," Ramsey responded lightly.

"Take plenty of breaks and drink lots of coffee."

"Yeah, yeah."

"Be careful."

"Listen, you'd better get going or you'll be late. You can bring the knives on board with you, but hand me the gun."

An elderly couple that was walking by at that moment stopped in their tracks and stared at Shane.

"Ramsey!" Shane protested.

"Don't sit near her," Ramsey told the elderly couple. "She's a little — " Ramsey tapped her head, crossed her eyes, and hung her tongue out of the side of her mouth.

The elderly couple gasped and quickly walked away.

Shane slapped a hand to her thigh. "Great! Ramsey, will do me a really big favor?"

"What's that?"

"Fuck off and die."

"And you have a nice trip, too," Ramsey grinned as she turned and walked out of the airport.

PART III.

SAN FRANCISCO, HERE I COME...UH...DRIVE

DICTATED ON THE ROAD ...

TO: Rita Hayes
FM: Ramsey Sears
RE: Additional entries, "I'm Just Wondering ..."

"I'm Just Wondering ... "

If today's thirty-dollar-plus jogbras had been invented in the seventies, would the feminists have burned them?

What Phil and Marlo talk about in bed.

Why gay people and gay-related topics are sought-after subjects for talk shows.

If a gay person could flunk a gay studies course.

What lesbian girls at a slumber party talk about.

Chapter 13

"Who said, 'San Francisco's a romantic city, and I want to go there with you'?" Ramsey asked herself about an hour after she had crossed the state line into New Mexico. "Someone said that to me once. I'm sure of it. 'San Francisco's a romantic city, and I want to go there with you.' It was just like that, one simple sentence. Actually, that's not a simple sentence; it's a compound sentence, but proper English doesn't matter right now. The point is, I can't remember who said that to me.

"But I do remember what I was doing at the time I heard that sentence. I was looking at a brochure from the Mark Hopkins Hotel. The voice continued, 'I want to make reservations for the suite at the top of the Mark, and I want to lie in bed with you all night, talking and making love and looking out over the twinkling lights of the city.'

"Who said *that*?" Ramsey tapped her forehead lightly with her hand. "How could I *ever* forget the face that made such an enticing proposi — Oh! I remember now." Ramsey frowned. "It was Sheila. That's who said those things to me. And *that's* why I forgot. I've still got a ton of guilt about that relationship and the way it ended, with me throwing a dinner plate against the wall and screaming, 'Get the fuck out of my life.' Which Sheila did."

Ramsey shook her head. "Sheila and San Francisco. God! I remember now how persistent she was, how determined she was, that we go to San Francisco together. All she talked about our last few months together was our trip to San Francisco." Ramsey sighed. "I wonder if *she* ever got to go? Well, Sheila," Ramsey declared, "*I'm* going to San Francisco now. The lousy lover who said she wouldn't go with you — the one who held out on you for weeks — is now going, but not because she really wants to and certainly not with anyone. Yes,

I'm going to that romantic City by the Bay, and I'm going there alone — but, hopefully, not to sleep alone." Ramsey grinned briefly, then shook her head. "I certainly will be alone. Oh, sure, I'll be with Rita and her fair Melissa, but I might as well be by myself. Wasn't it Sheila who also told me, 'San Francisco is for lovers?' Great. I'm going to be in a city that's for lovers, but with another couple. Why couldn't Rita have told me to get my ass to Maryland? I would've been more than happy to meet her in that state — the one that proclaims, Maryland Is for Crabs. But could Rita choose Maryland? Noooo. She's got to choose the city of romance, the city where people leave their hearts. Now, instead of looking forward to seeing the sights Sheila, my ex-lover, had wanted me to see with her, I can look forward to being subjected to Rita and her current lover giggling and cooing and staring into each other's eyes. Yuck! What fun," Ramsey deadpanned.

"Maybe I should've gone to San Francisco with Sheila after all. I probably would've had more fun with her." Ramsey paused for a moment to think about her statement, then shook her head. "On second thought, no. Now that I think about it, I wouldn't have. Had Sheila and I taken our let's-save-our-relationship trip, I would've had to struggle to keep things light and friendly while Sheila would've wanted to be deep and passionate and intense. Even though she never said as much, I know she believed that if we went away to a romantic place, we could rekindle the flames of love that had once existed for us. I think, deep down inside, she knew the relationship was over for me, but neither one of us admitted that. Instead, we ignored the truth and chose to argue our way around our frustrations — me, frustrated that I couldn't be honest with Sheila about my feelings and angry at myself for not being able to love the woman everyone told me was the greatest, and Sheila frustrated that there was nothing she could do to make things better." Ramsey shook her head. "*That's* why I don't want to get involved with anyone again, in that kind of committed relationship. There'll always be one person who wants more and one person who wants less. For the life of me, I can't see how women stay together for years and years." Ramsey shrugged her shoulders. "Aw, perhaps they just get so settled with each other and things in their lives get so intertwined — material things and finances and stuff like that — that it's easier just to stay together rather than break apart."

Ramsey sighed. "Well, then, with that theory in mind, I think it's best that I, Ramsey Sears — the answer to every lesbian's prayers — should continue to uphold the tradition of true bachelorettehood. So what if people around me — Shane, Rita, Justine and Bernice — are choosing to throw away their freedom for a lifetime — or six thousand miles, whichever comes first — of hearing 'it's your turn to take out the trash,' 'not tonight, I have an early meeting,' 'what do you mean, you're going out with the girls?', and other restrictive phrases common to lesbian married life? I may end up being the last living single lesbian on earth but, by golly, I'll probably be the *happiest* lesbian on earth."

Ramsey smiled. "So, go ahead, Rita. Be with this Melissa in the city of romance. I'll watch you two, and it won't bother me that you're together. Not one bit. *Not one bit*," Ramsey emphasized. "Because I can be with whomever I want to be while I'm there. You two can only be with each other.

"And what fun could *that* possibly be?"

"San Francisco and romance. San Francisco and romance. That's all Sheila talked about," Ramsey resumed, returning to the highway after a lunch break and fill up. "Sure, I wanted to see the city; after all, I had never been to San Francisco. But I didn't want to go with Sheila, not with the expectations she had of me — of us." Ramsey shook her head. "You know, I remember the first time she mentioned San Francisco. She had come home late from work. I had been watching the six o'clock news and eating reheated leftovers when she burst into the apartment, calling my name. I grunted a reply and continued watching the news and eating, but she flew into the living room, flicked off the television, and announced ...

"Have *I* got a surprise for *you!*"

"Later, okay? I was watching that, Sheila. Sports is up next, and I want to find out how Larry Bird is."

"Oh, who cares about Larry Bird? Sheila snorted.

"His wife, the team, the Boston fans, sports writers — and I do."

"Well, I think you'll find *this* much more exciting," Sheila smiled as she popped open her briefcase. "I'm sure you'll find what I have in here far more interesting than Larry Bird."

I sighed. "Sheila, your legal briefs always bore me. I'd much rather find out the status of Larry's — "

Sheila raised her eyebrows. "Who said anything about legal briefs? What I have in here is much more...hmmm...how shall I put it — exciting?"

I emitted a soft groan, recalling the time Sheila had come home and told me she had something exciting for me in her briefcase. She had bought slinky black lingerie and was clearly *in the mood.* But I hadn't been, and we had ended up in a big fight, culminated by her tossing my pillows out the bedroom door and locking herself in the bedroom for the night, thereby relegating me to the couch.

"Oh. Did you go to Victoria's Secret again?" I asked, trying to keep my voice light as I mentally scanned my body for some hint of sexual interest I could entice into action.

"Nope," she smiled, "but after I show you what I have in my briefcase, you might be interested in seeing me model my Victoria's collection for you."

I sighed. "Just show me what you have in your briefcase," I said as I thought, 'And let's get this over with.'

"Ta da!" she cried out as she tossed a packet of color brochures on my lap.

"What's this?"

"Our trip, darling. Our romantic, getaway adventure." She kicked off her shoes and sauntered across the living room carpet to kneel before me. "See? This brochure shows the hotel I want us to stay in — the Mark Hopkins. Isn't it fancy? Look at that lobby — and the rooms! And this brochure is about Fisherman's Wharf. We can eat at one of the restaurants there and take a walk along the water after dinner. And let me show you this — a picture of a cable car. Won't it be fun to ride on one? And look at those hills! Scary, huh? And here's a street called Lombard Street, the crookedest street in the world. See how it winds around? We can drive down it. And isn't it beautiful with all the flowers and the cobblestones? There's also a brochure I want to show you about — "

"What a minute, wait a minute!" I broke in. "I thought we were going to your parents' place at the Cape."

Sheila nodded. "I know we talked about it. But we never came to a definite decision."

"I thought we had. I thought it was settled."

"But honey, my parents will be there on the weekends and my brother is thinking about flying in to spend some time — "

"So? I like your parents. And you just said the other day that you hadn't seen your brother in over a year."

"I know, I know. But I want our vacation to be special this year. We've gone to my parents' place for the last two vacations."

"So? I like your parents' place. I like the beach. So do you. And we don't have to hassle with all this stuff," I said as I swept my hand over the brochures that were scattered over my lap and the couch.

Sheila grabbed a couple of brochures. "Hassle? What's the hassle with this? San Francisco is beautiful. It's somewhere neither one of us has been to and — "

"But we'll have to make plane reservations and book a room and — "

"I can handle that."

"We'd probably have to decide whether we want to rent a car and where — "

"Honey, we can do that when we get out there."

I shook my head. "I don't know, Sheila. I'll have to get time off from work — "

"What does it matter whether we go to the Cape or San Francisco? You still have to get time off from work."

"Well, we're talking about a vacation that'll cost us three or four times what we would spend at the Cape."

"Sweetheart, I've been saving for this for over a year. Remember the cosmetics injury case I won? I got a bonus for that. I banked the whole thing."

"You banked the whole thing? I thought you were going to buy clothes with that."

"I was. But I decided that a nice, romantic vacation with you was much more important."

"Well, I don't have the money right now. The only play money I have is what I make on royalties, and you know sales haven't been brisk."

"Honey, I don't mind paying for this. It's not just for me and not just for you. It's for us. And that's something we can't have at the Cape — just us." Sheila pushed my legs apart and leaned into me, pressing her breasts against the insides of my thighs. "Honey, San Francisco's a romantic city, and I want to go there with you. I want to make reservations for the suite at the top of the Mark, and I want to lie in bed with you all night, talking and making love and looking out over the twinkling lights of the city. I want to be close to you again, Ramsey — *really close* — the way we were in the beginning. I don't want to lose that, and lately it seems we have. I think going away on a vacation by ourselves, to a wonderfully romantic city like San Francisco, will help us get back to the way we were. I want romance with you again, Ramsey, and San Francisco is the perfect place to go ... "

Ramsey lifted her sunglasses as she steered the Wanderlust, rubbed eyes that were tired from driving, and sighed. "I don't know how Sheila put up with me for as long as she did. I think she kept hoping things would work out the way she wanted them to, but ..." Ramsey shook her head. "It's too bad I was such a schmuck at the end of my relationship with her, that I couldn't tell her my love for her had simply gone away. I was still grappling with feelings I had for my first love,

Paula, and I couldn't deal with the pressure Sheila was putting on me to try to save a relationship that I knew, in my heart, had run its course." Ramsey sighed. "*Now* it's so clear to me. But I didn't know it then. Funny, how things that once were totally confusing suddenly become clear."

Ramsey sat forward in the driver's seat and stretched her neck back and forth. "Sheila and I spent our last vacation apart. She kept pushing San Francisco; I kept refusing to go. I suppose, in retrospect, I could have gone and tried to make her happy while we were there, but I didn't think it would've been fair. Sheila wanted more from me than a day-to-day committed relationship. She wanted it all: the white picket fence, the joint savings account — perhaps children — but, above all, the future. She wanted to spend every day of the rest of her life with me. For her, I was *it*. How could I have gone to San Francisco with her under those circumstances? But I didn't know how to tell her what I was feeling, so we argued nonstop about the trip for weeks. Sheila ended up going to the Cape, and I rented a cabin in Lake Placid. Three months later, we split."

Ramsey stared out at the road ahead of her. "Every time I think of Sheila, I feel crummy inside. I hate that feeling. And now, thanks to Rita and her desire to have me in San Francisco, I get to relive those memories again." Ramsey suddenly stuck out her tongue.

"Pthhht! There! That's for you, Rita. That's what I think about this whole San Francisco trip!"

"Okay, okay," Ramsey said a few minutes later. "What an exciting drive this has been thus far. I've had my gee- I-feel-bad-about-how-my-relationship-with-Sheila-ended segment. And a very long, very tedious segment it was, I might add. I don't think I need to experience that any more. And I've had several moments of vocalizing on the topic of I'm-not- looking-forward-to-going-to-San-Francisco-to-meet-Rita-and-her-new-lover. So... what upbeat topics do I want to talk about now? I have a suggestion, Ramsey. Oh, what's that, Ramsey? Well, how about something light? Something light — like what? Well, there's Miller and Bud. Or there are houses and bulbs. Or there's by the dawn's early. Or — wait! I've got it. How about some jokes? Yeah! Good idea, Ramsey. You've always been able to knock 'em dead with your jokes. Then let's do it, okay? Spotlight on center stage. Let's hear the swell of music — Ta-da-ta-da! And now, ladies and lesbians," Ramsey shouted, "live on center stage, Kate Clinton's idol and role model — the fabulously funny ... Rrrrr-amsey Sears!"

Ramsey burst into a broad smile. "Hey, hey! How're all you ladies doin' tonight? Say! You down there — get your hand off that lady's leg — that's my mother. And she's not that kind of girl. Neither was my dad, you know. So how'd I turn out so *right*? They certainly can't figure it. Often I have to console them, tell them, 'It's okay, Mom and Dad. I don't think any differently of you, even if you are ... *heterosexual*! That makes my mother burst into tears. 'Stop torturing me with my heterosexuality,' she'll plead. 'I didn't choose to be this way, you know.' My poor mother. And she can't throw a softball to save her life. Isn't that amazing, how you can always tell the lesbians from the hets? Just toss 'em a softball and say, 'Throw it back.' The lesbian will easily move her arm back, then toss the ball over twelve buildings. The het will bend her arm back from the elbow, run forward three steps, hiccup, and thud the ball into the ground.

"'Yeah-but,' I hear some of you protest out there. You're lesbians and you can't throw a softball for shit. I often receive tongue lashings on that. *Very severe* tongue lashings. And you know how I respond to such protestations? I say, 'Hey, who cares whether or not you can throw a softball correctly — just keep giving those great tongue lashings!'

"Does anyone know why the dyke crossed the road? Because there was a softball game on the other side. Get with the program! Say, maybe I'm talking to the wrong crowd. How many of you are lesbians? Come on — I mean real, honest-to-goodness lesbians. You know, the kind that goes down on a woman for a half hour and doesn't come up gasping for air like a scuba diver with an empty tank. You know, the kind that doesn't reach for a towel the minute she's performed oral sex and grimace, 'Ewww — that stuff gets *everywhere*. And the kind that doesn't choke on one tiny pubic hair like it's a hair ball.

"If you're a real lesbian, you'll get this joke. How many lesbians does it take to screw in a lightbulb? None. Lesbians don't screw.

"Did you hear the one about the lesbian college student who hated to get straight As? But she loved oral exams! Stay with me, folks, I got a million of 'em ..."

Ramsey crossed the state line into Arizona late that afternoon. As soon as she did, she announced, "I'm so tired of listening to myself. Which cassette haven't I already heard a hundred times since I started this trip?" She flipped through her cassettes, hesitated over one — "I think I've only heard this one ninety-nine times" — then popped it into the Wanderlust's tape player. "Okay, folks, for your listening pleasure, a Ramsey Sears collection of those moldies, but goodies." A drum beat burst into the Wanderlust, followed by the sound of violins, castanets, and a black female voice proclaiming, "The night we met I knew I needed you so ..."

"Oh, yeah! 'Be My Baby' by the Ronnettes," Ramsey cried out, then sang along with the song. 'Be My Baby' ended, followed by 'She's a Fool' by Lesley Gore, which Ramsey sang at the top of her lungs. "And now, the Crystals!" Ramsey announced as the energized hand clapping at the beginning of the song motivated Ramsey's foot to push down on the gas. "Look out, Rita — I'm cruising along at a big six-five! Whoa, Nelly — I'm out of control," Ramsey chuckled as she banged her hands on the steering wheel to keep time with the music and sang her edited version of the song: "*She* picked me up at seven and *she* looked so fine, da do run run run, da do run run! Someday soon, I'm gonna make *her* mine ... " Ramsey sped along the highway.

"Oh, this is a great song!" Ramsey exclaimed as the Crystals version of "Then He Kissed Me" began. "But I'll have to change all the pronouns to make this come out right," Ramsey grinned as she sang: "I felt so happy I almost cried, and then *she* kissed me ..."

As Ramsey hummed, she let her mind drift. "Say, I just remembered something, something about that the last night in Fairfield, in my duplex, when the staff at *Woman to Woman* threw me a surprise going-away party. Something about that night has always stuck out in my mind," Ramsey remarked as she wagged a finger in the air, "and this song just made me remember. She *did* kiss me, didn't she?" Ramsey wet her lips. "Rita Hayes kissed me quite passionately, quite responsively, on the lips. But why? Everyone had left; Rita and I were alone. She was looped on champagne, but was that why she kissed me? I don't know. There was something strange about that whole episode on the couch. I guess it all began when she noticed me staring at her breasts and asked ...

"Do you like that?"

"I always have Rita. You've got a gorgeous chest and a beautiful body."

Rita began to unbutton her shirt. "Wanna see more?"

"Uh...Rita, I don't think you know quite what you're doing right now."

Rita sat up and leaned her body towards Ramsey's; her face and mouth were only inches away. "I know exactly what I'm doing. It's what I've wanted to do for awhile. It's just a little easier with the booze and with the knowledge that I won't face you tomorrow in the office, probably wanting you even more than I want you now."

"Rita, are you sure you want to be saying this?"

"I don't want to get rid of you, Ramsey. It is with great reluctance that I say goodbye." Rita's arms slowly circled Ramsey's shoulders, then she moved her head and met Ramsey's lips with hers. Ramsey put her arms around Rita and returned her kiss. It began slowly, tentatively, then built as open, unambiguous desire fueled their exploration. Their tongues danced together; their breathing intensified ...

"Did she ever kiss me!" Ramsey expelled a burst of air as she shifted position in the driver's seat. "But why? Just because we were alone? Because she was drunk? Because she wouldn't have to face me the next day? Hell, as soon as I see her in San Francisco, it'll be the 'next day' — the first time we'll be together since that kiss." Ramsey's eyes widened. "Hmmm. And if my memory serves me correctly, we didn't stop at just that kiss ... "

Rita reached behind her back to find Ramsey's hand. Holding it in her own, she gently guided it to rest on her right breast. Ramsey caressed the soft flesh, then her fingers unbuttoned Rita's shirt and slipped slowly into her bra. Rita gasped, then gently pulled away from their passionate kissing. They locked eyes.

"You're a very hard lady to resist, Ramsey Sears. I want you to know that I want you more than anyone I've ever wanted. It's been a long time since I've ... it's been a long time since I've thought of something — someone — other than the magazine and the employees. You are someone I have ... " Rita stopped ...

"I am someone you have what?" Ramsey yelled into the interior of the Wanderlust. *"What?* Why *did* you resist me, Rita? Is the reason you're with Melissa now, because of what we did on the couch? If that's the case, then why did you say all those things to me about wanting me and not feeling that way about someone else and — Aw, hell!" Ramsey slumped back in her seat. "What does it matter now? That night seems like years ago. I'm surprised I even remembered it. Hell, if I hadn't listened to that oldies tape, I *wouldn't* have remembered it."

Ramsey shook her head. "I hope Rita doesn't remember that embrace when I see her. I hope she doesn't bring it up, doesn't say something like, 'Uh, Ramsey, about that time at your party, after everyone had left ...' After all, there's nothing to talk about. Nothing happened. There's no need to discuss it or to even think about it anymore." Ramsey nodded her head. "I know *I* won't. It won't cross my mind again for the rest of this trip."

Ramsey continued driving through Arizona as the tape clicked off and silence filled the Wanderlust.

Woman *TO* Woman
MAGAZINE

April Issue

"Good morning. This is WLEZ, Lesbian Talk Radio, the all-talk station at 560 on your radio dial. I'm Jessie LaRoue, your hostess for the next three hours. All the lines are open. The topic this morning is whatever's on your mind. Caller from Jamaica Plain, you're on the air."

"Good morning, Jessie."

"Good morning. What's on your mind?"

"It's these mail order companies that sell those sex toys."

"What sex toys?"

"You know. Vibrators. Dildos."

"Yeah. So what's your beef?"

"Why do lesbians even need sex toys? I mean, we can do it without them."

"Yeah, but you can do it *with* them, too."

"Well, I never have."

"Maybe you should. Next caller. Car phone, you're on the air."

"Jessie, I'm a first-time caller."

"Welcome."

"I can't meet anybody, Jessie. I go to bars, but it seems the most popular spot in the place is the pool table. I don't know how to play pool."

"Nor do most of the women at the pool tables, either."

"Well, they certainly look like they know what they're doing."

"That's because they know how to hold a pool stick. Beyond that, it's just luck where they hit and what they sink."

"So what are you saying?"

"I'm saying not to be intimidated by a bunch of women who stand around a pool table trying to look like they know the game of pool. Those women are there because they don't know how to dance."

"I know how to dance."

"There you go. Forget about the pool players and get out on the dance floor."

"Wow! I never looked at it that way before, Jessie. I think that's what I'll do."

"Great. Next caller, you're on the air. Good morning, Boston."

"Yo, Jessie. I want ta tell

yah listenahs ta not forget ta tip the bartendah. Openin' brewskies is hard work."

"Okay, caller, you said it. Hear that out there, tight-fisted lesbians? Leave the change on the counter for the bartender. Next caller. Good morning, Allston."

"Excuse me?"

"I said, you're on the air, caller."

"Am I on the air?"

"You are on the air, caller. What's on your mind?"

"Jessie?"

"It's a three-hour show, caller, but I'd appreciate your picking up the pace a bit."

"Okay, uh, Jessie, I, uh — gosh, I'm just so nervous."

"It's just you and the telephone, caller."

What's on your mind, Allston?"

"What's on my mind, Jessie? I'll tell you what's on my mind. I'll get right to the point and cut right to the chase and let you know how I feel."

"When?"

"Well, right now."

"Go for it, Allston."

"I CAN'T STAND SOFTBALL! There, I've said it."

"Thanks for sharing that, caller. Next caller, you're on the air. Good morning, Cambridge."

"Good morning, Jessie."

"What's on your mind, Cambridge?"

"Well, I want to know whether you can answer this question. If a woman calls herself a lesbian but also says she's celibate, is she a lesbian? I mean, isn't our sexual expression what really defines us? So what does a lesbian who won't have sex with a woman mean?"

"What do you think it means?"

"I don't know. And how about this? I have a friend who calls herself a lesbian-with-a-boyfriend. What does that mean?"

"What do you think it means?"

"I don't know. And now this lesbian-with-a-boyfriend is pregnant and she's going to marry him. But she says she's still a lesbian. What does this mean?"

"What do you think it means?"

"I don't know. I'm seeing my therapist today. Maybe she can explain it to me."

"Maybe so."

"But I don't know. My therapist had affairs with women all through college, then got married, then got a divorce, and is seeing a woman right now, but she says she's not a lesbian."

"Maybe your therapist wouldn't be the best person to

help you with your confusion."

"Oh, I don't know. Perhaps I should move out of Cambridge. Things in this city are becoming too hard for me to understand. Last night I was handed a flyer when I walked by the Harvard Coop. The flyer announced a group being started for lesbians who support men's rights. What does this mean?"

"I don't know, caller."

"Isn't anyone just a lesbian anymore?"

"Are you?"

"Yeah."

"Well, there you go."

"Yeah, but I'm beginning to feel like I have to define myself more than that."

"Okay. How about you're a lesbian who has sex with other women, who doesn't have a boyfriend, who isn't pregnant and isn't going to get married, and who doesn't support men's rights?"

"Cool! That's what I am! Thanks, Jessie."

"Anytime. Car phone, you're on the air."

"Yeah. I'd like to order a large pepperoni with extra cheese."

"This isn't a pizza joint, sir, it's a radio station."

"What radio station?"

"WLEZ."

"Well, can you play 'Dancing in the Dark' by the Boss?"

"This is talk radio."

"Oh. What do you talk about?"

"It's lesbian talk radio."

"It is? Say, I've always wondered how you ladies do it. Do you — "

"Next caller, you're on the air. Good morning, Somerville."

"Yeah, Jessie. Do you know that if you play Holly Near's songs backwards, you can distinctly hear her say the phrase, 'I'm dying for a hamburger, medium rare?'"

"I didn't realize that, caller. Thanks for the info. Next caller, you're on the air. Good morning, Lexington."

"Jessie, do you think Kate Clinton is funny?"

"I think so. Why?"

"Don't you think she's a little heavy on the tampon jokes?"

"Do you?"

"Yeah. I don't see the humor in tampons."

"By the same token, tampons may not see the humor in us."

"Huh?"

"Never mind. Next caller, you're on the air — "

From Ramsey Sear's column, April issue, *Woman to Woman.*

Chapter 14

Ramsey screamed, reached out, and twisted the radio dial off. "Yak, yak, yak, yak, yak, yak, yak, yak, yak. That's all I hear on these radio stations — endless yakking. Yakking that sounds like quacking. Quacking — ha! Now that's an apt description. DJs are all ducks, ducks who quack, quack, quack, quack, all day lo — " Ramsey suddenly slapped the side of her face. "You're at it again, woman. Snap out of it. We talked about this only a few hours ago. We discussed your incessant chatter with yourself yesterday and how that wasn't going to happen again today. We decided that we were tired not only of the inane, pointless monologues we were having with ourselves but also of the questions we were asking ourselves — and answering. Weren't we? Yes, we were. And that's not healthy, is it? No, it isn't. What you need, Sears, is a nice, pleasant, *healthy* conversation with another human being — you know the kind — where one person says, 'So, what do you think about blah-blah?' and the other person responds, 'I'm so glad you asked. This is what I think about blah-blah.' Why don't we stop for lunch in a little while so you can practice such conversation with the waitress, a truck driver, the person sitting next to you at the counter — anyone! — so you won't end up two days from now walking down the sidewalks in San Francisco, muttering to yourself and laughing out loud at your own jokes."

Ramsey nodded her head. "Smart decision," she concluded. "So," she continued, "bearing that decision in mind, let's keep our sanity intact from now until lunch by playing a tape and singing along with it or by listening to the radio — even if it's a farm report — or by picking up that hitchhiker we just passed — you know, the one who looked like a dyke and was holding a sign that read SAN FRAN —

"HOLY SHIT!" Ramsey shouted as she quickly jerked the

Wanderlust into the breakdown lane, slammed a foot on the brake pedal, and came to an abrupt stop that emptied the contents of the camper's kitchen cabinets onto the floor.

Ramsey flipped on the Wanderlust's flashers, then slowly backed the vehicle towards the hitchhiker.

"I can't believe you're going all the way to San Francisco. Isn't that incredibly wild?" the hitchhiker asked she climbed through the side door of the Wanderlust, dropped two large backpacks on the floor on top of the kitchen cabinet clutter, and flopped into the passenger seat next to Ramsey.

"A human voice," Ramsey murmured as she signalled her intent to return Wanderlust to the highway.

"What an incredible happenstance, don't you think?" the woman asked. "I was just dropped off twenty minutes ago by a lady in a pickup who drove me all the way from Gallup. She said she would've driven me to the California border, but, you know, she couldn't."

"Oh," Ramsey responded, wondering whether she should act as if she *did* know why the woman in the pickup couldn't drive her to San Francisco or if she should ask why the woman — you know — couldn't. But before Ramsey could decide what to say next, the hitchhiker blew air out of her nose and shook her head back and forth, swinging a full head of frizzy hair around her face.

What *is* this woman doing? Ramsey asked herself, then noticed that the woman was smiling during the air-blowing, hair-swinging routine. Ah...she's laughing, Ramsey determined, then turned her head slightly to get a better glimpse of her.

The woman met Ramsey's questioning eyes. "Sorry, but I just had to laugh. This whole trip has been, well, quite a trip!"

Ramsey flashed her a half-smile. "I didn't know if you were hyperventilating or what."

"Nope. I'm incredibly fine," she responded as she settled back in her seat. "Incredibly."

"Good," Ramsey said and looked out at the road but kept her head slightly angled, noting that the woman, who was probably in her late twenties, early thirties, had a small blue bird's feather stuck in her hair above the ear.

Uh-oh, Ramsey thought. I may be stuck for the next two days with a hippie-dippie on my hands. I'll bet she's headed for Haight-Ashbury. Why did I ever tell her I was going all the way to San Francisco? That was pretty stupid. Now there's no way I can get her out of my life until we reach San Francisco. Oh, well, nothing I can do about it now. I suppose we could bounce around the theory that Janis Joplin really didn't die of a drug overdose, but was murdered by Bobby McGee. Or that —

"You got any water?" the woman interrupted Ramsey's thoughts. "I'm incredibly thirsty. And I mean, incredibly."

And I hear you, Ramsey mentally responded to the woman as she reached under the driver's seat and pulled out a plastic bottle of Evian water.

"Where did you ever get Evian around here?" the woman asked as she took the bottle from Ramsey.

"It's not Evian now. I keep filling it up because it's a good size to fit under the seat, where it stays pretty cool while I'm driving."

The woman guzzled half the bottle, then wiped her mouth with the back of a freckled hand. "I'm into recycling, too. I don't throw anything away. I'm incredibly earth-conscious."

Ah, Ramsey thought. I stand...uh...sit corrected. She's not a hippie-dippie but a Rhonda Recycler, environmentalist and friend of bears and gulls everywhere. That's why she has the feather in her hair. After all, why let it go to waste after the bird is done with it, when someone else can use it to ...uh...feather her own nest, so to speak? And that faded blue tank top, ripped gym shorts, and once-white socks she's wearing look like they're also part of her recycling philosophy.

"I'm so incredibly grateful for this lift," the woman said as she sighed and raised her arms above her head to pull bunches of hair away from her face. "There's just no breeze when you're standing on the road. The heat shimmers up all around you from the tar so you feel like some creature on a spit."

Ramsey turned her head to nod at the woman, noted the semicircles of perspiration under the woman's unshaved armpits, then got the whiff of a pungent scent in the air. What is that smell? Ramsey asked herself, then tentatively sniffed the air again. Hmmm. It's kind of like a locker room after a basketball game or my running clothes after they've sat in the laundry hamper for three days; Ramsey surreptitiously began lowering her window from half-open to fully open.

The woman glanced at Ramsey's action, then quickly brought her arms down. "Oops. Sorry about that. I probably smell incredibly bad. I hate to admit it, but it's been a couple of days since — "

"We don't have to discuss this," Ramsey broke in.

"Maybe sometime today we can stop at a gas station or somewhere with a bathroom so I could take a quick hand bath," the woman suggested.

"Sure," Ramsey answered casually, then thought, How about in two minutes? Ramsey laughed to herself, then frowned. Here I am, continuing to converse with myself, when there's no reason to. Am I getting loopy? Hmmm. I think I should do something about this — and fast. Now think, Sears — which would you rather have: two days of farm reports on the radio or talking with someone to pass the time? So what if the only person you have to talk to has a feather stuck in her hair? So what if her clothes could jump off her and walk unassisted to the nearest laundry bag? And so what if her body odor is enough to melt the — "

"By the way, my name's Nadine," the woman introduced herself.

"Uh...Ramsey." Gee, I think I'm on my way to becoming a sparkling conversationalist, Ramsey thought. Come on, Sears, pick up the pace or you'll...

"Pleased to meet you, Ramsey. And I sure am incredibly glad you stopped to pick me up."

Ramsey took a deep breath. "Actually, I don't think I've ever picked up a hitchhiker," she said. "That was one of those things you were told you weren't supposed to do. You know, like don't take candy from strangers and — "

"Oh, yeah," Nadine cut in with a grin. "And look both ways before you cross the street."

Ramsey nodded. "Yeah. And...uh...return your library books on time."

Nadine turned in her seat to face Ramsey. "I've got another one. Respect your elders. And...and — " she waved her hand excitedly, "Don't talk back."

"Do a good deed. Always say please."

"*And* thank you," Nadine added.

"You're welcome," Ramsey replied.

Nadine laughed.

"And how about this one — don't eat your paste," Ramsey grinned.

"Oh, I used to love that paste!"

"So did I."

"It came out of that big plastic jug. The teacher would tell you to line up with the rest of the class — "

"Single file," Ramsey broke in.

"Right. Single file. And you'd hold a small square of paper in your hands and when it was your turn the teacher would scoop out the paste with a tongue depressor and smear it on your paper. I'd always walk back to my desk with the paper an inch from my nose, just *inhaling* it, and then sit at my desk hunched over the paper until — "

"Until someone like me would come along and whap you on the back of the head so your nose would land in the paste," Ramsey grinned impishly.

"So you were the one!" Nadine smiled and wagged a finger at her. "That was incredibly naughty of you."

Ramsey shrugged her shoulders. "Yeah, well, I had my own set of rules back then, rules that were based on the principle of doing unto others as you *wouldn't* want them doing unto you."

Nadine shook her head. "Not me. At least, not until I got to high school and discovered the joys of the debating club. Then I discovered how much fun it was to break the rules. You see, I hadn't realized just how much anger I had kept inside all my life. When you're not real attractive, like I'm not, then you're often not the most popular person in the school. No matter who you are inside. Because if you don't have blonde hair and blue eyes or dark hair and dark eyes or fall into the category of being acceptably cute, you don't have too many friends."

"So how does debate fit into that?" Ramsey asked.

"I found out *that* was how I could excel, how I could get kids to notice me. Instead of looking at my hair or my freckles, kids I competed against *had* to listen to me, had to really hear me. They hung on my every word. You see, I was quite good at debating — in fact, I was the New York State Forensics Champion three years in a row. So you don't know what joy it gave me to make my opponents stammer and squirm and become genuinely flustered. Debate helped me realize the power I had as a person who had been invisible up to that point — invisible to everyone, including me."

"Wow," Ramsey stated. "You sound like you were a woman on a mission."

Nadine smiled. "I still am. And I do break those rules of the past, especially the rule that says don't take rides from strangers."

"That's a pretty dangerous rule to break," Ramsey pointed out. "You never know who's picking you up, even if they look as innocent as I do."

Nadine looked at Ramsey. "Who said you looked innocent?"

"I believe *I* did," Ramsey retorted.

"That's right," Nadine agreed. "Anyway, I know hitching is risky. But I don't have wheels or money. So this is my form of transportation," she said as she stuck out her thumb. "And I use my debating skills as weapons when I need protection."

Ramsey chuckled. "What do you do? Carry a stack of file cards that detail punishment for rape or murder and read them aloud when you're in danger?"

Nadine shook her head. "No. I just talk my way out of difficult situations."

"Oh, come on," Ramsey protested.

"I can prove it," Nadine stated. "There have been no less than ten men who have made overtures for sex after they've picked me up, but not one man got to even put his hand on me. I'll tell you about one guy who picked me up — a mister macho, mister rugged type — who drove a pickup with a rifle mounted inside the back window. Well, we're driving along and all of a sudden he cries out, 'Well, looky here.' Naturally I turned to look at him. He had his pants unzipped and his weenie was erect. 'Why don't you do something about this, sugar?' he told me, so I did. I embarked on a three-minute extemporaneous speech about the ugliness and lack of purpose in the male penis and literally watched him lose his erection. Of course as soon as he put his limp weenie back into his pants, he screeched the truck to a halt and kicked me out. But the point is that he didn't lift a finger to me and I didn't have to physically defend myself. I used my debating skills as my protection."

"But aren't you ever afraid?" Ramsey asked.

Nadine shrugged her shoulders. "Nah. I'm incredibly comfortable with hitching. In college, I did it all the time. After I graduated, I hitched cross-country with a friend. And now, well, it's my form of transportation." Nadine paused. "But what about you? You told me you've never picked up a hitchhiker before. What made you stop for me?"

"I guess I felt it was out of necessity. I figured I could either drive all the way to San Francisco and possibly lose my mind in the process, talking to myself and even answering my own questions, or I could pick you up. You were the lesser of two evils."

"Thanks," Nadine responded with a half-smile. "But I think I know what you mean. It gets incredibly lonely being on the road. I had enough money to take the good old Greyhound from Albany to St. Louis. Riding the bus is okay because there's always someone to talk to. But when my money ran out, well, it was thumb city again, with lots of time to be in my own head."

Ramsey turned to look at Nadine. "I've got to give you credit. I don't think I could hitch rides from strangers because I'd be afraid of who might pick me up."

"Well, it can be a double-edged sword, you know. What I mean is, when *you* pick someone up you never know what you could be getting yourself into."

Ramsey raised her eyebrows. "Yeah, you're right. That's why I'd never pick up a guy. But a woman, on the other hand— "

"Can murder you, rob you, beat you, or steal your car," Nadine pointed out.

"Well, sure," Ramsey agreed, "but *you* at least looked pretty —"

"Safe?" Nadine asked. "Like I was okay? Like I was harmless? Did I look like I was a nice person?" Nadine paused a few seconds from her rapid-fire questioning, then continued. "Tell me, Ramsey, have you ever heard what people say when police arrest their next door neighbor for multiple murders? They say, 'Gosh, he was just the nicest man. The kids all loved him.' Or 'She was such a sweet old lady. She never even killed a bug, so who would've thought she'd poison her tenants?'"

"Okay, okay, I get your point," Ramsey said. "Now stop it, because you're making me nervous."

"Sorry," Nadine apologized. "I guess I came on pretty strong. That's the debater in me."

"Well, a little," Ramsey declared. "But it was nothing I couldn't handle. However, if I had had an erect penis, I'm sure it would have shriveled up by now, just like that man's did."

"Listen, if *you* had an erect penis, I'd jump out this window — forget about my debating talents," Nadine said. "Anyway, I think I know why you thought I was safe to pick up."

"Oh?" Ramsey asked. "Why was that?"

"You thought I was a dyke. I'm right, aren't I?"

"Well, you are, aren't you?" Ramsey responded.

"And I'm right, aren't I?" Nadine persisted.

Ramsey nodded her head.

"And, from the looks of you, you are too."

Ramsey looked at Nadine. "From the *looks* of me?"

Nadine returned the grin. "Yeah. You look like a dyke."

"Well, I certainly don't try to hide anything, but I also don't go around advertising it. And look," Ramsey stated as she pointed to her hair. "I'm growing my hair out and I have braids. Now doesn't such femininity confuse you?"

"Nope. I thought you looked like a dyke. And you acted like a dyke, too."

"What do you mean?"

"Well, you looked at me when I sat down."

Ramsey flitted her eyes at Nadine. "I don't think dykes have the market cornered on that."

"No, but you were taking me in in the way someone who loves women takes in another woman. You know. The eyes ask: Is she or isn't she?"

"Only her hairdresser knows for sure," Ramsey quipped.

Nadine grinned. "And, chances are high *he* is!"

Ramsey laughed.

"Also," Nadine continued, "your look made me think that you might be wondering, 'Is this woman someone I might be attracted to, or will she be a buddy?'"

"I don't think I was thinking that at all."

Nadine shrugged her shoulders. "Well, maybe you weren't. Most dykes are incredibly good at using their eyes not only to check others out, but also to give signals to someone else." Nadine paused. "So what were you thinking when you stopped to pick me up?"

"The truth?" Ramsey asked.

"The truth."

"I wished you would hurry up and get in because it was hot

without a breeze blowing in through the windows."

Nadine nodded. "Fair enough."

"And what about you?" Ramsey asked. "Were you thinking, 'Uh-oh, this dyke wants to pick me up' or 'Hmmm, what do we have here and what might possibly happen when I get into that camper with her'?"

Nadine thought for a moment. "Actually, all I cared about was getting out of the hot sun and sitting down."

Ramsey and Nadine looked at each other and burst into laughter.

"So why are you going to San Francisco?" Ramsey asked above the clatter of dishes and mumble of voices as they ate lunch in a booth in a crowded truck stop diner an hour later.

"To be with my lover," Nadine replied as she swallowed a mouthful of a tuna fish sandwich.

"For a weekend? A week?" Ramsey asked, then bit into a hamburger.

Nadine shook her head. "For a long time, I hope," she said as she casually scattered the potato chips on her plate with a finger. "Even though it's been two years since we've seen each other, we've planned on settling down together all along."

Ramsey inhaled sharply, coughed on a piece of food that caught in her throat, then swallowed. "It's been two years since you've seen her?" she exclaimed.

Nadine gave Ramsey a sad smile. "Yup. She — Caroline, that is — wanted to get her master's degree, but couldn't afford school in upstate New York, where we lived, and couldn't get a loan at other colleges and universities she applied to. So she decided to move to San Francisco and establish residency. Once she did, she was able to attend the city college at a greatly reduced tuition."

"So why didn't you go to San Francisco with her then?" Ramsey asked.

"The timing was off. I had just completed a training program and had made a two-year commitment to direct a state-run program for inner-city kids. I had to stay to honor that commitment."

Ramsey furrowed her brow. "So you haven't seen...Caroline, is it?"

"Yes, that's right."

"You haven't seen Caroline once in two years?"

"Two years, three days, and a little over twelve hours," Nadine added as she glanced at her watch.

"So how do you know you're still lovers?"

Nadine stared at Ramsey. "Because we have a commitment to each other," she declared. "We were together two and a half years before she left, and we also called each other and wrote as often as we could."

"Yes, but you haven't even seen each other... haven't, you know — slept together in all that time — and I would think that you might — "

Nadine cut into Ramsey's statement with a sigh. "Believe me, I'm well aware of that. I imagine Caroline and I will be spending a great deal of quality time together in the bedroom for the first few weeks after I arrive."

Ramsey stuffed the last bite of her hamburger into her mouth, then wiped grease from her hands with a napkin. "So do you two have an arrangement where you've been able to see other people while you've been apart?"

Nadine's eyes widened. "Absolutely not!"

Ramsey leaned forward across the table. "Then how the hell do you...well...I don't think I've ever gone more than a couple of months not sleeping with a woman."

Nadine leaned across the table towards Ramsey until their noses nearly touched. "But *you* don't have a commitment to someone, do you?"

Ramsey jerked her head back. "No!"

Nadine sat back in the booth. "*That's* why you don't understand. A relationship is not just about sex or even just about sleeping together. It's about the emotional connection you have with another person. It's about the desire you have to be together because you love each other. It's about loving what the other person stands for and what she wants and having those feelings reciprocated. Caroline knew I had to honor my commitment to the United City Kids Project and accepted that, just as I accepted her need to go to a school she could afford. So we both accepted the two-year separation as a geographical and physical one, but certainly not as an emotional one."

"I've heard this emotional connection stuff before," Ramsey commented, "and I just don't know if I buy it."

"What's there to buy?" Nadine asked.

"Well, it doesn't make sense to me to make that kind of commitment to someone, to say you'll be there *only* for her, no matter what else. I mean, who knows if either one of you will meet someone else you'd rather be with?"

"Believe me, Ramsey, if I ever meet someone who I feel more strongly for than I do Caroline, I'll be with that person. But my love for Caroline and my connection with her is so solid that it would take a goddess to make me want to take my eyes away from Caroline for one minute — heck, for one second. Caroline's someone who...oh...I don't know — this sounds pretty corny — but she just takes my breath away." Nadine sighed, then looked at Ramsey. "Haven't you ever met someone who made you feel that way?"

"Nope. Never," Ramsey quickly answered.

"Someone who walks by you and makes thousands of butterflies flutter inside you?"

Ramsey shook her head.

"Someone who makes your heart pound faster just by hearing her voice?"

"Nope."

Nadine shrugged her shoulders. "That's too bad, Ramsey. But someday I believe you will." Nadine smiled at her. "And then you'll think back to this conversation and remember this diner and you'll — "

"Oh, no I won't," Ramsey declared as she pushed her way out of the booth. "And I won't call you, either."

"Huh?" Nadine asked.

"Private joke," Ramsey explained, then pulled money out of her pocket and tossed it onto the table. "Just suffice it to say that I plan on never having those feelings for anybody."

"That's too bad," Nadine responded. "Because even though these past two years have been extremely hard for me, Caroline's love and the love I have for her helped pull me through it. Someday I think you'll want to have someone there to help pull you through the difficult times in your life."

"Nope. Ramsey Sears does it alone," Ramsey declared as she strode out of the diner.

"I might as well admit it — I'm addicted to lust."

From Ramsey Sear's column,
Special Summer Fun issue,
Woman to Woman.

Chapter 15

"Now that was the best dream I've ever had," Ramsey sighed as she opened her eyes shortly before dawn the next morning and looked around her at the interior of the Wanderlust as a slow smile played across her face. "The very best dream," she murmured as she stretched her arms above her head with a soft, satisfied moan and rolled over on her side, closed her eyes, and drifted back into the dream world she had left...

Ramsey opened her front door. As Rita walked past her into the living room, her body brushed Ramsey's arm. Ramsey's eyes were glued to Rita's movements, to the tight black slacks that defined her shapely ass, to the sea-green camisole that shimmered under her sheer white silk shirt, casually unbuttoned to reveal the top of her ample cleavage, to the luxuriant dark hair.

"God, you look good, woman," Ramsey murmured, feeling a tremor deep inside herself.

Rita crossed the living room to the couch, and turned smiling to face Ramsey. Running her hands down her hips and thighs, she sank to the couch and patted the cushion next to her. "Why don't you sit over here, with me, sexy? I'd love to pick up where we left off."

Rita's throaty voice made Ramsey's heart pound, and her breath caught in her throat. She swallowed hard and closed the door, hearing the latch click as though from a great distance. Slowly, she walked to the couch and stood looking down at Rita.

"Kneel down," Rita commanded.

Ramsey dropped to her knees.

"Unbutton my shirt."

Ramsey moaned softly and reached out to release the delicate pearly buttons, one by one. Opening the shirt, Ramsey leaned her body forward against Rita's knees and ran her palms lightly over the nipples that were thinly veiled by the satin camisole.

Now it was Rita's turn to moan, and her nipples hardened as Ramsey gently pressed and fondled them between her fingertips.

"Harder," Rita panted.

"Soon," Ramsey promised, taking her hands away to pull the camisole free of her slacks. "Take this off," she commanded.

Rita shrugged out of the silk shirt and leaned forward to pull the camisole over her head. Then she tossed it on the couch. Her breasts, ripe and heavy, overflowed Ramsey's hands. She opened her legs and pulled Ramsey to her, so that Ramsey could bury her face in the hollow between her breasts.

Inhaling the scent of her — her perfume and powder and sweat — Ramsey ran her tongue lightly up and down and then in circles over Rita's skin, tasting and moistening the swell of her breasts and the delicate place between them, while fondling and stroking her nipples. Rita moaned again, and Ramsey slid her open mouth and tongue to the left, across Rita's breast to the erect and swollen nipple, leaving a wet trail. Taking the nipple in her mouth, she circled and teased it with her tongue, nibbling with her lips and then sucking hard, until Rita cried out sharply and her fingers tightened on Ramsey's shoulders.

Ramsey shifted to Rita's right breast, kissing and sucking it until Rita cried out again, panting and shuddering with pleasure. "Please," she gasped, "please ..."

"Yes," Ramsey answered hoarsely, sliding her lips down Rita's body, her hands moving down and back and under to clasp Rita's ass, even as Rita thrust her hips upwards against her...

"It's morning!" a voice announced in Ramsey's dream.

Ramsey was startled out of the dream, then decided to ignore the voice and turned her attention back to the dream. But when she did, Rita and the couch had vanished. She opened her eyes with a groan.

"Nightmare?" the voice asked.

Ramsey focused on Nadine's face. "Huh?"

"I asked if you were having a nightmare. I could hear you outside."

Ramsey shook her head. "Being woken up is a nightmare. I was having one of the best dreams I've ever had."

Nadine shrugged her shoulders. "Well, it didn't sound like a good dream. It sounded like you were being eaten alive."

"I might've been, but I'll never know that now."

"What's that?"

"Never mind. What time is it?"

"Seven thirty. Don't you think we should get going soon?"

Ramsey rubbed her eyes. "How about in half an hour?"

"Okay. I'm going to use the campground shower, all right?"

"Fine," Ramsey mumbled as she closed her eyes and drifted back into her dream world...

Ramsey was kneeling — naked — between Rita's bare knees. Rita was panting.

"Go inside me," she gasped.

Ramsey slid the tip of one finger into the slick wetness of Rita's pussy, then pulled back and circled the opening, slid in again, out again, in again — teasing, never very far — until Rita, in a frenzy, seized her wrist and pulled Ramsey's finger deep inside her. "Ahhhh — yes," she gasped, "more, more, deeper, deeper!" Ramsey inserted another finger, and then a third into the wet opening and, with her other hand, parted the dark curling hair and opening Rita's lips to expose her throbbing clitoris. Lowering her head between Rita's thighs, she slid her tongue over it, feeling the contraction around her fingers. Delicately, she circled Rita with her tongue, then took her between her lips and sucked gently while rolling her tongue over the clitoral head and sliding her fingers deep into Rita.

"Ohhh. Yes. Yes, Ramsey. Don't stop, don't stop. You feel so good...so good..."

"Ramsey?   It's eight," Nadine said as she shook Ramsey's shoulder.

"Not again!" Ramsey protested as her eyes fluttered open.

Nadine stood next to the bed in the Wanderlust in a clean set of clothes, rubbing a towel against her wet hair. "Sorry to keep waking you, but you told me last night that you had to get to San Francisco tomorrow. You mentioned that you wanted to get an early start today, so I'm only trying to — "

Ramsey sighed. "I know, Nadine. I appreciate your waking me. Let me take a quick shower, then we can grab breakfast somewhere and hit the road."

"Fine with me," Nadine replied as she stepped back from the bed so Ramsey could swing her legs out. "Oh, and I have something for you," Nadine said as she dug some change out of the pocket of her shorts. "Here are a couple of quarters. You'll need them for the showers, for hot water."

Ramsey shook her head. "No, thanks. Today I think I'll take a cold shower. A *very* cold shower..."

"So who's Rita?" Nadine asked as they each sipped from paper cups of after-breakfast coffee-to-go as Ramsey steered the Wanderlust up California Route 10 towards Los Angeles.

Ramsey choked momentarily on her coffee, swallowed with difficulty, coughed, then gasped, "How do you know about Rita?"

Nadine shrugged her shoulders and blew on her steaming coffee. "I only know her name. It's the name you kept calling out this morning when I thought you were having nightmares."

"Oh," Ramsey replied, then drove in silence.

"Oh?" Nadine echoed after a few moments. "That's all you're going to say? Ramsey, I don't mean to embarrass you, but now that I know you weren't having nightmares it's clear why you were calling out Rita's name."

"Oh? Why is that?"

"You were obviously having some erotic dream about this woman."

"Oh?"

"Yes, *oh*. You were calling out her name quite suggestively."

"Suggestively?" Ramsey pursued.

"Thank you for not saying oh one more time."

"You're welcome," Ramsey replied. "So what do you mean, suggestively?"

"You were moaning," Nadine explained.

"Moaning?"

"Moooaaannning," Nadine emphasized. "Yesterday in the diner you pretty much implied that you don't have someone special, but from the sounds of your moans Rita must be pretty special. So tell me about her."

Ramsey shrugged her shoulders. "There's nothing to tell."

"Aw, come on, Ramsey. I've been celibate for two years. Give me a thrill."

"There's no thrill, Nadine. Rita is my boss at the magazine where I work. And I guess I could call her a friend. That's all."

"Your boss, huh?"

"Yeah, my boss. She's my employer, I'm her employee. That's all."

"Well, if that's all, then why were you moaning her name?"

"I just had a dream about her."

"Well, it must've been some dream. Sounded like something pretty personal was going on, so I won't ask you to tell me about it."

"Good. Because I wouldn't have told you anyway."

"However," Nadine quickly followed, "I won't let you off the hook about Rita. Why don't you tell me what Rita's like?"

"What's she like?"

"Yeah."

"What do you mean?"

"What do *you* mean, what do *I* mean?"

"Just what I said. What do you mean?"

Nadine took a swallow of coffee. "You know what I mean, Ramsey. Tell me about Rita. What does she look like, for instance?"

"Okay, okay," Ramsey replied. "Rita is a very attractive woman."

"She is?"

"Yeah. She's... well...she's a knockout."

"Really?" Nadine grinned. "Tell me more."

Ramsey smiled. "Well, in my opinion, she could be *any* lesbian's wet dream. Everything about her is great. She's got a great figure and a really beautiful face. Her eyes are a smoky grey-green — they turn really green when she's angry."

"So you've made her angry, huh?"

Ramsey chuckled. "I tease her a lot, and she gets angry at me. It's a game we often play."

"Hmmm. Okay. Keep talking. Tell me more about her," Nadine encouraged Ramsey as she swung around in her seat, leaned her back against the passenger door, tucked her legs up on the seat, wrapped her arms around them, and propped her chin on her knees as she looked at Ramsey.

"Well, she's very successful. *Woman to Woman* is the only lesbian periodical in existence that's ever made money. And she's rich, too. Family wealth, but she also makes her own investments. I think they've paid off quite handsomely."

"She sounds like a real catch."

Ramsey nodded. "But do you know the greatest thing about her?"

Nadine shook her head.

"She's nice. I mean sincerely and genuinely nice. Someone like her, who has everything she has — looks, style, success, money — could easily act like a snob. But she's a down-to-earth person. She's generous and respectful and has always treated those who work for her quite well."

"So is she *your* wet dream?" Nadine asked.

Ramsey grinned. "She certainly was this morning."

"Sounds like you've got a bit of a crush on her," Nadine pointed out as she finished her coffee and crumpled the paper cup in her hands.

"A crush!" Ramsey burst into laughter. "That's the most far-fetched thing I've ever — "

"Then why did you dream about her?"

"How do I know?" Ramsey asked in a loud voice. "I don't preprogram my dreams."

"Then tell me about your dream," Nadine asked.

"Hey! You said you wouldn't ask me about that."

Nadine shrugged her shoulders. "So I changed my mind."

"Well, I'm not going to tell you."

"Ramsey, I can be very persuasive and extremely persistent when there I things I want to find out about. So you can tell me now or you can tell me later, but you *will* eventually tell me."

"Fine. It's no big deal anyway. I was making love to her."

"Was it nice?"

"Nice? Hmmm..." Ramsey thought for a moment. "It was *different*."

"Different? How so?"

"Well, it was intense. When I think about making love to a woman, I always think of it in terms of being erotic. You know, very sexual and sensual, very much a body-to-body contact type of thing. But in my dream with Rita, making love to her had another kind of intensity. Kind of passionate and consuming. Her body was turning me on, but in a way no other woman has before."

"How so?"

"What do you mean?"

"Like, why was it so intense?"

"Oh. Well, in the beginning of the dream, I open the door to my duplex and let Rita in. She walks by me, but instead of experiencing the usual reaction I've had before when she does that — which is to look at her body and think about how I'd like to jump her bones — I watch her walk by me in the dream and it feels like I've got butterflies in my stomach and my heart pounds so hard in my chest that it feels like it's going to explode. And when I start touching her in the dream, I'm aware of what she smells like and feels like, what it feels like to have her touch me, to have her speak my name..." Ramsey's voice drifted off as she dreamily stared out at the road.

"Ramsey?" Nadine asked.

"Hmm?"

"Have you ever thought about being with Rita? Not in a dream, but for real?"

"Oh, sure. I'm not the only one. I think a lot of women have wanted to go to bed with her."

"I don't mean just to have sex with her. I mean as a lover — someone you'd be with in a couple?"

Ramsey looked at Nadine. "Rita and me? Ha! That's like salt and pepper, fire and water, oil and vinegar — stuff like that. Rita and I are real opposites."

"How so?"

"I'll tell you. Rita Hayes is an elegant woman. She's refined. She's got style. Me? I'm into beer and basketball and rock 'n roll and wild sex. Rita's into champagne and lobster and Vivaldi and romantic hand-in-hand strolls on tropical beaches."

"Sometimes opposites work, Ramsey. Caroline is a very practical, rational woman — a decisive goal-setter and goal-achiever. I'm very emotional, can never make up my mind, and live my life one day to the next, without giving much thought to the future. Just because you and Rita are opposites doesn't mean that — "

Ramsey held up her hand. "Wait a minute, wait a minute! How did we ever get on the subject of Rita and me as a couple?"

Nadine tossed her empty coffee cup back and forth in her hands. "Because I contend, Ramsey, that you have a crush on Rita and that your having a dream about making love to her expresses your subconscious desire to — "

"Oh, spare me the psychobabble, Nadine," Ramsey cut in. "We wouldn't be having this conversation if I had told you I had had a dream about making love to a sheep or to a famous actress. So someone I happen to know was in my dream. I'm not surprised it was Rita; after all, I'm going to San Francisco to meet up with her. So I don't see any reason to psychoanalyze my subconscious desire in this — "

Nadine leaned forward in her seat. "But often there's more to dreams than — "

"Nadine, there's no point in discussing it anymore. And as for the possibility of a Rita-and-Ramsey combo, I might as well tell you that I don't do couples. And Rita has met — "

"So what do you do?" Nadine broke in.

"I go to bed with women."

"And then what happens? Do you stay with them a little while — have brief love affairs with them?"

"No. Then I leave."

"Well, no wonder you don't do couples. You don't stick around long enough."

"That's me," Ramsey grinned. "Love 'em and leave 'em — and always leave 'em wanting more."

Nadine rolled her eyes. "Hasn't there been anyone in your life you've wanted to settle down with?"

Ramsey nodded her head. "One."

"So what happened?"

"She dumped me."

"Oh."

"But I did have a relationship for two years," Ramsey offered.

Nadine gently patted Ramsey's arm. "Well, good for you! So you *do* do couples!"

"Did. I dumped her."

"Oh. Well, are you at all into Rita?"

Ramsey threw her hands in the air, then returned them to the steering wheel. "How many ways do I have to tell you? I've already told you that Rita is my boss, I'm her employee, I don't do coup — "

"And you have a dream about making intensely passionate love to her," Nadine added.

"Even if I were remotely interested in Rita, Nadine — which I'm not, by the way — "

"And which I'm not convinced is totally true — "

"Excuse me, but if you'd let me finish what I'm saying."

"Go ahead."

"Rita is out of my league," Ramsey finished.

"Has she ever expressed an interest in you?" Nadine asked.

"Absolutely not. She's all business with me. Very formal. Very professional. She's never once hinted...well...right before I left she kissed me — but," Ramsey held up a hand as Nadine opened her mouth, "she was drunk at the time."

"Ah-ha!" Nadine said as she nodded her head. "And what happened then?"

"It was no big deal."

"Uh-huh. Sure."

"Really," Ramsey insisted. "Rita threw me a going-away party before I left on this trip. She got a little looped. After everyone left, she felt a little...relaxed, I guess. She wanted to take off her shirt, then she kissed me and let me fondle her breast."

Nadine nodded her head. "No big deal."

"It wasn't," Ramsey replied defensively. "Nothing happened beyond that. She simply stated that she knew exactly what she was doing, told me she had wanted to do it for awhile, told me that she wanted me more than anyone she's ever wanted — you know — the usual drunken chatter. It was no big deal."

Nadine smiled and shook her head.

"What?" Ramsey asked as she looked at her.

"You don't strike me as stupid," Nadine replied, still smiling and shaking her head.

"I'm not."

"Ramsey, it doesn't take much to recognize that you and Rita have some chemistry happening between the two of you."

"Yeah, she sure lights my Bunsen burner," Ramsey grinned.

"Ramsey, I hate to wake you up out of your comfortable

hibernation from reality, but you've got a crush on Rita and she's got one on you."

"I do not. And she does not."

"Do too and does too. Listen, the woman kissed you and said some pretty direct and intense things to you."

"She was *drunk*."

Nadine shook her head. "There's something definitely going on for her about you. I mean, when someone has to get drunk just to say things like that — "

"She was saying them *because* she was drunk," Ramsey interrupted.

"The alcohol made it easier for her to say those things, Ramsey," Nadine pointed out.

"Well, she hasn't said anything to me since then," Ramsey stated.

"You two haven't talked since that last night?" Nadine asked.

"We've talked about business related things, but — "

"But not about what happened at your going-away party?"

"No. There's no reason to — "

"Now *that's* interesting," Nadine continued as she tapped a finger against her lips.

"Nadine, before you start off on another psychological interpretation," Ramsey broke in, "there's one thing you haven't let me tell you. Rita has met someone since I left. She's going to be in San Francisco with this woman."

"Really?" Nadine smiled, then rubbed her hands together. "Well, then, I can hardly wait to get to San Francisco."

"What do you mean?" Ramsey eyed Nadine suspiciously.

Nadine twisted in her seat to face forward. "Oh, I just think it'll be interesting when you meet up with Rita again — you know, when you both see each other for the first time after the things she said to you and did before you left, and with the obvious physical and emotional attraction you have towards her."

"I have no idea what you're talking about," Ramsey said.

Nadine turned to look at Ramsey. "You know, Ramsey, I really think you don't. But when you do finally figure things out — your feelings for Rita, I mean — oh, what I wouldn't give to be there then. But at least I'll get to meet this Rita when we arrive in San Francisco so I can have more than a mental picture of her."

"What do you mean? You're not meeting Rita. I'm dropping you off at Caroline's."

"Actually, Ramsey, Caroline is going to be meeting me."

"Where?"

"Where did you say you were meeting Rita?"

"At a place called the Inter-Continental, on Nob Hill."

"Oh, yeah. The Mark Hopkins," Nadine nodded.

"The Mark Hopkins?" Ramsey shouted. "No, that can't be right. I said the Inter-Continental."

Nadine furrowed her brow at Ramsey. "I know what you said. It's called the Mark Hopkins Inter-Continental. It's one of the fanciest hotels in San Francisco. They have the most elegant suites, with panoramic views from — "

"I know, I know," Ramsey moaned.

"What are you so upset about?" Nadine asked. "I'd love to stay at the Mark Hopkins."

"Not me," Ramsey sighed as she shook her head. "First Melissa," Ramsey muttered. "Now the Mark Hopkins. What else can I possibly *not* look forward to in San Francisco?"

"Do you want to hear something incredibly coincidental, Ramsey?" Nadine asked.

"No," Ramsey replied.

"The Mark Hopkins is where Caroline is going to be meeting *me*. Isn't that incredible? So I'll be able to meet Rita after all."

"Incredible," Ramsey mumbled as she slumped in her seat and drove the Wanderlust towards San Francisco.

Crossing the Golden Gate Bridge

"I can't believe this *isn't* the Golden Gate Bridge. I mean, I drive for decades   traverse the entire country from coast to coast — and believe that I'll arrive in San Francisco by crossing the famous Golden Gate Bridge. But instead I'm on the stupid Oakland Bridge. Who wants to be on the Oakland Bridge after driving thousands of miles? What a ripoff!

"I suppose the next thing you're going to tell me is that Joe Montana will *not* be standing at the end of this bridge, waving to people and signing autographs.

"You know, Nadine, I think San Francisco is highly overrated."

Ramsey's comments as she, Nadine, and the Wanderlust cross the Oakland Bridge into San Francisco

Chapter 16

Ramsey and Nadine stumbled into the lobby of the Mark Hopkins Inter-Continental Hotel on stiff legs the following afternoon, bleary-eyed after driving a day and a half with only essential stops.

"When is Caroline supposed to be meeting you?" Ramsey asked as she and Nadine crossed the lobby to the front desk.

"She told me to call her when I got in."

"Oh." Ramsey leaned against the front desk and waved her hand to attract the attention of a woman who was standing stiffly behind the counter.

"May I help you?" the woman pronounced perfectly.

"Could you ring Rita Hayes's room for me, please?"

"Whom shall I say is calling?"

"Ramsey Sears."

"Thank you." The woman sniffed once, scanned a computer print out, then punched three digits. "Is this the room of Miss Rita Hayes?" the woman enunciated into the receiver. "You have a Miss Ramsey Sears — "

"Miz," Ramsey corrected the woman, who shot Ramsey a sharp look, then immediately pasted a flash-frozen smile onto her face. "Excuse me, Miss Hayes, the — Hmmm? Oh, I beg *your* pardon, *Miz* Hayes. There is a *Miz* Ramsey Sears waiting in the lobby. Yes, I will. You're welcome." The woman replaced the receiver, then focused her attention somewhere above Ramsey's head as she stated, "*Miz* Hayes will be right down, *Miz* Sears." Then her frozen smile vanished and she resumed her rigid pose behind the counter.

"I wonder when *she* had her last orgasm," Ramsey whispered to Nadine as they walked away from the counter.

Nadine burst into laughter. Everyone else in the lobby, silenced by Nadine's outburst, stared at the two women for a few seconds before resuming muted conversation. "Oops," Nadine whispered.

"Apparently the rich and wanna-be famous don't like laughter," Ramsey muttered to her.

"That's because they think it's directed at them," Nadine replied. "And why not? They're trying hard to look like the minks, foxes, beavers, and seals they paid so dearly to have skinned," Nadine hissed.

Ramsey glanced around the room. "It *is* kind of like a zoo in here, isn't it? Do you think we're allowed to feed the animals?"

"Only macadamia nuts. Peanuts would be disdained."

Ramsey grinned. "Well, now that we've ripped the clientele here to shreds, I guess it's time to say goodbye. There's a bank of telephones over there if you want to give Caroline a call."

"No, I can wait."

"Well, I'm going to be meeting Rita in — oh no, you don't!" Ramsey declared. "You're not waiting around so you can meet Rita. I think you should just phone Caro — "

"Ramsey!" Rita's voice rang out across the lobby, instantly dropping a blanket of silence over the large room.

"Oh, as you were, people," Ramsey instructed the room. The murmur of subdued conversation resumed again.

As Rita walked across the lobby to greet Ramsey, Nadine tossed an arm casually over Ramsey's shoulder.

"What the hell are you doing?" Ramsey exclaimed as she tried to pull away from Nadine.

Rita's smile evaporated as she stopped in front of Ramsey, shook her head, and crossed her arms. "Well, Sears, I can see you didn't waste any time on the road."

"Nadine, let go of me!" Ramsey hissed as she tried to squirm out of the woman's grasp.

"Why don't you introduce me to your...uh...*friend*, Ramsey," Rita statedly evenly as her face grew flushed.

"She's...not...even...that," Ramsey explained with effort as she struggled to release herself from Nadine's hold. "There!" she declared as she finally succeeded in removing Nadine's arm from her shoulders. Then Ramsey readjusted her shirt and stared at Nadine. "What the hell has gotten into you?"

"Obviously she can't keep her hands off you," Rita commented as she tapped her foot repeatedly on the lushly carpeted floor.

"I can explain this, Rita," Ramsey stated as she stepped away from Nadine.

Rita rolled her eyes. "You always can."

"Rita, she's just someone I picked up."

"Of course she is. That's fairly obvious."

"No, no, I don't mean it like that. She's a hitchhiker. I *stopped* and picked her up. *To give her a ride.*"

Rita's left eyebrow began to twitch. "To give her the ride of her life, I bet."

Ramsey sighed in exasperation. "No. That wasn't it at all."

"Is that how you've been making this cross-country trip, Ramsey, by stopping and picking up any willing women along the way?"

Ramsey wiped sweat from her upper lip with the back of a hand. "Rita, she's the first woman I've ever picked up."

Rita clenched her jaw, then uncrossed her arms and jammed her hands on her hips. "Oh *please*, Ramsey, give me some credit. She's not the first woman you've picked up and she certainly won't be your last."

"Well," Nadine smiled, clasped her hands in front of her, then rocked back and forth on her heels. "I think I've seen enough. If you'll excuse me, I'm going to call my lover so she can come and get me. You see, Rita — I'm Nadine, by the way — " Nadine explained as she extended her hand to Rita, who briefly glanced at it, then looked away, "I was hitching from New York to San Francisco," Nadine continued as she lowered her hand, "to be with my lover when Ramsey kindly stopped to offer me a lift. Ramsey and I have had a fun time driving here together, except I'm afraid I may have bored her with my talk about Caroline. You see, Caroline and I have a lifelong commitment to each other. We lived together before she came here to attend school, but I couldn't join her because I had a work contract I had to honor. Anyway, the plan has always been for us to settle down in San Francisco and live happily ever after. So if you'll excuse me, I'll go call her now." Nadine turned to face Ramsey. "Thanks for the lift," she said. "And, by the way, Ramsey, everything I told you that I thought was true *is* true. Really. I see that now. Don't be dumb, and maybe you'll see it, too. Then maybe you'll want to do something about it. Anyway, Ramsey — ciao!" Nadine turned on her heels and hurried to the phones.

Ramsey faced Rita. "See? I told you I picked her up, in the *literal* sense. And she has a lover."

Rita stared at her. "Then why'd she put her arm around you?"

Ramsey shrugged her shoulders. "I have no idea. Gratitude, I guess. Maybe she's grateful for the ride."

"Well, I just want to be sure the magazine's money isn't being spent on financing escapades with bimbos you pick up in every state."

"Speaking of bimbos," Ramsey cut in, "when do I get to meet Melissa?"

"Ramsey, she's not a bimbo, she's a lawyer, and a very good one, I might add."

"I'm sure you might add that because I'm certain you'd know that."

"I do know, and so will you. We're all sharing a suite."

"The three of us are sleeping together?" Ramsey shouted, evoking another silence in the lobby.

Rita grabbed her arm and pulled her towards the bank of elevators. "My God, what these people must think of me!"

"Rita, I'm here too, you know."

"Ramsey, any semblance of a reputation you had was ruined years ago."

"Thanks, boss."

As soon as an UP elevator arrived, Rita pulled Ramsey through the opening, pressed the button for the top floor, and repeatedly stabbed at the CLOSE DOOR button until the doors sequestered them from the lobby listeners.

They rode up in silence.

◡◡◡

"I really can't believe this, about your relationship with Melissa," Ramsey said an hour later as she sat back in a chair that faced Rita and Melissa on the other side of the small meeting table in the penthouse suite. "I mean, I'm just stunned."

Rita smiled and looked at Melissa. "It kind of took us by surprise, too. It certainly wasn't something we had planned on."

Melissa returned Rita's smile. "Things like this are never planned. But they're once-in-a-lifetime opportunities."

"Mel knew all along it would work," Rita explained to Ramsey. "So I put my trust in her and let myself be swept away."

"Rita, this constitutes a *major* sweeping," Ramsey said.

Rita nodded her head. "I know. But Ramsey, *I really wanted it.* I really, really did."

"Then congratulations," Ramsey said as she extended her hand to Melissa.

Melissa took her hand and shook it. "Thank you," she said and smiled. "You know, Ramsey, Rita's told me a lot about you. I'm sure we're going to get along well."

"We'd better," Ramsey replied. "After all, we share a common interest," she said as she nodded her head in Rita's direction.

"I know," Melissa agreed. "That's why we wanted *you* to be the first to learn about our arrangement."

"I didn't even tell Shane before I left," Rita interjected.

"You're kidding!" Ramsey responded. "Why not?"

"I didn't want everyone to find out. It wouldn't have been right. Melissa said we should wait for the right moment."

"Well, the time is right now," Ramsey stated. "I think you should call her and tell her."

"Now?"

"Yes, Rita, now. The sooner the better."

"Will that be all right?" Rita asked Melissa.

"Fine with me," Melissa replied. "Anyway, it doesn't matter how many people know now."

"Great!" Rita exclaimed. "I really hated keeping this a secret, especially one as wonderful as this." Then Rita hesitated and chewed on a fingernail. "But tell me, Ramsey, what do you think I should say to Shane?"

Ramsey thought for a moment, then shrugged her shoulders. "Why not tell her exactly what you told me? I can't think of any other way to do it."

"Okay," Rita nodded. "So I'll say, 'Guess what, Shane? I have three great things to tell you. First, *Woman to Woman* has just signed an incredibly lucrative and exclusive deal to produce a mail order catalog that will offer a wide variety of women's products and services never offered by catalog before. The products and services will be offered by lesbian businesses, women-owned smaller businesses, and major corporations that make products for women. The terms of the deal call for ten percent of gross sales of the catalog items to go to *Woman to Woman*. We estimate a projected annual income from the catalog of — '"

"Tell her the name of the catalog, too," Ramsey interrupted.

"Right. I'll tell her 'We project an annual income from the catalog, which we've named By-Femail-Order, of between one and two million dollars. The second — '"

"Rita," Ramsey interrupted her, "you might want to pause then, to let the money aspect sink in. You might want to repeat the word *annual.* Or say something like, 'As I said, Shane, that's one to two million *every year.*' Then let her catch her breath before you tell her anything else."

Rita nodded her head. "You're right. That's a lot of money when you hear it for the first time."

"It is," Ramsey agreed. "Then, when you hear Shane breathing again, tell her the second great thing."

"Okay. Then I'll say, 'The second great thing I have to

tell you is that you, me, Ramsey, and the *Woman to Woman* lawyer I've hired, Melissa Chester, will be working together to produce this catalog. The four of us will work as equal partners to sign up advertisers and produce the catalog. Because we'll be partners, we'll each get a hefty bonus for every new supplier we bring on board. In addition, you will still collect a yearly salary as acting head of your department, but will promote your staff as necessary or hire new employees to relieve you of the burden of day-to-day operations.'"

"Good," Ramsey commented. "Remember to pause again before the third thing. You've just told Shane her earning and spending power has greatly increased."

"Let her catch her breath again, right?" Rita smiled.

"Right," Ramsey responded as she returned the smile. "And then you'll tell her the third great thing."

Rita nodded. "That's when I'll say, 'And guess what, Shane? You know that obnoxious gay male publisher from Thrust Publications — the one who wants to buy *Woman to Woman* but has been refused every time he approaches me, the one who accessed our mailing list and began a smear campaign against us, sending letters to our subscribers that informed them we were 'selling' our models to men, the one who began producing a competing magazine for lesbians in order to —'"

"Rita, Rita," Ramsey cut her off. "You don't need to tell her all that. Simply mentioning Thrust Publications will evoke the appropriate reaction from Shane — a loud 'ACK! I can't stand that guy!'"

Rita nodded. "Okay. So I'll just say — "

"'You know that sleaze ball at Thrust?'" Ramsey offered.

Rita laughed. "Okay. Well, he not only — "

"Say it, Rita," Ramsey cut in.

"Huh?"

"Say it."

"What?"

"About the sleaze ball."

Rita smiled and blushed. "Okay. 'Shane, you know the sleaze

ball at Thrust? Well — '"

"Shane's going to love that," Ramsey chuckled.

"*Well*," Rita broke in. "'We have a big fat lawsuit slapped on him, courtesy of Melissa Chester, attorney representing the new partnership of Chester, Hayes, Sterns, and Sears — '"

"Wait a minute!" Ramsey cut in. "Why is my name last in our partnership? If we're going alphabetically, Sterns comes after Sears."

"But it didn't sound right the other way," Rita explained.

Melissa nodded. "It's not good business practice to end a series of names with a name like Sterns. It sounds too severe."

"Then try it this way," Ramsey suggested, "*Sears, Sterns, Hayes, and Chester.*"

Melissa shook her head. "We can't. We already had the stationery printed."

Ramsey raised her hands in the air. "*This* is a partnership? How come Shane and I didn't get to vote on this?"

"There wasn't time," Rita said. "We couldn't do anything that would jeopardize our being the first to come out with this idea."

"We didn't tell you this, Ramsey," Melissa interjected, "but Thrust had originally approached *Woman to Woman's* advertisers with the idea of a by-women, for-women catalog. I only found out about it because my lover designs and sells her own cards at a shop on Newbury Steet in Boston."

"Your lover?" Ramsey echoed.

"Yeah," Melissa nodded. "Anyway, when I heard that Thrust wanted to capitalize on women's products, I contacted Rita right away and told her about Thrust's idea for the catalog. Personally, I think women's money should be used to support women's businesses, not to line men's pockets — even if the pockets belong to gay men. When Rita told me about some of the underhanded things Thrust had done, I encouraged her to pursue the idea of the women's catalog herself. In all actuality, Thrust could sue us for stealing its idea."

"But because of its past history with *Woman to Woman*," Rita added, "Thrust really has no case against us. Melissa says Thrust will probably offer us an out-of-court settlement for the lawsuit we have against them now — "

"And we'll probably take it, so long as Thrust agrees not to pursue its action against our catalog," Melissa finished.

Rita spread her hands out and shrugged her shoulders at Ramsey. "So, you see? I couldn't tell you anything about this, Ramsey. *I* made the decision about the stationery. I'm sorry you don't like it. If you want, we can order new stationary."

Ramsey shook her head. "Nah, that's okay."

"Well, that's agreeable of you," Rita commented.

"Well, actually, that's because I have some news of my own," Ramsey replied. "Maybe my name on the stationary won't matter."

"Huh?" Rita asked.

Ramsey sighed. "Remember that idea I had for a TV show?" Rita nodded. "Well, it seems something may come of it. Athena Broadcasting wants me to write a few scripts, just to see if it will fly."

Rita's elation disappeared. "What does that mean, Ramsey?"

"I don't know yet," Ramsey replied. "I'd like to write the scripts. I've never written for television before and I think it would be a great career opportunity. After all, you were the one who told me at the start of this trip that my writing for the magazine was getting stale."

"But I didn't mean to imply that you had to leave the magazine," Rita said. "I thought with the partnership and this new business opportunity — "

Ramsey took a step towards her. "It sounds great, Rita, really it does. But you have to admit, so does writing for television. Still, the bottom line is that nobody knows right now whether the series will be a hit. I could create a *Dynasty* or a dud. So I'm not about to up and quit my job — excuse me, my partnership — yet."

"Well I'm happy to hear that," Rita responded.

"Are you really?" Ramsey asked.

"Yes, Ramsey, I am. Really," Rita nodded. She rose from the table and walked to the window, where she turned her back on Melissa and Ramsey to look out over the city.

ᗡ♡ᗡ

"So you thought Melissa and I were lovers, didn't you?" Rita asked Ramsey as they sipped champagne at a table for two in a corner of the hotel's four-star restaurant.

Ramsey shrugged her shoulders. "Justine and Bernice were convinced "

"As were you," Rita broke in.

"As was I," Ramsey nodded in agreement, "that you and Melissa were an item."

Rita chuckled. "Melissa and Judy have been together for five years. Melissa's seeing Judy's parents tonight — that's why she couldn't join us."

"Oh."

"Although I don't mind, do you?" Rita asked.

"Not at all. I often eat dinner alone, so it's nice to have the company."

Rita looked at Ramsey. "It's been a long time since we've spent any time together — just the two of us — hasn't it?"

Ramsey sat back in her chair as a half-smile played on her lips. "I think the last time was...oh...let's see...uh...I think it was the night of my going-away party."

Rita raised an eyebrow in response, then quickly lowered her eyes. She set her champagne glass down and slowly began to run a finger around the top of the glass.

"Listen, Rita, about that last night," Ramsey began.

"About last night?" Rita quickly asked.

"No, I said about *that* last night," Ramsey corrected her as she leaned forward in her chair and placed her elbows on the table.

"What last night?"

Ramsey sighed. "The last night we saw each other. The night

of my going-away party. The night you kissed me and took my hand and placed it on your — "

"Oh, that night!" Rita said loudly, then raised her glass, drained it, and reached for the bottle of champagne that was chilling in the holder next to their table.

"Not yet," Ramsey said as she grabbed Rita's hand, held onto it, and pulled it back to the table. "I want to talk to you about that night and what happened before you end up as drunk as you were then. Now I don't know if you even remember anything, but — "

"I do," Rita interrupted her, then gently squeezed Ramsey's hand and rubbed her thumb along Ramsey's palm as she continued. "I remember everything about that night, Ramsey. I remember everything we did and everything I said to you."

"Look at me, Rita, not at the table," Ramsey said.

Rita shook her head. "I can't."

"Why not?"

"Because everything I felt for you that night is happening all over again — especially when I look at you."

"Oh? How much champagne have you had already?"

"Not enough," Rita replied, then raised her head to look at Ramsey. "It's not the champagne that's making me have these feelings, Ramsey. They've been there...they've been there for awhile. I keep thinking — hoping — that the champagne will make the feelings go away, but they're still with me, drunk or sober. I don't know what to do with them."

Ramsey shrugged her shoulders. "Why don't you act on them?"

"You want me to act on them?" Rita asked, then stared at Ramsey for a few moments. "And what about you? Did that kiss and what I said to you that night mean anything to you?"

"Of course they did."

"What did they mean?" Rita asked, then gripped Ramsey's hand tightly in hers. "Tell me. Then tell me I could be different, Ramsey. Tell me I wouldn't be just another quickie to you."

"Rita, I would never, *ever*, think of you in that way."

"How do you feel about me, Ramsey?"

Ramsey looked into Rita's eyes. "Rita, I'm so attracted to you. I mean, kissing you that night...well...I can still remember what it felt like. It was an unforgettable experience."

Rita smiled. "I feel the same way. Your lips were so soft, Ramsey. I never knew they could be so soft and so warm."

"I want to kiss you now, Rita."

"I want to kiss you, too."

Ramsey smiled, then began to chuckle.

"What's so funny?" Rita asked.

"Well, this is kind of gushy, don't you think? I mean, we're in a fancy restaurant, at a table lit only by the glow of candlelight, and I'm holding your hand and mooning on and on about your kiss — "

Rita yanked her hand out of Ramsey's and reached for the champagne bottle.

Ramsey instantly lost her smile. "What did I say?" she asked.

Rita filled her glass, shoved the bottle back into the crushed ice in its holder, and leaned against the table to bring her face closer to Ramsey's. "I can't believe you think this whole situation is funny, Ramsey. We're talking about feelings here — or at least I thought we were."

"I'm sorry," Ramsey said, then reached across the table for Rita's hand.

Rita sat back in her chair, pulling her hand out of reach.

Ramsey sighed. "Rita, I'm not laughing because I think anything's funny, especially your feelings. I'm laughing because I'm nervous. I don't know what to do in a situation like this. Normally this is no problem for me, being with a beautiful woman I'm attracted to. We'd just eat dinner and have sex. But you're...different. You make me feel all jumbled up inside." Ramsey paused, then again reached across the table for Rita's hand. "Please?" she asked. "I'm not comfortable right now. Holding your hand would help me."

Rita sighed, then placed her hand on the table.

Ramsey smiled, then covered Rita's hand with her own. "Thanks."

"So why am I different, Ramsey?" Rita asked.

Ramsey chewed on her lip for a moment. "I guess because I don't want to have one night with you and then leave it at that."

"Oh? Do you want two?" Rita retorted.

Ramsey stared at Rita. "No, I'd like more."

Rita raised her eyebrows. "More? What does that mean? Three...four...five nights? A couple of weeks? A few months? Stop me if I'm getting warm. Six months? A — "

"I don't know," Ramsey cut in. "Geez, Rita, you wanted me to be serious, so I'm trying to be."

Rita stopped and stared at Ramsey. "I'm sorry."

"Rita, I really don't know what I want. But one thing I do know is that...is that — aw hell — I like you a whole lot. *A whole lot.* And I don't quite know what to do with that."

"I like you a whole lot, too, Ramsey."

"You do?"

"Yes."

"Shit. Nadine was right," Ramsey mumbled.

"Did you say something?" Rita asked.

"No."

"Oh. Well, I know what I'd like to do in this situation."

"You do?"

"Yes."

"Then tell me."

Rita took a deep breath, then exhaled. "I'd like to take it slowly with you, Ramsey. I'd like to get to know you outside the office and outside our friendship. But — " Rita began, then paused.

"But?" Ramsey cued her.

"But — not if you're going to sleep with other women."

Ramsey squinted her eyes for a moment. "So what you're saying is that you want me to — "

"Take a chance on me," Rita finished for her. "*Just me.* How do you feel about that?"

"So you mean we'd be dating each other...uh...exclusively? Is that the term?"

Rita shrugged her shoulders. "I didn't know there was a term for what I want. All I know is that what I want has to be what you want too, Ramsey, or it won't work."

Ramsey was quiet for several seconds. "Okay," she finally replied.

"Okay, you heard what I said," Rita asked, "or okay, that's what you want, too?"

"Okay to both," Ramsey responded.

"Are you sure?" Rita asked.

"I think so."

Rita chuckled. "Well, coming from you, I guess that's a pretty firm response."

"I think so," Ramsey repeated as she raised Rita's hand to her lips and kissed it as the two women began their first romantic dinner at a table for two at the Mark Hopkins Hotel in the romantic city of San Francisco.

About the Author

ELIZABETH DEAN would love to report that she lives with her six cats and a life partner. However, she's allergic to cats and is also single; she often wonders if there's any connection between the two.

At any rate, she has built an outdoor cat condo that currently houses, year-round, a former abused cat, two brother cats that come from a dysfunctional home, and two aging toms. She's hoping that such kindheartedness will soften the heart of a member of the two-legged female species. When this happens, she promises that the woman can be an indoor lover who can share her spacious home in Maynard, Massachusetts.

THAT'S MS. BULLDYKE TO YOU, CHARLIE!

by Jane Caminos

Artist and illustrator Jane Caminos makes her debut as a Madwoman Press cartoonist with *That's MS. BULLDYKE to you, Charlie!* Ms. Bulldyke is a collection of 150 cartoons that record the ups and downs of lesbian life -- from baby dykes and lipstick lesbians to power dykes and older gay women.

The ever-blonde Caminos, who has been cartooning for more than twenty years, gives us a collection of hilarious cartoons that capture the lesbian communities she's seen while spending the last two decades in Boston and New York City.

That's MS. BULLDYKE to you, Charlie! (160 pages at $8.95) is another book from Madwoman Press, and is available at your local women's bookstore or directly from the publisher. Send your order to **Madwoman Press**, P.O.Box 690, Northboro, MA 01532. Please be sure to enclose $8.95 plus $2.50 for shipping and handling. Add $.50 for each additional book.